# LEAH'S PUNISHMENT

'I keep her nude as much as possible,' said Leah's master.

'Surely not in public?' asked the guest.

'Of course ... Men admire her singular beauty. Their attentions arouse her. But touch is strictly for the privileged few.'

'And punishment ... ?'

'Ah, yes ... Punishment hones a unique edge to any relationship. But mark this – without the commingling of pleasure, then all the pain in the world is rendered worthless.'

'I have some ideas of my own that I would like to try upon her – with her master's permission.'

'Be my guest.'

As Leah stared at him over the length of her prostrate body she was horribly aware of the way her pulse was beating in her naked belly. And the guest had seen it too.

# LEAH'S PUNISHMENT

*Aran Ashe*

This book is a work of fiction.
In real life, make sure you practise safe, sane and consensual sex.

First published in 2008 by
Nexus
Thames Wharf Studios
Rainville Rd
London W6 9HA

A catalogue record for this book is available from the British Library.

*www.nexus-books.com*

Typeset by TW Typesetting, Plymouth, Devon

Printed and bound by CPI Bookmarque Ltd, Croydon, CR0 4TD

The paper used in this book is a natural, recyclable product made from wood grown in sustainable forests. The manufacturing process conforms to the regulations of the country of origin.

ISBN 978 0 352 34171 6

Distributed in the USA by Macmillan Publishers, 175 Fifth Avenue, New York, NY 10010, USA

# Contents

Symbols key

 Corporal Punishment

 Female Domination

 Institution

 Medical

 Period Setting

 Restraint/Bondage

 Rubber/Leather

 Spanking

 Transvestism

 Underwear

 Uniforms

# 1

# Girl on a Boat

Of the many narrow boats navigating the mountain
waterway in the early warmth of that day, one was
special. Its line was sleeker, finer than the rest; it sliced
smoothly through the water; the horse towing it –
powerful and proud – held his head high. Any watcher
on the banks would have noticed these things first.
Then he would have seen the girl.

She sat astride the prow, dwarfed by the carved
wooden boss that crowned it. Her naked legs dangled
in innocent shamelessness and her toes flirted with the
warm wisps of breeze. She wore a broad straw hat and
an open shirt – too large for her and tied loosely at her
belly. Her countenance was angelic, yet her blue-eyed
gaze seemed open and knowing. Her delicate fingers
clung to the wooden boss in front of her; at intervals
her cheek or her lips would brush across its surface as
if she were daydreaming and echoes of intimacy were
caressing her mind.

But when she stretched her back, the watcher might
have glimpsed below her shirt the tell-tale fresh red
marks across her small nude buttock cheeks. Then idle
contemplation might next have drifted to that other,
most nude of places – between those tender open
thighs, so lithe and limp in their present pose and yet
so surely trained to adept gripping. Hidden from view

there nestled segments of a beautiful blue-jewelled chain that once linked those pierced pink inner lips, now plundered by repeated male wanting.

The watcher would not know this. Nor would he know how keenly the laying of those fresh marks of caring sexual punishment across her bottom had stirred female erection at the front; nor how her master had placed her in so aroused a state in this present pose, deliberately astride the prow, separating the two segments of her chain and pressing her female openness down; nor how he had spent productive time refining the positioning of her thighs, then caressing the sensitive hollow nudity at the base of her spine, whilst kissing her lips, yet at the same time searching out her keen erection, that special place, tip-touching it, softly pressing it back inside its lovely shell until her belly repeatedly tightened and her lips faltered against his kisses and softly but forlornly begged him for release.

Leah sat very still now, clinging to the prow, her breasts forced outwards by the polished wooden boss as she relived that deliciously prolonged touching. Merek had told her that he wanted her 'at one with the boat, fused to it almost'. Every slight movement, every swell in the water, lifted her belly on the sturdy waxed wood of the prow. The irresistible pressure between her legs slowly surged then swiftly dropped, imposing the beat of pleasure, slower than a heartbeat but fuller and more telling. The heavy tow-rope was anchored to a short mast some way behind her; as the rope tautened then slackened, a sweet forward pulse melded with the up and down.

Leah's breasts were smaller than those of most slaves that her master used: she was very conscious of this. But of late the surrounds of her nipples were becoming steadily more swollen. Merek had commented on this. He would stand Leah sideways and

2

pull her open shirt back, up under her arms, exposing her even in the presence of other men, and he would run his hands upwards under her breasts and the newly swollen surrounds of her nipples would stand out, puffed-up and hard. And he would gently pull and twist them and tell her he was pleased that they were getting fuller, with the fullness restricted to the sur-rounds of the nipples. Often, these other men would be watching and Leah's nipple-surrounds would puff up even harder because of this.

When her master had male guests at his table they would openly and frankly discuss her as they watched. Merek would sometimes offer her to favoured or important guests. Leah could never be sure which man, or which men, her body might be required to please – such was the duty of a Tormunite slave. The men always seemed to want to bundle her in their arms and carry her. When a man – her temporary master – did this with her he would usually already be in hard erection and Leah – if her hand was free – would try to feel this part of him through his garments, in part to judge in advance its girth and shape. It became her signal of assent to the sexual actions he might wish to take. If the acting master would permit, she would play with his flesh at length while it was naked: she enjoyed this, taking pleasure from imposing pleasure and taking brief control, provoking arousal but delaying spillage.

As Leah daydreamed, she put her lips to the wooden boss and gripped her thighs about its column until the soles of her feet pressed tightly together. Her open sex rode the softly surging prow as the tow-rope rose and dipped; she felt it, tugging the sluggish weight of the boat, tugging deliciously and remorselessly against the ball of arousal buried deep within her belly.

Then Leah heard her master's footfalls approaching. She tensed with anticipation but knew not to turn around. She clung in that same position, her feet pressed together. Merek had stopped short in order to look at her from behind. She knew he was studying her bottom and the marks that his guest of last night had put there. Then Leah looked up and saw a bridge ahead. There were men on it. They turned to stare at her. She so wanted to avert her eyes but knew she must not.

'Good girl,' Merek whispered. 'Keep looking at them. They want to see those generous eyes and those beautiful puffy nipples bared to the sun.'

Leah shivered self-consciously. Already she could hear the hungry murmurings, stirring sickly fear into the sweet arousal in her belly. As Merek crept up behind her, her upward gaze unfocused gently and her lips parted. The tips of his fingers touched the naked small of her back. 'Let go now – with your hands,' he said. Shuddering softly, Leah rode the surging swell of submission. 'Let your arms hang back – relax.' He cradled her by her shoulders. The sun's warmth bathed her quaking belly. Her thighs were still around the wooden column. The avid faces of the men on the bridge drew swiftly closer, with Leah now so sexually exposed. Merek deftly freed the knot fastening her shirt, which fell completely open. Her fingertips touched the decking. Her swollen nipples felt tight, her naked labia soft. In the pit of her belly was a nauseous desire – too sweet and cloying a burden for all her taunted longing. Her broken sexual chain had become so moistened that its segments lay enfolded within the limp flesh. She wanted Merek to put his hand between her legs and grasp her gently, or just press his fingertips against her knob as if to push it up inside her again.

The men were shouting and whistling. The bridge was almost overhead, coming nearer, faster. 'Make kisses to them,' Merek whispered. And when Leah did, he touched her, attempted softly to open her sex more

4

completely, and she came, briefly but so pleasurably, from the stretching and the lewd kisses she was making at the men.

Merek drew her upright with her legs still round the prow and her hat fell to the deck. The underside of the bridge raced over her head. 'Forward now ... Lean right over.' She leant round one side of the boss and he drew her shirt all the way up her back, exposing her from her shoulder-blades to her bottom. The boat emerged from under the bridge. The whistling and the shouts continued, for the men had run to the other side.

'Lean further,' Merek ordered Leah. 'I want them to see everything.' Her face and neck congested as she hung, head down, clinging to the prow by one arm, her shirt now over her head. The swirling water directly below made her giddy. Reaching under her from behind, Merek slowly unravelled the oily segments of her labial chain and stretched her sex fully open with them, stimulating pulsings that her body could not prevent. 'Beautiful ...,' Merek murmured as the whistling grew ever louder. 'The shafts of sunshine even reach inside you. Evidently my guest opened you well last night.' Leah shuddered sexually at the memory. Merek took one hand away and cupped her small breasts. He felt for the nipple surrounds and found them very swollen and hard. And he kept her in that exposed position until all the shouts and whistles had receded. Then he lifted her down and stood her unsteadily on the deck. She went light-headed and started to swoon. Merek held her gently upright. He did not pick her up nor let her sit but cradled her giddy head against his chest, her puffy nipples pressed against his taut belly. Leah tried to touch it. She snuggled closer – for her master was her lover and provider, not just her taunter and punisher – but Merek gently, firmly drew her arms away.

5

He looked down at her, searching her eyes. 'Did the pleasure come – when I spread you open?'

'Oh, master – yes . . .,' she murmured. Again her fingers came up to caress his torso but he would not allow it.

'Put your arms behind you!'

When she did this, her breasts pressed deeper against his belly and her nipples stood harder. Momentarily Merek closed his eyes and, to Leah, that small signal was itself beautiful. She pressed her puffed-up nipples against him. She wanted them to pierce the cloth of his shirt and the points to puncture his skin and burrow beneath it like little goads that would blister within him and from which he would never be free. Her open lips touched his chest and she felt a shudder move through him. She was excited that she had made this happen.

'Let me look at you,' he said more gently. Once again he stood her sideways to assess her breasts by hand for weight and girth. 'They're definitely getting more swollen around the nipples. It must be the good living – plenty of fruit and plenty of admirers.' He kissed her fully on the lips while his fingertips lightly grazed the undersides of her nipple-surrounds, setting erect every skin-hair down her back. He rolled her sleeves up. Then from behind he drew her shirt-tails tightly up underneath her arms and tied them in a knot above her breasts. The downward pressure made her breasts more swollen and left her whole body naked from her shoulders down. The rolling up and tying of the cloth made goose-pimples spread over her exposed skin.

'Turn around.' He wanted to look at the new marks that had been put across her bottom the previous night.

Whenever Merek examined Leah's marks, he would hold her in this special way, one hand between her

6

thighs at the front while the other rubbed and pinched her reddened buttock cheeks. 'Stand up straight,' he ordered, for her knees were sagging under this fresh stimulation. Merek would never permit the excesses of whipping to lead to perforation of her skin but the marks were always long-lasting. His fingers swiftly found the most punished part of the cheeks and worked them. Fiery needles stung that skin. In the flesh beneath, a dull ache stirred, as if the warm firm fingers had plunged into the cheek itself, burrowing through the very flesh, making her anus tighten guiltily, triggering a strange sensation in the back of her throat. And at the front, where he was holding her lips and now gently milking and teasing her knob, there was a much more direct pleasure. Her legs began to tremble and her knees again went weak. The two segments of her labial chain slipped down and dangled free; her sexual lips were swelling. She wanted him to bend her over his lap and finish her. Moist sounds were coming from her front. 'Oh, it feels so warm and good,' he murmured. 'Open it.' He suddenly held the lips fully back and made her push until she felt her inner flesh gently erupting into his taunting fingers.

When Leah had first come to Merek, she was newly deflowered: her broken chain was the external indication of this; the frayed tenderness inside her body was the living proof. Merek had vowed to make her more open still. He had tied the broken strands of her labial chain to leather garters at the tops of her thighs and had stretched her sex repeatedly. 'Your inner beauty shall henceforth be visible at all times to all men,' he had told her. He would make her sit, open and unclothed below the waist. Her thighs were only permitted to close around an object or a human part. When she sat, he instructed, she must do so with her open sex fully visible to any onlooker, or she must sit with it open and pressed against the seat.

7

Merek now lifted Leah from the deck, her crotch cradled in his hand and her sex still wide open, his other hand clutching her punished buttock cheeks: her climax came as her toes left the decking. The inner flesh of her sex was still pulsing out between his fingers – she could feel it and could sense that he was studying its performance. He carried her back to the prow and put her legs either side of the short column supporting the wooden boss. Once again, her inner flesh pressed against its waxed surface and the short lengths of chain hung down on each side. Then he kissed her while this intimate conjunction of girl and boat was maintained. He told her that he was pleased with her progress and learning. He continued to kiss her and to touch her between the legs very gently, and as the boat drew towards a wharf, he whispered: 'There is a gentleman whom I would like you to meet.'

# 2

# Hides and Skins

As soon as the boat had docked, the loading began.

'Do you want to accompany Asgal?' Merek asked Leah. Asgal was unharnessing the tow-horse for stabling. 'There's no hurry – our guest is not expected yet,' Merek added, stroking her hair. 'In fact, we shan't be leaving today.'

Leah feigned indifference, hoping that her master would not realise why she did not want to go with Asgal. Asgal made her uncomfortable – his desire was hidden and barbed; it carried jealousy of the master and Leah avoided Asgal whenever she could. So she answered that she would wait aboard with her master.

'Then you can supervise the loading,' Merek said and Leah smiled. But in truth she was curious to watch.

Each port along the waterway was different; in the smaller ones like this, the labourers might be rough but they were mostly open and kind. Even so, Leah kept her distance. As part of her training, Merek deliberately tied her shirt-tails up under her breasts so as to leave her belly and bottom quite naked, knowing that the freedom of nudity in itself aroused her. He did not force her to approach the men but he expected her not to hide. It was a test, a fine line of gentle flaunting that Leah had to tread. She knew that seeing her thus before the men excited Merek; she tried to conceal how much it excited her too. The men worked bare-chested, carrying aboard the heavy bales of hides and skins without pausing for rest until Merek called a halt and told Leah to bring beer for their refreshment.

Leah approached them timorously, dispensing liquor from the heavy jug as the men sat about the deck. But there was nothing to fear: they thanked her and said only kind things and that she was very pretty and asked where she was from. Then one of them playfully asked her why her sex was nude of hair. Leah immediately retreated to her master, who put his arm protectively about her head but did not take umbrage at the labourer's pointed question. Leah's cheeks and neck glowed with hot embarrassment as her master quite freely explained to the whole group: 'The Tor-munite girls are routinely kept naked there. Their training-masters see to it. It is central to their practice for the females, either by shaving or by depilation with salves.' Then he drew her closer. 'But Leah needs neither: no hair has ever grown upon her in that place. In that respect, as in many others, she is special.' He paused, cupping his hand around her naked belly as he kissed her publicly.

Murmurs of appreciation from the men turned to sighs as Merek seated himself amongst them and lifted her on to his lap so that all could see the bareness between her legs. 'Push out,' Merek whispered lewdly to her, kissing her ear lobe. The men gasped as Leah felt the segments of her labial chain sliding down and dangling. Merek now bared her breasts by unknotting her shirt and the shiver took them, as if cold lips had closed about each nipple. Through half-closed eyes Leah beheld the men watching her and the skin-shiver fed a shudder of desire through her core as she imagined what it might be like, were they to take her now, on deck, all naked and erect and besprinkled with fresh male sweat. And she would want it deep yet gently, after the first strong insertion, and she would want it to be prolonged. Such was the nature of Tormunite training.

That evening, with the loading completed and the labourers gone, Leah was told that she was to be put to the 'feeling'. The 'feeling' was a session in which Merek would test his slave, in the presence of another man or other men, normally without penetration occurring. Merek told her he would do this to her at a time convenient to himself. Then he left her to contemplate this in the cabin, where he placed her astride the corner of the bed. 'Your thighs must remain open,' he explained as he tied her wrists behind her, so that she could not touch herself, then he tied her ankles individually to iron rings in the floor. Then he opened her body, not too widely but enough to put sensual pressure to the opening and he told her to push – 'to keep yourself open, to begin the swelling'. Then he thrust a cool, oval swatch of soft leather – 'a gift from our guest' – a little way under her sex before kissing her, softly and long. For the duration of the kissing he pressed the pad of his middle finger directly against her tender pink inside, which through her sexual pushing, was already swelling out.

He left a candle burning in the cabin. When he had gone Leah strained to hear the voices beyond the door, wanting to know who had sent the strange leather 'gift'. After a while she stilled herself and focused on the flickering candle until its flame appeared disembodied and seemed to swell and pulse in rhythm with her breathing. Each fleshly push that Leah exerted seemed to make the flame bloat until its licking cusp, in its slow writhing, seemed to cause a dull tickle in her knob, which began to stand up, yearning for cool, cruel pinching fingers to snuff the burning gnawing at its tip.

11

Leah, ankles fastened, sank back upon the bed until her knotted hands behind her back made her belly arch lewdly and her clitoris project and throb almost painfully keenly. She wanted someone to come through that door now and suck her very quickly, suck out all restraint then go inside her body very deeply, with his cockhead straining at her womb until it made her come so strongly that her sex would squeeze him red and purple round his rim.

She did not have to wait much longer – the voices suddenly got louder and now she wanted to sit up but was too terrified to move. While she lay prone and open, the door of the cabin abruptly swung wide.

'Stay still,' her master said but Leah was already frozen with fear as the guest advanced towards the bed.

'I keep her nude as much as possible,' said Leah's master.

'Surely not in public?' asked the guest.

'Of course ... Men admire her singular beauty. Their attentions arouse her. But touch is strictly for the privileged few.'

'And punishment ... ?'

'Ah, yes ... Punishment hones a unique edge to any relationship. But mark this – without the commingling of pleasure, then all the pain in the world is rendered worthless.'

'I have some ideas of my own that I would like to try upon her – with her master's permission.'

'Be my guest.'

As Leah stared at him over the length of her prostrate body she was horribly aware of the way her pulse was beating in her naked belly. And the guest had seen it too.

'My, my ...,' he whispered gently, stretching his large hand across the drum-tight skin, causing a shudder through her body. He leant over her. 'My hand – is it too cold?' he asked softly, raising it. Leah was shaking her head and still trying to regain composure, when her master interjected: 'She thinks you are putting her skin to the test, assessing its saleability, like one of your hides. Always the merchant . . .'

'Oh no, my lord,' Leah whispered up to the guest then saw that he was smiling. He was much older than Merek – round in the face and silver-haired. She knew that sometimes it could be nice with older men but not always. She was staring at his hands. Merek untied her then lifted her in all her nudity, apart from the little oval swatch of soft leather that came with her, and put her directly into the guest's broad arms. Her heart-surge immediately came again and the guest noticed it, seemingly more than Merek, and drew her close. She remembered to keep her thighs open. The guest noticed the leather and his first sexual act was to place it against her inner flesh where it had opened. 'See, Merek – it adheres.' It was so thin that she could feel the coolness of his pressing fingertips and could count their number. 'So hot, she is, inside . . .,' he murmured. The intimacy of his touching would become his measure and already she was well aroused.

When they took her into the living quarters of the boat, the guest insisted on carrying her, with her knees tucked up and his fingers still attentively in place, steadily drumming against her leather oval. He seemed to sense the beat of her pulse and he mimicked it with the steady thump of this sexual patting. She was already light-headed when Merek broke away from watching and said quietly: 'I have explained to our guest the rules.' He came close and stared into her eyes, searching for assent, which Leah now gave by the merest flicker. 'Good – then we continue,' he declared, and sat down to watch.

An hour-glass was used to gauge the duration of the session of touching during which Leah was forbidden to come. Tonight Leah would lose count of the number of turnings of this glass. When the guest himself at one point suggested she be given a pause for sleep, Merek said: 'I have observed through long practice that exhaustion does not preclude erection in a girl,' and then the guest himself proved this maxim true, for Leah's climax nearly came out – through the soft film of leather and against his fingers – before she managed, at the very last second, to blurt out her pleading. Thus the swapping of the slave between the protagonists had been effected without the crisis of pleasure precipitating and without her feet ever touching the floor. But Merek had first insisted on checking her body closely to ensure that she had not come. He laid her on her back on the table to examine her. 'Please leave her leather undisturbed, if possible, my lord,' the guest whispered. His collusive gaze never left Leah. Her gaze never left his generous hands.

Sleep had now been swept aside by the early nearness of the crisis and by the ensuing fear of Merek's intimate checking after such sweetly knowing touching by this stranger's fingers. The guest then said: 'Pass her again to me – if it please . . .'

During such passing, Leah would normally be kept with her feet off the floor but the guest this time made her stand unsupported. 'Stand astride my lap. There . . .,' he instructed her. Her legs were unsteady after being bundled up yet their very unsteadiness seemed to please him. Leah faced him very nervously indeed, not knowing what to do with her hands, where to look or how to cope with the deeply sexual feelings as he began again to tease and then slowly to peel the thin sticky leather from the mouth of her sex. He set the oval pad carefully aside. 'She glistens . . . I see her virgin's chain is broken in two. Yet my lord does not remove it?'

'No,' Merek answered.

'She is still delightful,' the guest went on, 'still narrow here.' His little finger entered her on a slight up-curve. 'See – the inner lips remain firm and pouted. Very firm . . .' Then he whispered: 'No my dear, you should not close your eyes. I want to look at them.' The tip of his finger, now within her body, began lifting, as if beckoning her to lewdness. Her open legs began shaking quite strongly. She broke the gaze, looking over her shoulder to Merek, as if pleading for help against these feelings. He must surely know how near she was to coming. The guest gently turned her head back, drew her chin forward and softly kissed her, while his finger inserted in her was still lifting and drawing the teetering pleasure slowly out. Leah's hands, which had not known what to do, were now upon the guest's naked forearm, as if to stay the delicious progress of the belly-pulling fingertip. During the long kiss, her tongue in uncontrollable complicity slid into his mouth. His fingertip drew a pleasure too far. Leah moaned and froze; her back arched down so deeply that her belly touched his wilful wrist. Her head sank sideways against his shoulder, her tongue still darting. Soft precursors of this unwanted yet keenly yearned-for climax sucked upon his finger. He tried to lift her on to his lap with his finger still inside her. At that point – when her toes started to leave the floor – she began the urgent pleading that so aroused the two men.

The guest did not really want to hand her back to her owner, did not want that pointy tongue, which had delved so impishly yet lovingly inside his mouth, to poke inside her proper master's. But he too obeyed the rules and Leah now sat sideways on Merek's lap, her thighs still beautifully open, those inner lips still standing stiff – a pouting little cup of flesh in which a quicksilver droplet of her fluid was clinging.

'Come – join in. Do something to her,' Merek invited him. 'She can plead again if we go too far.' And

15

he sucked her ear lobe and turned the hour-glass and the sand again started running.

The guest could not prevent his erection showing through his clothing; Leah was looking at it as he approached her. He knelt – perhaps to hide it – while he spread her legs fully open. He pressed the thin wet oval of leather against the inner surface of her pouting sex, bursting the quicksilver droplet, then smoothing the leather until it moulded to her shape. 'See, Merek – how her knob stands visibly through it.' Leah lay back, gasping softly against her master while the two men gently recommenced touching her. One strand of her chain had become enfolded in the crease between her inner and outer lips. The guest teased it out. Its blue jewels sparkled. Leah watched him and watched Merek's hands round her breasts, his fingers squeezing her nipples; she watched the guest spreading the inner lips of her sex wider with his thumbs, until the edges of the leather pad lifted. He pulled it off her; she moaned. Her inner lips stayed wide open, filmed with glistening silver. Merek turned her head and kissed her lips – a crushing kiss, desirously harsh – and the guest simultaneously started smacking the hot, fully exposed internal flesh of her sex, which pulsed like a bright red beating heart. She felt the tips of his fingers steadily snapping down just below her clitoral knot until it grew as hard as stone and little warm splashes of her liquid silver showered her inner thighs.

The crushing kiss stopped and Leah gulped for air like a drowning person. 'She has beautifully puffy-nippled breasts,' the guest said. 'See how they shake each time her vulva is smacked.' He took one in his wet fingers, rolling the swollen nipple-surround while Merek still cupped the main body of the breast. 'It's soft on the outside, firmer within, as if there is a pithy core.' Then he grasped it as if it were a cow's teat that he was milking. Leah's legs made as if to close. Merek, stroking her ear lobe with his lips, admonished her with a whisper. When the guest's other hand went between her legs and the fingertip pressed that special place, halfway between knob and pee-hole, Leah again pleaded.

'It is all becoming too difficult for her,' Merek sighed. 'Her need to capitulate is too strong. She needs a distraction.'

The two men stood her up, with the guest's hand now coming from behind and under, his fingertip – now the middle one – regaining the same sensitive place, still pressing as they made her walk. Her knob protruded strongly; the mouth of her bottom was hot against the heel of the guest's hand and kept tightening; he could surely feel its tension. After a few paces, Leah stopped, her knees half bent, and began trembling with the want of deliverance. Merek had gone ahead. 'What is it?' the guest whispered. 'Is the pleasure very near?' Leah could only nod, gasping softly, as the delicious trembling in her thighs continued. Then she felt his thumb against the mouth of her bottom, searching out the tight velvet hollow, by turns softly stroking then pressing it. Her bottom wanted to open to take the thumb but she knew that would make her come. The guest waited patiently but did not stay the sexual pressure of his fingertip under her knob or the pressure-stroking of her bottom. 'Fight it,' he coaxed gently as she leant further and more limply forward. His other arm slipped under her hunched nude body to lift her tenderly upright, his hand slipping across her erect nipples, bringing delicious transitory pleasure, eliciting a moan, his fingertips finally lodging in the softness under her arm.

'Please . . .,' Leah begged him, not knowing whether she pleaded for deliverance or delay. The fingertip pressure under her knob retracted but in doing so pulled upon the tender flesh to which it had for so

17

many minutes adhered. The sensation seemed to draw down through her womb and she moaned louder. He thought that he had hurt her and drew her close against his breast. Leah felt a luscious wave of warmth engulfing her and fought back the tears of warmth lest he misinterpret them. She buried her face in his shirt.

'Can you go on, my little one?' the guest-master whispered tenderly and, in answer, Leah reached up and kissed him entreatingly. Realising that he too was trembling, she felt emboldened and kissed his warm belly through the cloth and sensed his breathing change. She wanted to kiss his penis and stir desire there but he drew her up and held her gently at arm's length by her shoulders. Sighing, he looked at her – her face, her breasts, her belly, then back to her face. Voice wavering, he said: 'Stand open.' She edged her feet apart. 'Open . . . more so . . .' She could scarcely hear him. She was watching his face, watching for his gaze to falter. His voice came as a strained whisper: 'Put your hands behind your head.' She heard his deep sigh then felt his fingers, trembling but between her legs again, teasing, then his whole hand enveloping her there – the outer lips, the inner, the knob and all the sensitised flesh within – and very gently squeezing, pulsing, finding her heart's rhythm, taking all the sexual warmth and softness and lovingly kneading.

She heard Merek ahead on deck, calling for Asgal the steersman to assist him. At the mention of that name in such a context, Leah froze.

'What is it, my dear?' the guest asked.

'Nothing . . .,' she murmured. But the guest was not worldly-wise enough to understand the cryptic plea in her voice.

On deck in the warm night air, under his master's direction, Asgal stretched two thick ropes tautly, horizontally, one at belly height, the other at arm's length above it. The guest, with recovered confidence, remained attentive and kept Leah in sexual readiness through gentle provocation while the ropes were being tightened. 'Stand open,' he repeated gently. But it was not sufficient that her thighs obeyed. He worked upon her gently until her body opened too – until the inner lips gaped and his fingertips were able to effect freely sliding pressure-strokes up the smooth wet inner walls. The stimulation induced by being stroked inside her body was intense. She tried not to make a murmur in Asgal's presence and tried to conceal the guest's actions under her hands. 'I want your bottom open too,' he whispered. 'Now, and in your master's presence.' Leah closed her eyes as the finger and thumb of his other hand softly invaded the crease of her bottom and gently pinched the lower rim of the smooth, pouting mouth, which tightened involuntarily. 'Keep your feet flat down. Stretch your toes. There . . . let all the tightness slip away.' The inveigling finger and thumb, gaining surer purchase, gently pinched the fleshy rim until Leah moaned and opened. But the thumb did not go fully in. The lower rim was simply held in an ever-tightening pincer-grip, inducing a delicious, dull, strong pressure-pain, like a swollen blister being squeezed. And all the while, the pleasure of the precisely focused masturbation just below her knob was coming keener and keener at the front. Leah quaked on the verge of faintness or coming, clasping her hands about the hand that bestowed such pleasure at the front, not to stay it but to be as one with it. Then Merek's voice broke in: 'Thank you, Asgal. I'll call you, should you be needed further.' Leah opened her eyes to see Asgal leering at her then sneaking off into the darkness.

Merek turned and saw his guest with Leah slumped against him, her hands still enfolded weakly about the hand invading her belly. For a moment, as Merek

19

hesitated, Leah feared reproach. She had not intended to conceal herself from her master but rather from Asgal. She beckoned with her eyes and opened her hands and Merek came to her, bestowing ardent kisses on her face, breasts and neck, even as the guest's finger and thumb, in her crease, still gripped her flesh as if it were a swollen blister.

'She is very near to climax, Merek,' the guest observed.

'The rope will fix that,' Merek answered calmly. 'It will numb her and allow more time and scope in our investigations.' Leah shivered; her flesh was frightened by these threats. Merek simply put his arms around her even as his guest still gripped the throbbing rim of her bottom. Her rigid nipples poked through Merek's shirt.

Over Merek's shoulder she glimpsed Asgal, shifting in the darkness. She dreaded that throughout her tortured pleasurings he would still be there. But she dared not warn her master for fear of drawing unwanted questions. There was nothing she could do to prevent Asgal's witnessing all that followed, hearing every moan of shameful pleasure that Leah uttered and discovering all the ways of intimate touching that her body openly craved.

The two masters lifted her astride the lower rope, tying her wrists over the rope above her head, and tightening the lower rope so she was balanced with her feet just off the decking. While the rope pressed into the saddle of flesh between her anus and her sex, the guest paid homage to her puffy nipples by sucking them into elongated teats. Soon the numbness came between her legs, then a feeling as of soft needles being pushed into her sex and bottom. After a few minutes, Merek asked: 'Can you feel this?' He was touching her.

'Yes, master,' she murmured.

'Are you sure?'

She nodded uncertainly. For his fingers, which seemed to be touching her at the front, felt like thickly gloved thumbs probing clumsily into the burgeoning numbness.

'Let me touch her bottom,' the guest said. Merek relinquished his place and Leah saw that his fingers were saturated with her wetness; so numb was she that she hadn't felt it coming out. She shuddered as he ran those same fingers up her belly to her breasts, already sensitised through the sucking. 'She can feel that,' the guest observed. Then she felt the guest's fingers pushing down against the resilience of the rope that she hung astride, then smoothly, numbly, up into her bottom, which did not tighten. The pushing fingers forced her belly forwards, forcing the tight rope against her knob, forcing soft long needles of numbness through it and up into her womb. Her bottom started to tighten against waves of fine hot needles.

'She's coming,' the guest shouted.

'Help me lift her off the rope.'

Still impaled on the fingers and tethered by her wrists, Leah, stretched and moaning, was lifted to the deck. She could not stand but only slumped forwards against her master. Electric needles of pleasure moved in continuous waves up the insides of her legs from her knees to her crotch. The guest's fingers adhered to the tightly spasming muscle as they slid out of her bottom. Merek unfastened her wrists then carried her quickly below deck and laid her on her back on the bed but did not close the door. Despite her whimpers of protest, the guest massaged the needle-prickled flesh of her inner thighs until it felt as if the needles had shortened and blunted and the waves came fainter and these sensations retreated from the surface but seemed to have lodged within her womb, as if warm spice-water was being gently flushed inside there.

21

The men asked her more than once whether the pleasure had been triggered. Leah murmured that she did not know for sure. Then the guest spread her legs out properly. 'How does it feel there?' he said gently. Leah shook her head, unwilling to admit that the feeling of anticipation was coming back. When his tongue approached her knob enquiringly – even before it touched – she moaned again. When the touch came, her shudder told that all the feeling was back; in fact it was stronger. He tried to pace the touches – making little licks, not true sucking kisses – and every time her knob pulsed or retracted or her belly cramped, he would pause while Merek simply kissed her on the lips or breasts or under her arms until the licking could resume. Then, at a nod from Merek, the guest disrobed completely. Leah looked sidelong from the bed at his very swollen penis and cast quick glances at the open doorway, for fear of Asgal's presence.

'Ah – the glass needs turning again,' observed the guest, misinterpreting Leah's glances.

Her first definite climax was achieved soon afterwards, during the stretching of penetration by the guest's penis, sheathed in soft, oiled deerskin. The second came when the strap of punishment was laid precisely on the bridge of flesh between her sex and anus, where she had been put astride the rope; Merek used it until the imprint of the rope had disappeared beneath the swelling. The guest was all the while touching her at the front as she lay belly-down upon his palm; it was the touching during punishment that made this second pleasure come. At the moment of coming Leah glimpsed Asgal on the stairs beyond the open doorway but this did not stop her pleasure – to her shame it only made it stronger.

Afterwards, she could not stand and could not close her thighs but did not need to. Instead the guest lay with her, kissing her swollen bridge of flesh. 'She reacts

22

well to punishment, Merek,' he said. Then he said that he wanted to explore this reaction further. 'Let me whip her buttocks.' He used his personal crop; its fine elastic stem was wound with a strip of thin leather. He made her lie face down with her sex on a pillow. 'Open your thighs about the pillow. Now grip it – yes, as if you are making love.' He whipped her bottom in that position. Then he rested while she whimpered softly. 'Now, spread your cheeks with your hands. Wider – let us see this precious place.' He whipped there too, until her anus burned. 'A little wine, Merek. I fear I may have gone too far. Thank you – just the jug.' He sat beside her trembling body on the bed and dripped the cooling salve against the burning mouth of her bottom, smoothing each drip with the tips of his fingers. She felt his other hand sliding beneath. 'It's still up – and bigger, I'd say, and harder too, like an unripe seed-pod.' Leah felt his tongue licking her naked shoulder and his cool wine-wet finger-strokes on the hot mouth of her bottom and his gently rolling grip upon her slippery clitoris and suddenly she grunted and thrust, belly-thrust his hand into the pillow, tried to thrust it through the bed and then the climax came that felt so wet and burning and so cruelly intense.

'Perhaps we should let her sleep now, Merek?'

'Not yet.' She knew from his tone that her master was irked by her coming. Three times it had happened – each time with the guest and each time with less resistance. Leah's hand reached for Merek but he kept back and it was left to the guest to stroke her body very gently till her tears were quelled. He turned her on her back with the pillow still beneath her. 'Let me look at you. There ... You are beautiful in form and deed. Were I a younger man ...' He sighed. 'But it is fortunate your master is not jealous.' He glanced enquiringly at Merek.

'She shall continue to please you – it is her privilege, while I will it.'

'She pleases by her very existence – I am the privileged one here, Merek, by the generosity of your acquaintance and by the bond of trade that ties us. But I never, even in my keenest imaginings, dreamt of treasures such as these.' He ran the tips of his fingers down Leah's body and made her shiver.

But Leah would pay for her lapses of self-control.

Her master did not wait for his guest to leave. Under the pretext of a passing-over he lifted her from the bed and whipped her with the guest's own crop while she stood bent over the cabin table with her open sex astride the corner. She was forced on to tiptoes, her back hollowed and her buttocks projecting. Merek whipped fiercely, in jealousy, through her gasping tears of supplication and almost too far.

His guest finally intervened. 'May I touch her, my lord?'

'But of course . . .' Merek, his nostrils still flared from the cruel exertion, suddenly seemed to apprehend the depths of his excesses and stood aside in an attempt to regain composure. Leah's tear-stricken face was pitiful and pleading. The guest, now seated on the other side of Leah, tactfully encouraged her to stand straight and turned her to face him before putting his arms around her waist as she stood there sobbing. He simply held her till the sobs subsided. Then he kissed her burning belly very lightly, inducing another shiver. Then he turned her round and kissed the livid, still-swelling weals that her master had just put across her bottom. He kissed very slowly and lightly, causing shivers to mingle with the burning stinging. He called for more wine and Leah thought he meant to apply it to her weals or even to the mouth of her bottom again; instead, he offered the cup to her. 'Take it, my

24

dear. There . . .' As she took it in both hands he turned her fully facing him again and as she drank he eased apart her thighs and spoke across her to the sullen Merek: 'I sense – indeed I see – that there is good arousal yet within her, my lord, though I fear the hour is late.'

'The glass is not beyond another turning, my lord.' But Leah sensed resentment in Merek's tone.

'Did you hear that, Leah? There – give me the cup before you spill it.' He took it from her then clasped her round the waist with one arm and slowly tongue-kissed her umbilicus while he touched her between the legs. She made droplets of liquid on his milking fingers, which he gently reapplied to the aroused fleshy parts that had escaped the whipping. Then he squeezed firmly the two places where her jewelled chains passed through her inner lips, increasing their swelling steadily and deliberately to the point of pain.

Merek's attention gradually returned. He came closer to Leah, without warmth but with interest in what his guest was doing. Then he said: 'You were telling me, my friend, of the little instrument that one can use to develop the clitoris to a surer protrusion.'

'She does not need it,' the guest answered without taking his eyes off Leah.

'Nevertheless, I would like to see it shown.'

'So be it.' The guest sighed. He moved his chair nearer the table then moved Leah back until her buttocks touched the edge, instructing her: 'Thighs open . . . Lift up a little, on to your toes. Now, Merek, I shall need your assistance.'

Leah shuddered when, under the guest's direction, her master's fingers, up-curved, thrust inside her, pressing up behind her knob until it stood out. 'Now, Merek, draw back her foreskin – all the way, if you will.' The stretching nearly hurt Leah. She pleaded with her eyes for Merek to kiss her then – just one sweet kiss while she was so stretched and pushed out, all for him. But it was the guest's lips that pressed their moist envelopment briefly round her knob and the pleasure almost came.

Then the guest took from a little case a tiny instrument like a toothpick but with a smooth pad at the tip. This tip he first dipped in a tiny bottle of oil then brought up to her quivering knob. She gasped as it was rubbed slowly, gently all around the root of her extended knob and into the juncture with the drawn-back foreskin. The sliding pressure of the tip was gradually increased until all the oil had exuded from the pad, whereupon the tip was soaked again and reapplied. Such precisely focused pressure fed a peculiar arousal that was specific to this form of stimulation – she wanted to escape it yet when it drew away she wanted it even more. The pointy tip, pressing and circling the root of her knob, imparted such exquisite feelings. The oil had a warmth like unguent; the scent was like cloves.

'It grows – though little by little and slowly. Can you see it?' She could now feel her erection standing stiffly like a rod.

'There is no hurry,' Merek whispered, while Leah's chains were quaking. All the while, Merek had two fingers hooked within Leah's sex, applying the steady outward pressure behind her knob, thrusting it forward for the treatment that his guest was meting. Through his clothing she sensed Merek's erection brushing her thigh and this caused a pulse of pleasure far deeper within her than the root of her knob. She tried to push out her erection still further, to please her master. He commented on its jumpy movements when the oil-soaked tip of delicious torture touched it again. He baited her gently, through his guest, telling him that his slave's pleasure often came too swiftly and needed further control. The expelled oil from the repeated treatments ran down her shaking labia to the lower lobes. One large drop splashed between her toes and made her tense and moan. Had they touched her at that moment then, for sure, she would have come to climax. Merek recognised the signs. 'Stop, my friend, for a little while,' he said then whispered something further to the guest, who took Leah into his arms directly and kissed her.

Her lips were desirous; her kissing was deep; she did this for herself and for Merek's pleasure too because she knew her master now wanted it. Within his tense expression, she saw desire steadily surmounting rejection. She could feel the guest's erection and as she fingered it she could feel warm dampness coming anew from its tip, for he was leaking just as she was.

Later, as Leah lay face down across the guest's lap, with the swollen glans of his leather-sheathed penis just within her sex, keeping its entrance stretched, he started masturbating her bottom very skilfully with his fingers. The tightness he induced in her sex made his penis squeeze from its sheath, come out of her body completely, slip and jump in sexual nervousness, skin to skin, and pump semen against her naked, engorged knob. She climaxed very strongly, very pleasurably. The guest turned her over to look and found her erection standing like a little trembling penis drowning in his cream. Her wanton fingers sought his sticky glans and, squeezing, found it still rich with issue.

Merek left the two of them together: he liked her to be had by other men but Leah knew he could not always bear to witness it. Leah was still playing with the guest's penis; she could not stop now, the desire lay so ingrained within her. The heat from its bulb made the stickiness turn to silken smoothness as its yield of semen quickly dried. Left alone with this man, she felt empowered. She did not put the smooth bulb in her mouth but peeled the film of dried semen from it in

27

small morsels and consumed the flakes while her lover watched. The flakes melted back to pungent stickiness on her tongue. The protracted peeling and progressive eating of his semen made his penis swell anew, as Leah knew it would. She proceeded systematically until all the dried issue was removed and consumed. Then she crouched and kissed the junction of his sac and rigid penis. The skin there was smooth and hot against her lips. His fingertips rubbed her swollen clitoris through the dense film of spilled semen, which would not dry there for she herself was still leaking. She put her fingers under his sac and the flesh there felt firm and shiny hard as if he were swelling inside, as if the yield that she had drawn out of him and massaged dry and eaten was not the limit and even more was building up inside him.

Leah coaxed him in this rigid state; she kissed his stem, kissed under his sac and gently, nervously pumped just the glans of his penis, as if she were unsure quite how to do it. She put her fingertips round the rim of the glans and gently tugged, repeatedly, as if it were bedded through a tight fleshy ring from which it could not be retracted. The erection hardened as she knew it would. Then she remembered the collar. Leaving hold of the penis she leant across to the bedside drawer and found the little strip of leather, with its sliding bead and adjustable loop at one end. From a distance, she had once seen Merek using this, fastening it round his flesh when he lay with another girl. But Leah was uncertain exactly how this collar should be applied – whether round both sex and sac or simply round the base of the stem. She chose the latter. Even as she began to tighten the collar, his sex began to swell very hard; the bead pressed into the base of the fleshy tube on the underside of the stem. Her lover's breathing suddenly changed and Leah knew this instrument must be working its spell.

She now kissed below the sac, and the flesh felt even harder and hotter than before. She considered trying to put her fingers into him – up his bottom, as some men liked – to try to squeeze this hardness from inside. Then she realised his penis was still swelling – and now jerking as if it wanted to come – but she was not touching it and the guest was no longer touching her. His fingers had bunched as if in spasm. Leah kissed them then laid her cheek against the burning stem of his penis. She could feel the swollen tension, like a cord inside it being drawn ever tighter and being plucked deeply and strongly and repeatedly. When she drew her cheek away, the penis followed; deep ripples shook her lover's belly; his stem, swollen very fat above the constriction of its collar, jerked as if an invisible stick were smacking it. Leah took part of it in her mouth – just the head – and held it warmly and tight, waiting for the invisible smacking to deliver up its yield.

A deep wrenching groan shook the guest's whole body; his belly thrust his penis deeper into her mouth; Leah sucked and the head was racked with jerky spasms. But no discernible fluid came out, no taste of semen, and her mouth finally released it. Her lover lay helplessly, his penis pulsing but nothing emerging, and Leah watched, transfixed by delicious arousal tinged with awe. Then she remembered the collar. Swiftly she released its potent grip. There was a groove round the base of the penis and a deep impression where the captive bead had pressed into the tube. The penis was still hard, jerking at intervals, but still with nothing coming out. The guest lay exhausted, his eyes closed tight. Leah kissed his breasts then laid her cheek upon his belly and shyly fingered the groove that she had made in the base of his penis. She put the tip of her finger into the round indentation in the tube beneath and gently tried to rub the mark away. He gasped softly and the awed excitement that Leah had at first

29

felt was now swamped by her arousal. She again took
the head of his penis into her mouth; there was but a
faint salty taste of semen, yet his pleasure had been
wrenching. Leah sat up and clasped his swollen sac,
squeezing it gently, half hoping it would force the
issue. 'What was it?' she whispered, turning to look at
him. His eyes were still closed. She kissed him on the
lips and squeezed his sac again. 'What was it?'

He shook his head.

'Was it good, the collar?'

'Oh, yes,' he sighed.

'And is all the fluid still inside – for me?'

His strength of swelling told her it was. Yet his body
bore the languor of exhaustion. 'Make spoons,' Leah
whispered. She snuggled on her side, her back against
him. She took his hand and put it around her belly.

'Shall my lord be travelling with us?' she asked: that
would be nice, and she could work upon his pleasure.

'I must leave before dawn. I have a journey –
business to engage, that will take some days at best.'

'Has my lord a special slave, at home?' she ventured
boldly.

'Not a slave . . .'

'Then a lady?'

'Yes, my wife.' He sighed.

'And you love her? Is she beautiful?'

'Too many questions, my child . . . Yes I love her
very deeply. She is not quite so young as you but she
is very beautiful – high-born and graceful. And men
admire her. Yet she accepted me – a common merchant.'

'And does my lord admire me?'

He turned her to face him. 'You know the answer.'

Leah smiled warmly and kissed him and climbed
upon his torso and made him kiss her bud that he had
rendered so swollen. Then she made spoons with him
again and milked his naked penis with her hungry

body, wriggling, intensifying the feelings for him, seeking to milk out all the fluid she knew was bottled up inside him. When she felt the edge of pleasure tighten hard in his penis, she drew it out trembling and, making a claw of her other hand, used that to grip just the glans. Suddenly she felt the force of all the pent-up semen spurting hotly against her fingers. She kept her hand in place until his gasping had subsided and the pulsing had stopped completely, then she clenched the shaft and masturbated it quickly, tightly, with the slippery goo squeezing through her clenched fist, not stopping until the wrenching groan came again, as of a creature in the throes of torture. And then her lover of this night was truly spent. Before she had finished licking her fingers he was asleep and he did not stir until dawn was breaking.

While Leah lay with her lover that night, another tryst was taking place a half day's journey away, in a sumptuous bed in a stately mansion. It was a congress of a young woman of sophistication – now a trades-man's restive wife – and a highly fortunate head groom.

Through repeatedly denying her pandering old hus-band whenever he was home, Lauren's passion smoul-dered unchecked within her. Whenever he was away she had Kapler shed the necessary spark to make that passion burn. It mattered not that her head groom might privately use the servant-girls in fleshly fashion. It gave him panache; it strengthened what he brought to bear; and it endowed him with experience. And now there was a new and younger groom to be subsumed into Lauren's expanding circle of illicit learning.

# 3

# Lady Lauren

Lady Lauren arose from the bed – her husband's bed – in which, in her husband's absence, her head groom now reclined, tired but not yet exhausted by her attentions. Despite the delicious tell-tale marks of their joint emissions upon the pillows and sheets, he still retained the erection she had induced at the start of their evening's tryst. In this respect, as in many others, Kapler was a quite different article from her husband. Lauren prided herself in having made him so – or rather, in having forged his latent prowess into its present impassioned state, for one cannot fabricate a silken bolster from an old boar's scrotum. Her husband was living proof of this. And she took quiet pleasure in the thought of a relationship at once kept secret from her husband but acknowledged quite openly in his own servants' quarters.

Nude and smiling, curling her silken blonde locks coquettishly around her fingers, Lauren tiptoed across the room and tugged upon the sash that summoned her chambermaid. 'No – don't cover yourself, Kapler. I want her to see – why shouldn't she? She must learn these things at some point. Lie back. Put your arms under your pillow. There . . . expressive, beautiful and proud.' Lauren sat on the edge of the bed and leant over him, kissing his lips, tonguing them, feeling her nipples coming erect again with the weight of dangling in her breasts, the nearness of his chest hairs, the tightness in his belly under the light stroking of her fingertips. It is a good way to kiss a man – with his hands imprisoned, out of the way, so he cannot take you in his arms and you remain in control and he can do nothing but react passively to the stimulation. She had had men ejaculate simply through the act of her kissing them while she was naked, nervously touching their naked supine bodies but not touching the penis in any way. This phenomenon was beautifully rewarding – for the man's belly would be flooded in semen while his pride was drowned in shame. And Lauren could then make amends by licking and drinking every pool and globule from his flesh then tonguing her victim deeply in the mouth, returning his yield to him, smearing it slowly and sexually round his tongue. And his erection would never wane. Her tongue now laved the last traces of shared semen into Kapler's mouth and she glimpsed his erection bobbing harder and straighter. Then, after a barely audible knock, the bedroom door opened.

A petite, dark-haired and quite pretty girl entered. Lauren retained her position, naked on the bed beside the equally naked Kapler, and she watched the girl freeze then, trembling, begin to turn back towards the door. 'No, stay, Deneca,' Lauren said. 'Come here, girl.' She waited until the young girl shuffled closer, eyes downcast in embarrassment. 'Did I not ring for you?'

'Yes, mistress,' came the murmured reply.

'Look at me, please, when you answer.'

The girl raised her terrified eyes to the stark scene. 'Yes, ma'am, you did.' After that first instruction, Lauren was pleased to observe that the girl's gaze, when it faltered, only did so after nervously inquisitive glances towards the head groom's naked midriff, crowned by that blatant erection.

33

'The sheets have become soiled – a little accident . . . You understand me?'

'Yes, ma'am.' The girl was barely audible.

'Then you know about such things?'

'Oh, no, mistress.' The girl looked mortified. Her cheeks glowed a beautiful, youthful red.

'But you said you understood how my sheets had become soiled.'

'I meant only that . . . only that I would change them, directly, ma'am.'

'Wait.' For the girl had taken a half-step forward and had slightly raised her arms, almost as if to encourage the naked pair to vacate the bed. Evidently she was quick-witted – Lauren would allow her that – but that alone would never save her from the present inquisition. Her eyes were an uncommon shade of green – quite attractive. Undoubtedly she was a virgin; her demeanour spoke it; the below-stairs tittle-tattle confirmed it. Virgins – of either sex – are always the best for training: since their experience is so restricted, their imagination roams wild. Lauren could see some of that suppressed waywardness in those eyes.

'Deneca – your gaze is quite brazen, for one so young. Have you never seen a male disposed in such a state?'

'Only the horses, ma'am,' the girl responded un-blinkingly, and Lauren inadvertently laughed out loud.

'Thank you, miss – young madam: you may go now, Deneca. Attend to the laundry later.'

Lauren waited until she had curtsied and left. Then she turned to her accomplice. 'I like her, Kapler.'

'She has a cheek.'

'Surely she flattered you?' But his demeanour hinted at some ill-feeling towards the girl. Perhaps he had already attempted approaches? No matter . . . She would need Kapler's assistance in what she was planning, so she tested the water: 'I thought I would pair her with Ean, the new groom – Ean and Denni,

34

what do you think?' Kapler looked away. Lauren stealthily ran her fingertips across his torso and clasped his erection round the base, steadily increasing the pressure of squeezing. Kapler did not resist. Smiling wickedly, Lauren watched the glans swelling. 'We could train them together,' she whispered. 'You could deal with young Denni if she becomes fractious. And I with Ean ...' And, maintaining her merciless grip about his swelling stem, she reached down and sealed the bargain by kissing and licking him very lewdly on the lips.

'Ean! Ean – wake up!'

Ean opened his eyes, blinked and gradually took in his surroundings – the hayloft where he had finally fallen asleep after shifting so many sacks of feed.

'Ean!'

His vision slowly focused on the urgent face of the girl who was shaking him back to reality. 'Denni – what is it? What's happened?' He scrambled to his knees, brushing the hay from his tunic.

'The mistress wants us – all the servants – assembled in her drawing-room. Now!'

'All of us – why?'

'I don't know. It must be important. Don't look so worried – just make yourself presentable. And be quick about it ...' Denni began pulling away the stray strands of hay, then started to smooth his hair, until she caught his stare, when she suddenly stopped, embarrassed. 'Come on,' she mumbled, turning, and disappeared swiftly down the ladder, leaving him wondering more about her than about the mysterious assembly. Why had she troubled to find him and show concern for his appearance? He paused at the slatted window to watch her hurrying back across the yard and glancing behind her as if suddenly fearful he might catch up with her.

Ean was the last to arrive at the drawing-room. He crept in quietly, controlling his breathing, for the room, though crowded, was completely silent. The servants were arranged in little groups – stable-hands, kitchen-staff, chambermaids. Some of the women were seated – uneasily, self-consciously. Denni was standing by a window. Her cheeks were still flushed with the exertion of hurrying; her gaze met Ean's for a moment before she looked away, staring expectantly at the mistress, who stood grave-faced by the great fireplace with Kapler beside her.

Lady Lauren took a step forward and began to speak in a soft but measured tone: 'I thank you all for assembling so promptly in response to my request.' She glanced pointedly at Ean, who bit his lip and uneasily looked round to see if the others had noticed the reference to his tardiness. When he looked back at his mistress, he caught a transient smile – again directed at him – before her expression returned to solemnity. 'As you will know, my husband and I value loyalty in our servants. For me it rides above all the virtues. So when there is breach of loyalty, it is a matter of the utmost gravity – in fact, it is a poison for which the only remedy is excision.' Lady Lauren's determined gaze swept across the anxious, silent, trembling faces. Then she said: 'I shall come directly to the point: there is a thief among us.'

There were gasps from some of the women; the men stood silently exchanging guilty expressions. Ean was fearful now, since he was the only person to have been singled out by his mistress's gaze. In fact she was looking at him again when she declared: 'My emerald necklace – the treasured betrothal gift from my husband – has gone missing from my bedchamber.' Again there came gasps from the women, and whispered exchanges, abruptly cut short by the mistress's next remark: 'But now it has been recovered . . .' And to

36

prove it, she held up the beautiful necklace of bright gold set with glowing green stones, as she again surveyed the anxious faces arraigned before her. 'And it was found, where . . . ?' She stepped back. 'Please tell them, Kapler.'

Kapler too looked pale but his voice was firm, though his hands seemed unsure – whether to clasp together or enfold with his arms or reach out to the assembly. In the end he stood almost to attention as he spoke: 'On your instruction, my lady, I searched the maids' quarters first. I found the necklace in your second-chambermaid's box.'

Amid the gasps and hubbub, Ean felt as if he had been pole-axed. Denni . . . How could it be? All eyes were now upon her and she stood as if turned to stone.

'Come forward, girl,' the mistress beckoned. Denni didn't move. Some of the women began shaking their heads; others bit their lips. The assembly parted to let Kapler through to Denni. He dragged her by the arm to her mistress, who addressed her with a trembling voice: 'Why did you do this, Deneca? You could never show such jewels. Was it from spite?'

'Mistress – no!' But Denni looked at the floor.

'Then why?'

'I didn't take it. I didn't take anything.'

'Then how did it come to be with your things?'

Denni just shook her head and bit her lip. Murmurs of disapproval came from some of the other servants. Denni turned on them. 'I didn't take it!' she cried out. Ean saw the tears running down her burning cheeks. He looked to the mistress, who seemed almost as distraught as Denni as she sealed the maid's fate. 'It is a matter of loyalty and trust. I do not see you as a bad girl. But whatever your reasons, your loyalty stands gravely tainted by the issue. Trust between us is gone. Is there anyone here who will gainsay this?' She looked slowly around the room. Ean's tongue cleaved to the roof of his mouth. 'Deneca, I am afraid you must leave my service forthwith.' A gap opened between Denni and the door. Ean's heart sank to the soles of his boots as he watched the poor creature turn to go.

'Wait!' said the mistress, clasping her by the wrist. She took the necklace from Kapler and pressed it into the girl's hand. 'Take it. I want you to keep it, notwithstanding. It matches your pretty eyes.'

'No!' Denni cried. 'I never took it before nor shall I take it now!' And she threw the necklace to the floor and ran sobbing from the room.

Kapler began ushering out the servants. 'Stay behind, Kapler . . . and Ean, too, if you will,' said the mistress. Ean, jarred by the mention of his name, felt his heart pounding as he waited guiltily for the room to clear. His mind raced to fathom the reason for his singling-out by the mistress. When she looked at him he glimpsed compassion in her gaze before he was compelled to look away; so many emotions raged within him.

Lady Lauren walked over to him. 'That was very unfortunate,' she said gently. 'For the world, I would not have wished it. You liked her, I understand?'

Ean could not easily answer. He hardly knew Denni; she was attractive and warm-hearted and she was honest – of that he felt sure, but until today the thought that he might feel anything deeper for her had not really occurred to him. He glanced up at his mistress without replying.

'Thank you, Kapler,' Lady Lauren said and Ean heard the door closing behind the head groom before she continued in a soft voice: 'It is difficult to speak of such matters of the heart – I understand this. But Deneca often spoke of you.'

'She did?' Ean was surprised and bewildered by this revelation.

'Very warmly . . . and I could see in your face your concern for her just now.'

'I cannot believe she would do such a thing, my lady.'

'Nor could I at first. But the evidence is compelling and the denial was weak,' she said firmly. 'This household cannot suffer such a blighting of trust. But your friend shall not go empty-handed: I have instructed that she be paid her dues and more besides. One must hope that she learns from all of this and that loyalty rates better with her in the future.' Her expression turned from firmness to kindness as she looked at Ean again and sighed: 'You need the air, Ean. We both do. Saddle my horse. Come with me. Take the bay.'

They rode for perhaps an hour, in short gallops interspersed with canters but mostly at a walk, moving ever deeper into the woodland bordering the estate. The mistress appeared to take no obvious route but Ean was content to let her lead, for that allowed him to ponder the day's cheerless events. He searched his mind for anything over recent days that might have betokened Denni's interest in him. He recalled little incidents – glances perhaps, and cheeky remarks, and always her heart-warming smile. She had spoken of one day leaving service and seeking work along the waterways; it seemed a strange thing for a girl to want: perhaps she was not at ease here. But she was always kind and generous to him. The more he thought about her now, the more clearly he pictured her lovely face – her black, black hair, her soft warm lips and eyes as green as jade. It was true – that emerald necklace would indeed have suited her beauty. Why had he not returned her interest or spoken to her more often? Perhaps events might then have taken a different turn.

When he looked up he saw that they were emerging into a small glade with a shallow, sun-dappled, reed-filled pool at the end. The place was unfamiliar to Ean but the mistress seemed acquainted with it. She dismounted, allowing the reins of her stallion to hang loose. Mistress and stallion went forward and stooped to drink from the pool. They made a pleasant scene – the horse arching his strong neck, Lady Lauren crouched, back-lit by the softened sunbeams, scooping the dripping water into her delicate hand and drinking, careless that it spilled in dark blotches over the breast of her tightly buttoned tunic. She too was beautiful – older than Denni but finely-featured, and very elegant. Her tunic top had an extra, belted fastening that served to accentuate her breasts by constricting her waist. As she turned and he saw her in full profile, Ean could not help but imagine her nude.

Unlike Denni, the mistress seemed well aware of her own beauty, but that did not diminish it. All the male servants were envious of the master's choice and even more so of the special status that the head groom seemed to hold with her. So Ean felt pleased and a little proud that his lady had chosen him rather than Kapler to escort her on her ride.

Lady Lauren looked up at him. 'Ean, come and drink.' Self-consciously he dismounted and led his horse to the edge of the pool but kept hold of her reins with one hand as he stooped to take water. Lady Lauren gave a little chiding laugh. 'You fear her escape?'

'Habit, my lady.'

'Leave her free a moment and come here.' Docilely he submitted, finding himself on one knee before his mistress and suffering the unfamiliar pleasure of re-ceiving ice-cold water tipped from the slender bowl of her cupped palms. Her small cold fingertips touching his open lips sent shivers down his spine. He had never been so close to his mistress; in fact he had never touched her and now she was touching him in this intimate way, deliberately touching his lips as she administered the water. He closed his eyes then suddenly felt a shock – the beautiful sweet arousing wanton sensation of her lips, so small and soft and deliciously cold against his open mouth, closing now upon his lower lip and then upon the upper, sucking it as if it were a warm fruit, and then her tongue, a little darting urgent hot tongue exploring inside his mouth, and then her sigh of satisfaction as her hand came so expertly upon the captive flesh now straining against his breeches.

'There – I have the upper hand and you shall do my bidding.'

He felt something being slipped around his left wrist and he looked down to see a loop of rope encircling it. He threw a questioning glance at his mistress, who only kissed him again while she tightened the loop. She then stood up and tugged the length of rope. 'Come, my captive groom, that we might begin your grooming.' Aroused and spellbound under the sexual promise of the unknown, Ean rose and allowed his mistress to lead him as she chose. She was desirable and evidently experienced; he was a novice but a willing participant in her game. Her allure was intense; already he craved more of those deeply sensual kisses. But as she tugged the rope again, he was shy of moving, so evident was his state of arousal. Lady Lauren only smiled and whispered: 'Perhaps I should have tied the loop around that . . . great thing . . .' She stepped closer, took hold of it through his breeches and, as she kissed him on the lips again, squeezed the glans of his penis with a slow sensual pressure. He felt his erection subside a little then swell again even harder. When she drew back, still stroking it, her teeth were gritted and her eyes flashed wickedly.

Still holding the end of the rope, she went to her horse and took an object from the saddlebag. It was smooth and cylindrical. 'I had it fashioned of soapstone, of a sort denser than the norm, and of a girth between a man's and a horse's.' Then Ean saw what it was. Lady Lauren carefully deposited it in the chill water at the edge of the pool. 'Now – over here with you.' She drew Ean by his tethered wrist to an old, low-branched tree, stopping at a place where a fallen log lay immediately beneath one of the horizontal branches. She made him step over the log and then turned him to face the pool. In a moment she was standing on the log, tying his left wrist up to the branch then using the excess rope to tie the other wrist similarly. Ean made no move to resist, no verbal protest. He was under the spell of those sensual kisses, the like of which he had never experienced before.

A peculiar yet intensely pleasurable feeling pervaded his being as he watched this beautiful sexual creature freely working upon him with such purpose while he remained so tamely submissive to her whims. His mistress plainly understood the effect of what she was doing. 'Good boy,' she murmured, gripping his shackled wrists while she kissed his ear lobe and blew softly into his ear, making him shudder until his erection hurt. 'Good boy . . .' He felt her excitement too as she began unbuttoning his tunic and shirt. Her lips caressed his neck as she fumbled with the buttons of her own tunic top, then wrenched it open to the waist-belt.

He gasped as her pert hot breasts with cold little nipples pressed against his chest and she clung to him and bit his neck – bit hard, with a sucking bite that went on and on. She reached down to try to free his penis but could not without breaking breast contact, which she seemed not to want to do, so she squeezed the glans mercilessly through his clothing until he could feel the warm wetness leaking. Then she shivered as though a small paroxysm of pleasure had moved through her body. When she drew back there was a smear of blood on her lips, so intense had been her

42

kissing. He glanced down to where her neckline plunged to the opening of her tunic but the two flaps had almost come together again, concealing her breasts. All that remained in the tantalising gap beneath was a delicious glimpse of an ivory-smooth swell of belly and a peep of perfectly oval umbilicus.

'Your gaze is very forward, young man.' Lauren smiled, stepped down from the log and stared at his midriff. 'And your demeanour is brazen. Let us see if this brazenness stands the test.' She began to unbuckle his breeches. Ean's gaze lifted skyward from self-conscious shame as the cool air bathed his exposed loins. He felt his breeches being dragged to his knees and the flaps of his shirt being drawn up and tied through the restraints at his wrists. Lauren had climbed back on to the log and, as she did the tying, his erection brushed her tightly leather-clad upper thigh. When she moved across to tie the other flap, his naked penis briefly rolled against the delicious cool tightness of those leather-clad thighs and slipped into the gap between them. She evidently felt its sudden pulse, for she immediately stopped and, opening her tunic, slid her arms around his back, her hands under his shirt, her fingertips lightly exploring his shoulder-blades, even as her upper arms squeezed him captive and those cold, lovely nipples pressed into his bare chest again and the cool pressure of her smoothly clad thighs slowly increased around the hot shaft of his penis.

Then she kissed him, with a long slow sucking biting of his lower lip as she held him tight, unmoving now, apart from that sucking and the steadily strengthening pulses she provoked in his penis. He could feel them coming from deeper and deeper within, like a swelling ache that seemed to burgeon low down against his backbone. He knew that, if she were to move against him, the pleasure would surely come and, so nakedly pressed against her, so clamped between her tight thighs, he would never be able to control its emission, which would surely besmirch the shiny leather. He closed his eyes tightly and gritted his teeth. Then suddenly the contact was broken; her fingers and arms slid away; he felt cool air all around him and, when he opened his eyes, Lauren was standing on the ground just watching him. She smiled as the tremors in his erection slowly diminished. He knew then that his mistress would be merciless in the way that she administered pleasure.

With mounting sexual apprehension and a delicious dryness in his throat he watched her turn and walk calmly to the pool, then retrieve the dripping instrument and return to him. She paused, her fingertips running repeatedly over the rounded tip then testing the smoothness of the shaft, then clasping it, barely able to encircle it at its widest girth. 'It's cold, Ean, very cold now – just right.' He felt the muscles of his abdomen tighten involuntarily, causing his erection to pulse. Smiling again, Lauren slowly dribbled spittle round the crown of the soapstone instrument. Then she stepped over the log and stood behind him. Ean held his breath. Though she was his mistress, he might have cried out for her to desist; he might have struggled against his bonds; he might have kicked back at her. He did none of these things: his mouth opened for a timid cry that never came; and still he did not dare to breathe.

The smooth slippery crown of the soapstone phallus nosed between his buttock cheeks. Simultaneously he felt his mistress's slim cool hand reaching round but not touching his penis, instead taking hold of the sac, her finger and thumb gripping one of the highly sensitive fleshy balls within and slowly increasing the pressure as the slippery head of the phallus mated to the tight funnel of flesh in his bottom. She pushed and pushed, until Ean gasped and the funnel-muscle yielded to the will of his mistress, yielded girth until he felt that he would split, and the dense cold smooth object slid and slid inside his body – such coldness and such an intense thrill as he had never experienced. His mistress murmured: 'There ... Do not stint, now. Take it all.' Her cool, soft lips dabbed little kisses upon his back. 'I can feel your special tightness in the shaft I have implanted; it will not lift or move sideways; it knows only one direction ... up and in ...,' she whispered, pushing again, still squeezing excruciating pleasure-pain into the fleshy ball trapped between her finger and thumb, until the cold smooth sliding sensation came again, ever deeper, distending him, seemingly relentlessly swelling inside him. He shuddered as the widest girth of the phallus began to slide very slowly against the seminal gland buried within him, exerting pressure on a gland already swollen, overfull. 'There – think of Denni now, taking your flesh in this very manner – hard and full and deep inside her, stretching that lovely bottom, whilst you squeeze her little cunt-lips and make the pleasure ache.'

Ean shuddered and moaned as the irresistible tightness squeezed the seminal gland in belly-wrenching pleasure-pulses against the smooth cold unyielding phallus. His ejaculate spurted, then poured. Only then did she release the pressure on the tortured ball in his sac and cup her hand to catch the emission. She stepped over the log, faced him and slowly slurped the fluid from her hand. Then she clambered up and kissed him, laving his tongue with his own semen, in a prolonged kiss, her lips sticking to his, her hand clasping his still-erect penis in a singular manner, at the very base, between her finger and thumb, which pushed hard down, stretching the skin of the wet shaft, putting tightness all around the sensitive head, causing a harshness of constriction yet extreme pleasure while the salt kiss continued.

He felt deliciously overawed by her sexuality; she instilled anxiety and overwhelming desire. Most of all he wanted to see her nude and to touch her in the ways that she was touching him.

The removal of the soapstone phallus was more torturing than its insertion. Lady Lauren's fingertips searched the sac beneath Ean's shaft and, finding the same tender swollen ball of flesh as before, gripped it tightly between thumb and finger, squeezing ever harder, and slowly forced the withdrawal against the muscle spasm. A deep throbbing pulse came in his penis and continued even after the withdrawal was completed. The mistress watched it in fascination. 'Will it come again, your semen? If it comes, I shall make you drink it, every drop.' The muscles of his abdomen cramped and Lauren smiled wickedly. She waited until she was sure no emission would come, then she said: 'Good – you are learning control. Thus far, you have done well, my groom. But it is time for our return.'

His erection did not wane whilst Lauren was untying him. Afterwards, on horseback, it kept coming on hard each time he thought of her and what she had done – that wicked streak of causing pleasure laced with humiliation for him, without his ever being able to touch her. His desire for her now was all-consuming.

Near the edge of the woods, his mistress halted, dismounted and led the horse to a small rise above a gap overlooking the ride down to the house. Ean quietly dismounted and followed her. She seemed pensive now, quite unlike her earlier self. He felt confident enough to venture gently: 'What is it, ma'am?'

'Nothing, Ean.' Then she said: 'I hope Denni will be all right, don't you?'

'That I do, ma'am. You are very kind.'

She turned to face him and he saw her eyes were moist and she suddenly looked so forlorn that on impulse he moved forward to put his arms around her.

'What are you doing?' She glared at him. 'Don't ever do that again!'

'I . . . I'm very sorry ma'am.' He backed away like a beaten dog.

Then just as swiftly her mood swung and she came to him and said very softly. 'Remember your place – that is all I ask – and all shall be well between us. I mean it, Ean: I hold you in the highest regard. But speak of our tryst to no one; in the house, show no sign that we have loved and kissed. Understood?'

He nodded, his heart leaping at the words 'we have loved'.

'But think of me – desire me – always. Just as I desire you . . .' So saying she stepped back, slid her hand down the front of her breeches and closed her eyes. Her nostrils dilated. Hypnotised, Ean watched his mistress's fingers writhing under the leather, listened with bated breath to the rhythm of her breathing, wanting so desperately to see her nude and to watch what her fingers were doing. Her eyes slowly opened. 'Kiss me,' she murmured. Shakily his arms encircled hers but did not attempt to grip. When his lips touched hers very lightly he felt her shudder and a near-gasp came against his mouth, then came a more powerful shudder and an open-mouthed groan, which deepened as Ean, encouraged now, slid his tongue inside her unresisting mouth. He held her limp body for a beautiful few seconds, fending off the temptation to lift and carry her. Then she drew back a little, withdrew her hand from her breeches and very slowly pushed two slick musky fingers into his mouth. 'Suck,' she whispered. 'Suck . . .' Afterwards she hungrily pressed her lips to his, to share in the delicious female musk that she had shed.

47

The return journey was for Ean a turmoil of arousal and desire. He knew that he must never make any advance to his mistress but would have to await her call; already she seemed aloof. On arrival she handed him the reins of her horse without a word, then ignored him, sent for Kapler and went to her rooms. In a daze of uncertainty and rebuff, Ean retreated quietly to the servants' quarters, where all now seemed to have returned to normal following the upset of the dismissal. 'What news of Denni?' he asked the scullery maid belatedly and rather guiltily.

She stared back reproachfully. 'Denni's gone. She was looking for you; she wanted to say goodbye but it seems you were off with her ladyship.'

'I was obliged to do my mistress's bidding.'

But the reproach was still there in her eyes, triggering a still keener reproach in Ean's unsettled heart.

Lady Lauren stared across the room at her head groom. 'I understand Deneca has already departed.'

'Yes, ma'am. I believe she left with good grace – without fuss.' Kapler looked up to see his mistress still staring at him.

'Then you didn't attend to her departure personally?'

'No, ma'am. The head chambermaid –'

'But I asked you.'

Irked, Kapler looked away, which only drew his mistress nearer. 'Do you think she took it, the necklace?'

'It was in her box.'

'But someone else might have put it there?'

'Why should anyone want to do that? And she was the only one daily in your bedchamber.'

'Surely not the only one, Kapler?'

'My lady . . . ?' A slight smirk crossed his face before he managed to check it. He glanced at her, trying to

48

judge her mood, then said: 'No, it was Denni, all right. She was a wilful girl.'

'Exactly so – wilful . . . Perhaps especially so in the face of unwelcome advances?'

'My lady, surely you are not suggesting –'

'I know you well enough to guess. And I may choose to tolerate some things, provided there is no disruption to the smooth running of this household. But I do not care to have to furnish excuses to my husband. Do not jeopardise the very things you are privileged to enjoy.' Then her voice softened and, reaching, she touched his hand. 'What was it, Kapler? Were you jealous of my interest in her?'

He shook his head without conviction. After a long pause, he said: 'Is that all, ma'am?'

'No, Kapler, it is not. Through your machinations I am now denied a girl to assist with Ean's training. I don't want any more complications with our servants. I want simplicity, and I want you to arrange it. Now come here.'

# 4

# The Initiation of the Groom

Beautiful thoughts of desire and clinging caressed
Leah's mind as she perched next afternoon in her
customary place astride the bow of her master's boat.
Merek's hands, strong but gentler now that the visiting
merchant had gone, once more extended protectively
round her belly from behind and held her in the way a
lover should. All trace of jealousy had left him: she had
lain with him that morning and ensured it.

'My guest was pleased with you last night,' he
whispered appreciatively. Leah turned and kissed him.
'Do you want to ride the tow-horse again?' he asked,
stroking her hair.

'Oh, please . . .' Leah nodded eagerly. Merek whistled once and the horse slowed almost to a halt.

'I'll relieve Asgal at the tiller. He can help you.'

Leah's smile faltered.

'What is it?' Merek lifted her chin and studied her
face.

'I can manage by myself,' Leah whispered guiltily.

For a long moment, he stared questioningly at her,
for Asgal was a servant, not a guest, and there must be
no transgression of that threshold. Then he smiled and
nodded. 'Go on, then.' He lifted her down. 'Take care.'

The boat had drifted closer to the bank but Leah
still had to leap. Without stopping she got a high

foothold on the heavy leather tracery round the horse's flanks and clambered quickly on to his back. She dug in her heels and the horse set off again, Leah waving proudly and her master still smiling.

The horse was handsome – sturdy, steady and gentle. His back was broad and dappled black and brown. Leah opened herself to its warmth. His coarse hairs prickled inside her body, making shivers that felt good. She stretched her thighs until they ached, until the tightness came. She leant forward till her bared breasts lay against his back and, clinging to his head-collar and mane, inhaled his scent while the warmth of his sturdy body steadily seeped inside her. She closed her eyes, swaying upon this huge, warm, rippling, prickling, redolent living bed while the sunshine gently basted her naked lower back and tingling buttocks. And she fell asleep.

She woke shivering. The boat was tied at a wharf and Asgal was unshackling the horse. There was no sign of Merek.

'Shall milady dismount or shall she go with him to the stables?' Asgal asked coldly.

'Where's master?' Leah asked anxiously, averting her gaze.

'Why, "master" is here.' Asgal folded his arms and stared up at her with a wicked grin. 'Is milady's memory that short?' Leah's heart sank to the pit of her belly. She tried to cover her breasts from his loathsome gaze. 'Oh my – look at that . . .' He shook his head mockingly. 'Milady has acquired a rash. And what a rash – all down your front. Tut, tut . . .'

Leah was in dismay: from her neck to her thighs, her skin was covered in dreadful, raised blood-red blotches. She started shivering uncontrollably. Asgal, less certain now, lifted her quaking body down. 'Calm yourself, girl.' He examined her then declared: 'It's just a reaction to the horsehair. It should go away. But

51

look – it's even marked your lips and cheek.' He smiled thinly.

'Oh, no . . .'

Two men emerged from the stables. 'What's up with her?'

'Too intimate with the horse, I fear. See to him, would you?'

The men laughed. 'Better see to her.'

Though Leah hated Asgal, she let him carry her, clinging to him to avoid her blotches being seen by anyone. She did not realise what was in store.

The mistress of the wharf-side lodge brokered the transaction, which was unusual in that the principal patron, though accompanied by two men, was female. It therefore seemed unnecessary to stipulate limits. The minder merely handed over the girl and skulked to the card table with his proper reward. The girl, overawed by the eyes now fixed upon her petite, half-naked body, looked to the lodge-mistress for reassurance that her master would soon arrive. But the lodge-mistress, perceiving the extent of the raised red blotching that besmirched the girl – disfigured her, even – fended off that naïve supplication with narrow-eyed disdain. 'Your master is busy but has left clear instructions,' she lied. 'Attend them lest you come to regret it.'

She directed the girl past the men to a quiet corner where the lady, her face still veiled, was ensconced. 'A bonny girl, a little headstrong perhaps, but my lady must understand that fever or wanton ill-practice may have rendered her unclean. Had I known in advance –'

'No matter,' the lady said curtly, raising her veil with her gloved hand. She was significantly younger than the veil had implied; her blonde hair hung in soft, loose ringlets; her face was small; her eyes glittered as she assessed the girl.

'It is only that I am fearful for your good men as much as for the sheets,' the mistress wheedled, eyeing the handsome younger master until the lady's stare upbraided her.

The lady turned to the second master. 'Kapler – pay the mistress her premium.' Then she arose, veiled her face and, taking the girl softly by the arm, led her back to the middle of the room. The two masters followed. When the girl became aware of the many boatmen now staring at her, she moved closer to her new guardians. They seemed to respond in kind: indeed any heart would have gone out to that vulnerable, anxious, nubile girl. The lady put her gloved hand gently about the girl's head, drawing her against the folds of her heavy cloak. She then nodded to the younger master who, after a moment's hesitation, took the girl's slender hand – almost timidly – and gently kissed the livid blotches on her arm. The girl's lovely saucer-eyes then looked up expectantly at the second master, the one called Kapler, seeking reassurance about the final link in her protection from the crowd.

She looked beautifully vulnerable in her open shirt. She had closed her thighs to try to conceal her naked sex and its broken chain from the gaze of the onlookers but this stance served only to accent the taut profile of her buttocks. When Kapler turned her to face away from the throng, her shirt rucked up under his hand and the brief vision was delicious, of those female dimples and that lovely, smoothly sculpted hollow above the base of her spine. Every tongue-tip in the room surely craved to lick that girlish hollow and delve lower and deeper, between those tight smooth cheeks, probing the dusky velvet secret mouth and slipping up the fertile female pinkness nestling beneath. Every pair of hands craved to clasp that narrow warm ribcage from the front – for the simple pleasure of feeling it. Then, perhaps with the thumbs slipped under

53

those deliciously puffy breasts, those hands might lift her small body high in the air, with the tongue-tip up between her dangling legs, slowly milking precious musk from her female pinkness, testing her restless rapture through the quavering of her breathing, until that tight nude belly was racked by iniquitous shivers.

The lady's expression remained impenetrable beneath her veil as she surveyed the room and held the nearly naked girl gently close to her breast. Then she turned to the younger master, who seemed suddenly ill at ease as she nodded towards the stairs.

The three patrons kept tactile contact with the young girl – at her neck and wrist and against the hollow of her back – as they directed her up the stairs to the highest landing and the quiet seclusion of the room under the rafters.

Over the course of the night, the requirements of the lady were exacting; and, to the chagrin of the lodge-mistress, the first of these requirements was an immaculate damask sheet.

Leah, manoeuvred forward by her guardians, crept up into the secret bedroom: whatever trial Merek had arranged, she would do her utmost to endure in compliance with his will.

Bare-boarded and windowless, the room extended the length of the building. Its walls sloped to make a ceiling, buttressed by heavy beams. The newly lit lamps smelt smoky. When the door was closed behind her, the sounds from below were deadened: no one would hear her. The lady intercepted her anxious gaze. The veil had been completely removed; the lady was handsome and her gaze was determined. Her heavy cloak was now cast aside to reveal a sylph-like figure in a slender gown. Purposefully she removed her gloves. The younger man appeared very nervous as her gaze returned to her hireling girl.

Leah already felt naked – more naked than simply in front of men, for women were more knowing and were harder to please. She put her arms behind her and tried to stand correctly for inspection, exactly as she had been trained to do. Her shirt was already unbuttoned; its soft, creased flaps were now drawn back by her arms; she wore no trousers – in fact no other clothes of any kind; her sex was sheltered only by the shadow from the nearest lamp. She was acutely conscious of the itchy blemishes made by the horsehair all over her skin; nevertheless she remained true to her training, eyes downcast, exposing herself, submitting her flesh to whatever scrutiny her new guardians might employ.

However many times it happened, the initial dread was always with her when she was put to new men. In the Abbey she had confessed this to the nuns, who had told her that such dread was meet, since it kept the fleshly feelings keen. The presence of the lady only compounded this fear, for she seemed to be the architect of this encounter, and a person of such elegance would probably be disparaging of a girl of Leah's station. Sure enough, the lady continued to stare without even approaching to test Leah's nudity. Leah's breathing was uneven and shallow; her tongue clung to the roof of her mouth; under that critical gaze her flesh shivered as if a thousand spiders were crawling over it; and her belly felt as if it were filling up with squirming snakes. The ugly raised blotches tingle-tightened across her skin; her upper lip felt horribly swollen on one side.

The lady finally moved, walking self-assuredly to the bed and seating herself there, still staring at Leah, whose heart continued to sink into the pit of squirming snakes. The younger master hovered anxiously near the lady while the elder master began single-mindedly checking the contents of the secret bedroom, his shadow looming ominously across the rafters.

'Do you know why you are here?' the lady suddenly asked softly. The elder master stopped moving and everyone's attention fixed on Leah. She tried to take a breath but could not; her belly tightened, forcing her heart to her throat, slowly choking her as the apprehension mounted. She sank to her knees.

'Ma'am, please ... She is frightened,' the young master whispered unexpectedly.

'Thank you, Ean,' the lady replied without looking at him.

'It is fitting that he shows some interest, Lady Lauren,' the other master said.

The lady pursed her lips then nodded. 'Come a little closer, girl. Head up, so we can see you.' Leah, still on her knees, edged forward, keeping her arms behind her as she knew she must. 'Your name is Leah? Good. Now, Leah – there is nothing to be afraid of.' Lady Lauren looked up. 'Kapler – I had expected a more experienced one; she is shaking. Evidently your boatman was economical with the truth.'

'Not my boatman, my lady – I only met him on your –' But her sharp glance cut him short, so he changed tack, stepping forward and touching Leah's forehead. 'I can feel no fever. A little nervousness on the girl's part can be good.'

'Leah?' Lady Lauren said. 'You are well? No sickness is upon you? Good – a healthy, loving young girl; I could see it from the start – in the eyes, lovely eyes. Raise your chin – let me look again. Now, these marks ...' Her long finger traced the blotch extending down the side of Leah's breast and Leah shivered. 'Does it hurt as I touch?' The lady's eyes shone.

'It's like ... an itching, mistress,' Leah murmured.

Lady Lauren's attention now turned to the place where a cruel blotch traversed Leah's lower belly and intersected her sex-lip. 'Beautifully hairless pubes. The perfect adjunct to learning ... Ean, feel here,' she said simply and the younger man jumped as if stung. 'Come here and do as I say.'

Under her coaxing, the shy younger master hesitantly but gently pulled Leah's fragment of chain and the lip slowly unfurled. The very nervousness of this touching accelerated the arousal in so sensitive a place. Leah could feel her flesh responding to the intimate contact and she was afraid the lady, more than the men, would recognise its significance. Ean began to touch the blotchy swelling itself and the lady watched, taut-lipped as Leah gently squirmed. Leah's eyes, seeking escape, only met the elder master's interested gaze. 'Keep your arms back, Leah,' Lady Lauren reminded her, for her arms were becoming restive. 'Kneel up straight – and continue to offer.' The lady surely understood the sensations that Leah was now experiencing.

'Her nipples are nicely puffy,' the elder master, Kapler, said. 'As if there is a fresh surge of growth.' He began to touch the surrounds of her nipples as the lady continued.

'You will get to know our little group: Master Ean, getting gently acquainted down here, is my newest groom; Master Kapler is his senior; and you may call me Mistress Lauren. And you, my dear Leah, are here to teach young Master Ean all he needs to know about girls. Master Kapler and myself are here to give assistance where needed.'

There was a knock at the door, then the lodge-mistress entered bearing a folded white sheet. Ean's fingers immediately faltered and Leah tried to twist aside to shield what was being done between her legs. Lauren quickly got up from the bed and made the kneeling Leah face the woman. She deliberately drew down the chained lip that Ean had been touching, making blatant the extent of Leah's arousal. The mistress glowered at Leah as she laid the sheet over everything – pillows and cushions – that lay on the bed then smoothed it down as best she could. Leah now felt like a leper. She turned to Lauren, who put her hand in mock reassurance about Leah's head. Kapler began arranging some of the lamps ominously closer to the bed.

'Thank you, mistress,' Lauren said.

'Maria will bring refreshments directly, my lady,' the mistress said.

'She need not knock: I want no distractions.'

'I understand, my lady.' The mistress curtsied and departed.

Lauren looked down into Leah's upturned face. 'Well, my dear – on the bed . . .'

Leah gasped when Kapler's strong arms gripped her under her breasts and swung her on her knees into the middle of the hummocked sheet. Ean now sat tentatively facing her at one corner of the bed; Lauren sat on the opposite edge, a little nearer. Kapler, still standing behind Leah, leant forward with one hand slung over a beam. Then Lauren said gently to Leah: 'You are used to men?'

'Yes, mistress,' Leah whispered.

'How many have you had inside you?' Lauren's eyes dilated with arousal as she put the question.

Confounded, Leah shook her head. If the lady meant at the front, Leah might be able to guess the number, but if she meant inside her bottom, or in her mouth . . . 'You are young – surely you must know?' Lauren insisted insidiously.

'Her eyes look hunted,' Kapler said.

'Show your chains properly,' Lauren said abruptly. Still on her knees on the bed, Leah leant back, spreading her thighs for the masters and the mistress. Kapler brought a lamp close. 'She's still shivering. My, but she is lovely, there – and not too opened, I'd say.'

But the first testing fingers that actually entered her body were Lauren's. They took Leah by surprise and made her gasp. 'Lean back. Lie still: let me show him.' Leah kept glimpsing Ean's face, daunted yet fascinated as his mistress used Leah to explain clinically to him how girls were broken in. 'Her virgin's chain has been cut – or snapped, it would appear. And see, in here, the hymen – the tissue inside her – ruptured, beautifully ragged, yet if I open her wider, each tattered attachment still has life.' Leah murmured as the female fingers probed and exposed it. 'Her first lover was too keen . . . Push out, Leah. Push it all out.' Lauren's eyes glistened with perverse excitement. 'All must come to light, here. We need to see it. I can feel the lovely warmth rising out of it – all hot and moist and shiny and pink . . . Now touch it, Ean.'

There was a pause. Then Ean touched it; Leah thought he wouldn't but he did and, after that first fear, his fingers did not recoil and Leah experienced little pulsing shivers, because her ragged inner flesh was pushed out and these strangers – all three now – were touching it and discussing what might be done.

Kapler took her trembling torso in his arms while she was still kneeling open, kissed her lips and face – sucking the very blemishes – and tongued her puffy nipples while his fingers rejoined the others between her legs – three people's fingers again – opening her like a living love-flower and drawing out her silken nectar. Kapler kept her arms pinned back; her nipples and their surrounds stood out further with each sucking that he gave them. A long, slow finger slid inside her sex as Lauren urged her protégé to touch the entrance to Leah's womb and to describe exactly what he could feel.

'She's so hot in here, mistress,' Ean murmured reverently. 'There's a little bump, like a nose, right up at the back.'

'Press it – gently. Harder . . .'

Leah moaned into Kapler's mouth. He drew back to look at her with her arms still pinned behind her and Ean's fully extended middle finger deep inside her. 'These blemishes, Lauren,' Kapler said. 'They look darker and more raised now. She looks as if she's been splashed all down her front, with every splash inducing swelling; they're on her neck and lip and even on her cunt.' He sucked Leah's swollen upper lip then asked: 'How did you get such blotches?'

'This afternoon, on the boat-horse, after I fell asleep . . .'

'Her skin must react to horsehair,' Lauren said, running her fingertips over the itchy marks and gritting her teeth as Leah winced. Lauren then stared knowingly at Kapler, whose eyes suddenly widened with understanding. He stroked the marks very lightly, until Leah's shudders came strongly, whereupon he sucked her swollen upper lip again before getting up and heading for the door.

'Mane-hair or tail-hair will be best, I think,' Lauren shouted after him. Leah started to whimper. Lauren protectively stroked her hair. 'Don't cry, Leah. Not yet, at least. We've a long way yet to go.'

Ean's finger slid gently out of Leah's body. He seemed mesmerised as he murmured: 'She's like a beautiful flower, her petals fully opened.' Lauren surreptitiously laid her hand on Ean's thigh but he continued to look at Leah whilst asking his mistress whether the petals would cool if they remained pushed out like that. Lauren said: 'Discover by testing.' While he did so, Lauren kept her hand upon his thigh and whispered to him about kissing girls between the legs and about the female climax.

Ean was gently teasing out the small inner sepal-like remains of Leah's plundered virginity when the door opened and a serving girl entered with refreshments.

Lauren intercepted the girl's gaze but kept her hand on Ean's thigh and made the girl witness the testing of the coolness of Leah's pushed-out petals with the tip of Ean's tongue. 'Well, Ean?'

'She's seeping warmth from inside. It's fragrant – like honeydew but not sweet.'

'Good – then she's ready,' Lauren answered. 'Sit her up – on the sheet. Keep her open – thighs wide and this part nicely open. Always . . .' Then Lauren quietly reached across and kissed Leah, gently, with warm soft lips and a tongue that languidly probed inside her mouth but with the strained, held breathing of deep excitement. All the while, Ean was helping keep Leah's body open as Leah, her belly softly rippling, was obediently pushing out, exposing her inner self to the sweet attentions that would come there.

When the long kiss from the mistress was completed, Leah saw that the serving girl had retreated, ruddy-cheeked and wide-eyed from the headiness of such a scene. With no hint of embarrassment, Lauren gave her leave to go. Then her attention returned to her young groom and Leah. She began by pulling Leah's shirt off her. 'No blemishes on this beautiful back . . .' Lauren kissed it, lightly and lovingly – making Leah shiver into the hands that were helping her stay open at the front. Lauren, teasing, contrasted Leah's small breasts with the serving girl's. Ean said he liked Leah's exactly as they were and that they were not that small in proportion to her frame. Then he took a nipple and its puffy surround very gently into his mouth and sucked it. Lauren simultaneously held Leah's head back and stretched her arms out behind her until she began to go dizzy. 'Is she still making wetness?' Lauren asked.

They held the white sheet against her body – Ean put his hand under it and Lauren urged Leah's sex forwards against the cloth. 'I can see my fingers through the sheet,' Ean said after a short while.

Lauren released Leah's arms. 'Leah, show my groom where your pleasure comes keenest.'

Leah obediently turned over on to her belly and spread her bottom cheeks.

'It comes keenest here?' Lauren whispered, suddenly unsure. Leah nodded uncertainly, wondering if she had done wrong by telling the truth. Lauren's fingers faltered. 'No,' she whispered in renewed excitement, nervously stroking Leah's lower back. 'So be it. Hold your cheeks open. It is good – especially good – when a girl likes it here.'

Leah closed her eyes, waiting for the singular pleasure of being touched there. When it came, it made her shudder – a sweet lovely pleasure, deep and strong. 'Ean – now you touch it – in the middle, the very rude middle, where it wrinkles. Gently poke that pushed-out little wrinkle up inside her.' Leah shuddered before the touch even came. Lauren turned Leah's face towards her. 'Open your eyes, my love. Let me look at you as he does it.' The moan came and then the female kiss, softly, urgently and continuously while Leah's trembling fingers held her buttocks open and Ean's nervous fingertips centred themselves in that special place then gently pushed those sensitive wrinkles of velvet very surely up inside her.

His fingers gently withdrew, leaving intense arousal still swelling inside her. 'Mistress – see, she has stripes across her bottom, like bruises.'

Lauren answered: 'Move the lamp closer . . . I had thought them shadows. Ah, now I see – marks from a whipping. Even better. But see how she tightened in there when that word was uttered?' Lauren's face came very close to Leah's. She laid her hand against her throat. 'You must not tighten that lovely place while we still explore. Understand?' Leah nodded, swallowing gently. Lauren's eyes suddenly narrowed wickedly. She deliberately took hold of Leah's swollen, blemished upper lip between her finger and thumb and slowly increased the pressure of squeezing. Arousal squirmed in Leah's belly; her mouth lay open but her breathing became shallow. 'Relax. Spread your arms above you on the bed. Relax your hands, each finger too. Now spread your legs more – more – with this knee bent a little . . . Good. For Ean needs to see both of these lovely places from behind.' She still gripped Leah's upper lip tightly. 'There . . . Stillness is a virtue at times such as this.' She lowered her voice. 'If pleasure comes while you remain quite still – absolutely motionless – then you are blessed.'

Lauren's other hand continued to stroke Leah's throat as if the girl were a distraught creature she was quelling. 'Look at me, Leah, with those generous eyes. I mean to hold this upper lip, squeezing very hard until the blemish on it spreads into your cheek and still keep squeezing until the pleasure comes. And you shall stay still for it and I shall feel it only through the pulsing of the bruise within this lip. Open her bottom again, Ean. Stretch that muscle nice and wide – be very firm in your fingering.' Leah moaned and shuddered. 'Good . . . Now hold it so it cannot close. We really need Kapler here to give her a whipping.'

Leah's climax came when that was said: it felt like hot water rushing up her bottom and somehow flooding her womb. Lauren squeezed her upper lip ever tighter until it felt like it must burst and the pulses of pleasure came without mercy.

'The honeydew's coming out of her at the front,' Ean said. She felt Lauren's other hand going under her belly, catching the fluid and smearing its sticky warmth all round her throbbing sex. The oily rubbing, the fingertip invasion of the sensitive furrows, almost made the pleasure burst again.

Lauren turned her over. 'Her lip . . . Look at it,' Ean said anxiously.

'It's nice to do that sometimes to a girl – like you do with ponies – putting on a twitch. It doesn't have to be on the lip: it works with the nipple; anywhere between the legs; sometimes an ear lobe; in her case, doubtless, the rim of the anus. But when you do it right, you can always tell. See – it's made her ejaculate.' Lauren stretched Leah's thighs wide as she lay on her back.

'I didn't know that girls –'

'Then you are learning, Ean. Hold it open, Leah – yes, your precious flower. Now pull back the sleeve at the top. Show off your little cock.' Lauren then explained the function of the clitoris.

'But it's tiny and there's no hole.'

'In a girl, there's a separation – it provides an extra place for pleasure. Show him, Leah. Let him touch the tiny hole. See, she likes that too.' Lauren gently sucked her nipples while Ean pressed and teased her pee-hole, making Leah want to come. The stretched muscle of her anus throbbed hot, as if still held open. Ean started to pluck at the segments of her chain adhering to her labia. Lauren sucked the bruised swelling on her upper lip, inciting it to grow. Then Leah felt the segments of her chain being used to draw her further open. 'I want to see her . . . ejaculating,' Ean murmured, 'how it actually comes out and what brings it on.'

'And how it tastes,' Lauren added, 'surely that too. And how often it can be made to come, and whether she can be drained before exhaustion – either hers or her lovers'.' Lauren sighed dreamily then stared down at Leah, who was breathing shallowly, the pupils of her eyes dilated to blackness. And for the first time, unprovoked, Leah reached up, her fingers tentatively caressing the lady's neck, wanting to be kissed again while the touching between her legs went on and on and wanting in turn to kiss a female breast or a swollen penis. Leah longed to explore as intimately as she was being explored; especially she wanted Ean, as the least

64

experienced; she wanted to play with his penis, to force it to come in her mouth and to drink its salty spillage.

They sat her up again. Lauren allowed Ean to take temporary charge of Leah. His fascination now turned to her breasts: he wanted to know what made girls swollen there, why the nipple-surrounds were broader than a man's and why the nipples were fatter. Lauren simply said it was to do with making milk. 'But Leah's breasts don't have any milk,' Ean said. He sucked them hard, to make quite sure, and her nipples came fatter still. He kissed the blotches of raised, angry, itchy skin from her neck to her belly; he put his tongue inside her navel and made her squirm.

While his mistress left the bed and began pouring drinks, Leah tentatively touched his erection through the thinness of his trousers. She had not realised how close he was to spilling: under her touching he suddenly froze and she could feel the lovely warning tremble through the tips of her fingers. Then, sure enough, a small patch of his pre-come darkened the cloth. Leah kissed it, allowing the heat of her lips to seep through the cloth. Ean half restrained her by her shoulders; his whole body was trembling now. She took the fat glans – still sheathed in cloth – gently between her teeth, held it for a moment, then drew back and watched him teetering on the brink. She was about to put her hand down his trousers when Lauren returned with two goblets of drink.

Ean sank back on the bed to hide his erection. He took deep swift draughts from the goblet that his mistress gave him. Then Lauren offered Leah some but insisted on taking Leah partly on her lap to administer it. Leah could feel the warmth of her mistress's body as Lauren fed her little sips of what tasted like grain wine. Then she made her open – sitting fully astride her mistress's lap, facing outwards. Then Lauren dipped her fingers in the liquor and began anointing Leah's clitoris, making it shiny wet with repeated applications and gentle rubbing. Then, edging Leah forwards, she asked Ean if he wanted to lick it off.

Leah sat very open astride Lauren's knees. She felt Lauren's hand, hot against her back. 'Rest your head back against my shoulder,' Lauren whispered. Then Leah felt the liquor being trickled very slowly between her breasts, down the band of itchy, blotched skin and over her belly in tickling wavy lines that converged between her thighs in little pulses against her throbbing wet clitoris, kept erect by the fleshy warm licks of Ean's tongue.

'I think she's coming, mistress,' he murmured through the lickings.

Lauren urged Leah's legs even wider and thrust her bottom forward so that her groom might witness the spasm in detail. But Leah's come stopped in mid-execution; she wanted it but either the wine had dulled it or the licking had been too keen. Lauren took her by the strands of jewelled chain and made her labia gape. 'Push out again,' she whispered in her ear.

'Let me see his nakedness,' Leah pleaded.

Ean then self-consciously unfastened his belt and Leah took his hot erection in her trembling fingers as Ean closed his eyes.

'No, master groom,' Lauren chastised him, 'you cannot now abdicate. The male must earn his deliverance. Gently – put your moistened finger into her – up behind her pee-hole. Now rub upwards, firmly, as if you mean to lift her bodily on your finger.'

Under this inner caressing, Leah moaned and shuddered, still clutching the fattened glans of Ean's penis and now drawing it towards her taunted sex. Her deliverance came: the rubbing, lifting digit steadily pumped the come from Leah's body and it squirted over the tip of his penis. Still shuddering, Leah squeezed the eye of the penis open and the last squirt filled the end of his tube. She tried to seal it with the pad of her thumb but most of the liquid exuded. His climax had not come, though she could feel its imminence in the slippery cap of his trembling glans.

Under Lauren's provocation, Ean grew bolder. He laid Leah on her side on the bed with her arms drawn back. She felt Lauren settling behind her. 'No, mistress – let me look at her first.' Ean's voice was guttural with excitement as he sought to take command. He walked round the bed to Leah's front, his penis poking from under his shirt, its cap still glistening with her come. She saw his sac – like a heart, it always seemed to her, a second heart that men have underneath, that pumps their semen into girls – and she wanted to reach to squeeze it but her hands were still behind her. Lauren grasped her restless wrists and drew them back. Ean now straddled Leah's narrow waist while she was lain on her side. His hot, heart-like sac sank into the hollow of her narrow middle. She felt the balls inside the sac, rolling against her, and the hot length of his penis stretching up her side. His knees trapped her ribcage tightly. He courted wantonness. She struggled for breath as his fingers began to twist her nipples and to pinch the swollen blotches down the side of her breast. His toes probed under her belly and buttocks, seeking heat and moisture.

Lauren revelled in this coarseness. 'Open for him,' she urged Leah. 'Open properly . . .' Leah tried to raise her leg. 'Wait, Ean . . .' Lauren made him dismount, then she held Leah's ankle high and started to smack her between the legs. 'It gets them ready,' Lauren said. Ean watched, taking tense pleasure from Leah's reaction. 'She's coming more open,' he murmured. Lauren continued smacking, concentrating now on Leah's sex, regardless of the presence of the chain, smacking the itchy blotches, making the pink flesh red, making the swollen inner lips vibrate with each smack that she delivered.

The door opened and Kapler came in. 'Leg up high,' Lauren warned Leah. 'And keep it up: don't make me keep telling you.' She continued smacking between Leah's legs, the smacks now falling directly upon her anus, which kept tightening though her mistress expressly forbade such contractions. Kapler approached the bed. In his hand was a dense hank of horsehair. Leah, shuddering under the sexuality of smacking, buried her face in Ean's lap. She put her open lips against his swollen sac where it fed into his penis and she shut her eyes and sucked – just as she wanted her sex to be sucked, while it was so achingly smacked to arousal and her labia felt so swollen with taunted pleasure.

She heard his gasp and felt the pulsing start and realised she had gone too far. She felt hot semen, not spraying but dripping like melted wax upon her ear lobe, inside her ear, running underneath and down her neck. Then she heard hollow sounds as if her head were under water. Now she kissed the balls more gently – they were still very hot and very fat. Her tongue laved the crease at the side. She loved licking men in these smooth ticklish places. Ean shivered in a way that told that he had never experienced this licking. His cock still stood up, hard and lovely. Both men were now naked. Leah twisted round to look at them, her arms still trapped behind her, her legs still open, her belly streaked bright purple with the itchy rash. Below it she glimpsed the reddened, aroused swollenness between her legs. Lauren was watching the men but now began touching Leah where she had been smacking her. It felt to Leah as if a wide warm bandage swathed the flesh there, and fingers were pressing blunted pleasure through it.

Kapler joined in the examination, asking specifically about Leah's ejaculation. Lauren was telling him as she toyed with Leah's semen-slickened ear lobe. The bubble of semen suddenly popped inside her ear and she felt hot liquid coming out and the sounds in the room got louder. Lauren bent over her and kissed her mouth, sucking the swollen lip that she had earlier cruelly pinched and twisted. At the same time Leah felt Kapler's heavy fingers trying to open her smacked sex as he spoke with Ean about her chains. Kapler then nipped the puncture points in her labia very hard whilst Lauren put her semen-coated fingers into Leah's mouth to hold her tongue, to quell her and stifle her gasps.

'See the clitoris, Ean,' Kapler was saying, 'becoming harder when I squeeze these piercings? Now – take hold of its foreskin and push it right back.' A hand came against Leah's belly, pressing. Then she felt her clitoris being forcibly extruded. 'There – like a little hard cock.' None of its sensitivity had been lost in the smacking; she felt the hot moist tip of it against the cooling air. Then something touched it, rasping stiffly, rubbing back and forth. 'See it twitching?' She shuddered and bucked. 'Now sit her up. Let's see if it swells.' Wound round Kapler's finger was a strand of horsehair.

'Oh no – please . . .,' Leah begged him.

'The reaction may take time,' Lauren said sultrily, putting her arm about Leah's shoulder. 'So sit up now, Leah. Put your knees up high. Push your little penis out while Kapler tries to make it bigger. Good girl . . . Let me touch her first. Let me touch it. Mmm . . . It feels so good and flickably stiff. Oh, you dirty little fat-cocked fuck.' And Leah groaned as Lauren flicked it. Then Kapler took a dense hank of horsehair and began to dab it gently against all the inner flesh that was pushing out. It made an itchy tickle wherever it touched. There was no stronger reaction at first. But the tickle continued even after the touching had stopped and when the same flesh was dabbed again, the itchiness deepened. It was like the tickle that you get inside your throat and cannot stop, but this tickle was spreading inside her sex. The more gently Kapler rubbed with the horsehair, the more Leah's toes clenched and the more she moaned.

'See, lad – two sets of lovely lips,' Kapler said. 'These inner ones, where she is punctured, are the more sensitive. They're erect but you can still feel a thin edge to them because her arousal is honing them keen. Now let's see what happens with the horsehair.'

'Let me,' said Ean, his voice strained with excitement. Leah looked at him with baleful eyes; she had thought him kinder than this. He did not meet her gaze but neither did he desist.

Lauren held her shoulders down. Kapler held her frightened knees tucked up and bundled her across his lap. His burning naked penis touched her spine. 'Use the long ones – they're tail hair,' he told Ean, who knotted the small hank into a shiny black bow. He rubbed the tightly curved end of the bow back and forth on Leah's protrusive knob until even Lauren shivered. Then he took a length of twisted strands stretched tightly between his hands and pressed it far into the crease between Leah's inner and outer lips. Leah gasped as her knob thrust out and tilted over to try to meet it. Quickly he pulled it away only to thrust it back on the opposite side. 'Careful. Go slowly,' Kapler warned him, gently pressing her tilted knob against the taut wiry strand.

'She's making honeydew from inside,' Ean said.

'And look – the inner lips are already swelling hard; the edge is disappearing.'

'Stop for now, Ean,' Lauren whispered huskily.

For Leah could feel her labia pumping up with fluid and tingling as if newly bruised, and it felt as if her tiny labial punctures instead had broad pins pushed through them.

'Give me one of those long hairs,' Kapler said. He wound the hair tightly round each of Leah's nipples, fastening them together, then he laid her on her back on the bed. 'Keep your knees up: our young master might not have finished in there.' He started to get off the bed then changed his mind, gathering her under the shoulders and knees, bundling her tightly then kissing her, sucking the itchy crimson swelling on her upper lip into a blister. Then he held her shoulders down on the bed and pushed his erect penis into her mouth and rubbed the blister with his thumb while Ean brushed the coarse points of a little sheaf of horsehair slowly back and forth across her pee-hole.

'She's a lovely one, Lauren,' Kapler said, carefully withdrawing his penis from Leah's mouth, rubbing his curved palm over her pulsing tight belly and plucking the puffy, tied nipples that crowned her young breasts.

'She's a good choice for him to learn with,' Lauren sighed.

'Then I'll get the ropes and things, now,' Kapler answered. And he began to dress.

'Go and help him, Ean,' Lauren said. The young groom appeared surprised; nevertheless he clambered into his clothes and followed Kapler from the room. Lauren remained with Leah, whose eyes were hunted and whose breathing had tensed. Lauren gently stroked her cheek. 'It seems we are alone,' she whispered wickedly. 'Turn over.'

# 5

# The Ties That Bind

'So beautiful . . .,' Lauren whispered. 'So swollen . . .
Perfect, dirty, precious, wanton little trollop . . . How
I wish you could be mine.' Coarseness tumbled from
her lips as she examined Leah intimately while the men
were gone. Leah lay on her front while Lauren opened
her and touched inside her sex and bottom. She asked
about Leah's virgin's chain and who had put it there.
Leah whispered of her training by the monks and of
how they had used her bottom sexually while she
remained a virgin and could still be shown as such to
the visitors. When Leah mentioned their use of sack-
cloth to train her to anal pleasure, Lauren became very
excited indeed. She pushed a thick knot of horsehair
up Leah's bottom then slowly twisted it whilst stimulating Leah's swollen clitoris with very precise fingertip
pressure – adding little dabs of spittle, keeping it
moving, sometimes scraping it very subtly with the
fingernail – until the men returned with the equipment.

When Kapler started hammering the iron tethering-
pin into the floor-beam, the lodge-mistress arrived at
the door to discover the cause of the commotion.
Lauren went to explain to her what was about to be
done and to press a gold coin into the woman's hand.

'Oh – apologies, my lady. She looked a minx when
I saw her.' The lodge-mistress stared at the knot of

horsehair in Lauren's fingers then, appeased by the gold, left.

Kapler screwed the rest of the pin firmly home and tested the eyelet by pulling. He had positioned it under a cross-beam in the roof. Lauren was back with Leah, rubbing her bottom and clitoris gently with the horsehair, then examining the progress of the swelling as the men undressed. Lauren's finger, soothingly cold, went inside Leah. 'You feel tight inside, my darling. Does it hurt?' She thrust deeper, forcing Leah's sex into a soft spasm against the feeling of penetration and the coolness, where she was so itchy and swollen. Her inner lips stood out from her body. The men, already bearing powerful erections, came to feel and to squeeze them. They made her kneel up while Ean tied long lengths of horsehair to her labial chains. Then they made her stand on the bed, her feet in the patch of warm new dampness that she had yielded, the long strands of irritant horsehair dangling to her knees.

Ean funnelled his lips tightly round her shiny, hard erection then, with a hard suck, drew away. 'It's like a blister now,' he said excitedly. His lips reached again. With her flesh so tightly engorged, his tongue-tip could not find her pee-hole. He drew her as far open as possible using the lengths of horsehair, tying them round the tops of her thighs. Then he teased the exposed inner flesh with a fresh fistful of horsehair until Lauren warned him: 'Gently – she's still swelling inside.' Then Lauren's own gentle palpating of the inner flesh now bulging out only made the prickling pleasure worse. Leah remained standing open but her wriggling under Lauren's teasing drew the men into touching her even more.

They roped her wrists together and slung her under the cross-beam so her feet dangled over the metal eyelet screwed into the floor. They put a single loop of rope round her ankles and drew it down through the eyelet then horizontally to a pillar, to which they tied it with a slip-knot. As Leah's muscles stretched, Kapler gradually increased the tension with the slip-knot.

'She's sweating,' Ean whispered, standing before her, studying her skin minutely.

'It's from the stretching,' Lauren said. Ean's lips nuzzled under Leah's arms. 'Feel her belly now – racked ever so tight,' said Lauren, crouching, and brushed her lips over it while surreptitiously slipping her fingers round Ean's shaft.

Kapler wanted to whip Leah directly; Lauren wanted her masturbated first. In the end they did both together. They decided that Ean should hold her sex while Kapler whipped her bottom with a switch. The stretching had made her thighs so tight about her swelling sex that Ean had to force his fingers round it, to get a proper grip. Then Kapler started whipping.

At that very moment, just beyond the door to the secret bedroom, the servant girl, Maria, returning for the tray, was about to lift the latch when she heard those sounds – the grunts of male exertion, the sharp, snapping thrashes and the gasping female moans. They were sounds that Maria immediately understood, though she had witnessed such an event only once – a traveller, fully dressed for riding, wielding a crop upon a pretty girl who lay naked and face down on his bed. That vision remained with Maria, feeding dreams from which she would wake wet with desire. The other girls would often speak of such practices, describing what they had seen in the rooms and in the stables; sometimes they would enact them in play. Maria would watch; she had the desire but never the courage to join in. And afterwards her dreams would be fraught with whipping pleasures. Tonight in this room, already she had witnessed a young man kissing a girl between the legs; her belly tumbled as she wondered what it might be like to experience that special sensation. Quietly, shakily, she opened the door.

The scene confronting her burned into her soul. The girl was strung up naked and the two men were touching and punishing her – whipping her bottom and touching her at the front. They too were naked, their male parts standing stiff as wood. The beautiful lady was watching and directing. The girl was covered in raised red and purple marks, as if a paintbrush had splashed her. Her skin looked deathly pale, as if all the blood was drawn into these stains. Her upper lip and her nipples were swollen bright red.

Maria was terrified and fascinated, wanting to withdraw behind the door and peep. But the lady had spotted her, so she must go in. Quietly, with eyes averted, she crossed the room. Hurriedly and fumblingly she tried to collect her tray. The lady said something and Maria looked up, her pulse pounding in her ears, her cheeks burning at the sight of the naked stiff parts of the men. Before she could escape, the lady grasped her by the wrist. 'Don't go. Would you like to watch?' she whispered, drawing her nearer to the painted girl. The men moved aside and the older one leant against a pillar, the birch switch in his hand, not hiding himself, smirking, causing her to look away. The younger man seemed almost self-conscious, yet he was the one whom she had earlier witnessed kissing the girl between the legs. And now he had only been touching the girl in that same place, exciting her during the whipping. In truth that thought excited Maria too.

The girl's eyes were half closed and she was whimpering, but very softly, almost as if in trance. There was black thread tied between her bright bulging nipples and there was more round the tops of her thighs. The lady explained: 'It's horsehair, there to make her itch.' Then she whispered: 'And we have rubbed it between her legs and I have pushed it up her

75

bottom so now she is swelling everywhere, with her thighs drawn tight to keep all the delicious pleasure sealed inside.' Then she took Maria's frightened fingers and directed them between those thighs to the girl's tortured red swelling. 'Have you ever caressed a cunt so swollen?' It was heart-stoppingly exciting for Maria. Though the lady cajoled her wrist, her fingers sought the heat, trembled against the female slipperiness and in shocked excitement felt metal links buried in the flesh. Still she continued to touch, explore and squeeze. The girl's shudder made her fingers withdraw.

'Don't stop,' the lady murmured. 'Hold it properly. Get a finger up inside if you can.' Then she turned. 'Here, Kapler, hand me the switch. Now, girl, you use it on her. Reach round.' There was something in the pale girl's compliance that spurred Maria to obey; in her heart she wanted to do it; the very prospect triggered a giddy sweet pleasure. 'Here – across these cheeks. Good. Hard. Harder! And get that finger in deep.' Maria's fingertip, far inside the girl now, was pressed against something hard there, like the stone inside a soft fruit. It started stabbing her fingertip and the pale girl began to groan, breasts shaking, belly drum-tight. 'Oh, sweet fuck,' the lady whispered in Maria's ear. 'She's coming. Oh, beautiful, dirty, precious creature . . .' The whipping stopped; the switch dropped to the floor. The stabbing of the stone inside the girl softened to a beating pulse. And the lady's lips, moving ever closer, moistly closed about Maria's burning ear lobe. Maria, dizzy with the pleasure of forcing female pleasure through sexual penetration and pain, gazed in awed arousal and mortified dismay at the girl's glaze that now coated her fingers so thickly.

'Ean, take charge of Leah for us, would you?' the lady asked. She led Maria across the room, standing her beside a chair on which the lady now seated herself. Maria's gaze was drawn back to the girl and to the young man named Ean, still naked, still hard. The girls were right about this part of a man: it looked as if a curved bone had been pushed up it from inside his bottom. The head was glistening as if leaking.

'See – he's masturbating her, like you did, but not so well,' the lady whispered. Maria watched in deep arousal, and she watched the young man's stiffness bobbing. Then the lady took her hand and stroked her palm with very gentle fingertip swirls. She felt her nipples tightening; the sensation of falling kept coming in her belly. Then the man called Kapler started whipping the suspended naked girl on the cheeks of her bottom. Maria felt the lady's other hand slowly sliding under the hem of her skirt. She shivered as the fingers ventured up the back of her leg, then round the side, searching for the draw-string of her knickers. Her knickers dropped to the floor. 'Open your thighs,' the lady whispered almost imperceptibly. Maria complied and felt beautiful shivers as the lady's fingers and thumb gently reached up and lightly grasped between them. She heard the lady sigh and settle to touching, softly fingering, besieging this nudity, trying to coax it open.

Maria's shaking gaze was fixed upon the shuddering girl being whipped, and the naked young man's hand prising under and around her swollen female part, gathering it up, lifting and squeezing. Maria felt her own pleasure building as the girl's taut body hung so lewdly in his hand. 'She's coming – again. Sweet fuck . . .,' the lady murmured and Maria, trembling on the verge, stepped completely out of her knickers as the hand between her thighs, finding unfettered access, began clutching in sexual rhythm with the punished girl's tortured breathing. When the girl looked pleadingly across the room, directly at Maria, the lady lifted Maria's skirt at the front and the whipping paused and

77

Maria felt her sex bursting open like a swollen fruit, spilling its juice all over the lady's fingers, which sank deeper as the thumb slid up her bottom. This vision of Maria's coming to climax on the lady's fingers drew the other girl's come so harshly and deeply from her body that she bucked until Maria heard the young man's knuckles crack between her thighs.

The lady then dismissed Maria. 'Leave your knickers where they lie; I doubt you shall have need of them henceforth. But take your tray, girl.' The lady's face was stony. Maria, at first stunned, rushed sobbing from the room.

Afterwards, the cruel callousness of that dismissal remained with her, but so did the other memories – the unbearable sensations of lewdness and pleasure, the images of the naked men, but most of all, the intimacy of that contact with a restrained nude girl and – once the sexual touching is combined with whipping – those powerful, heady feelings of control. After that day a marked change befell Maria: no longer content just to watch the other girls in their fake enactments, she thrust a new edge of craving into their girlish games; instead of recycling tales of the lewdness of the guests she fell to instigating the antics. As for the present, there was a score to settle, starting with some enquiries at the livery yard.

With Maria gone, Lauren was staring at Leah, whose belly was still quaking after the powerful surge of pleasure she had spilled into Ean's hand. The intense climax had started in her bottom under the probing of that middle finger. Then the thumb sliding up her sex had triggered the feeling that his whole hand was inside her, back and front, and was squeezing her womb.

'You can't leave her too long like that. Take her down – carefully,' Lauren finally told the men.

Leah was unfastened and bundled on to the bed. She could not move her fingers because the tendons in her wrists felt so stretched. She murmured with the pain as Kapler worked them. 'Free her nipples, Ean.' They had swelled so much that the horsehair was bedded. Goose-flesh spread across her breast as Ean unwound the buried strands. When he sucked her nipples, she felt as if they would burst; her trembling fingers clasped his head and her nails dug into his scalp. He nuzzled the sides of her breasts and under her arms, causing shivers that made the feeling in her nipples more sexual and keen. When she looked up again, Lauren was standing, waiting. Very gently she touched the horsehair bindings at the tops of Leah's thighs. 'Puffy lips and puffy nipples . . . Is she not beautiful, Ean?' In Lauren's other hand were two thongs of leather, like bootlaces. 'Leah, do you know what these are for?'

Leah knew well, for she had used something similar only last night: they were to make the penis bloat to fill a girl as completely as a girl could take. Lauren made her tie them on the men. She sat her on the edge of the bed and made her begin with Kapler. Leah's fingers were weakened and clumsy; his penis, already powerfully erect, bobbed in front of her face. 'Take the cord under the balls,' Lauren corrected. Leah looped the thong under his sac then over the root of his penis and round. 'Take up the slack, Leah,' Lauren encouraged. She ran her fingers, redolent with Maria's musk, under Leah's hair. 'Now tighten it . . .' Her trembling fingers pulled at the thong and pulled again and Kapler gasped. His penis had swelled so fat that its veins stood out blue. As Leah touched it in adjusting the cord, Lauren began to kiss Leah and to fondle her breasts very softly, in the way that women do. Leah began to shake, not simply from the fondling, but also from the pleasure of forcing the male arousal to come on stronger, against the burgeoning pain of such rigid swelling. It felt burning hot now; she could feel its heat on her face, though her face was not quite touching it.

'Keep wrapping the cord round the root,' Lauren murmured, kissing her ear. Kapler shuddered. 'Round again,' Lauren whispered hoarsely. 'Keep it tight – tuck the end in. Pull again – make certain. Now look at it – so fat now. Kiss it.' Lauren was now touching Leah between the legs, masturbating her swollenness very gently and Leah was staying open for it, as best she could, the horsehair cords chafing the tops of her thighs, her slit so narrow in all her swelling, desiring the bulging penis yet sure that it could never fit. She took the burning male flesh in both hands and kissed it like a lover, all the way down its rigid underside to the bedded cord and the bulging sac. As her head tilted to suck the stem she glimpsed Ean's jealous gaze. Then she moaned, for Lauren was teasing out her engorged clitoris, pushing the sheath back. And the heat of all the blood, pumped up inside the penis, seemed to burn her lips; the veins stood out like whipcords. She imagined it inside her body, its hot shiny cap up against her womb, and she almost came on Lauren's probing fingers that were trying to widen her constricted slit to make an oval, prior to penetration. Oil came out of her. 'No – don't close your legs,' Lauren whispered to her. 'We all want to see and I want to feel . . .' Her thighs were shaking as Lauren pulled her head back and held her slit open and the warm trickles came, glistening against the damask sheet.

Leah was then put to binding Ean's penis. It was the larger after tying and its flesh was smoother; it turned bright cherry red and the glans was shiny purple. During the binding, Ean's climax almost came; Leah felt the signs and she slowed and waited. 'Good girl,' Lauren whispered. 'Treat it gently – save it up. We shall very soon need it.' She made Leah lie on the bed,

80

clasping the two erections, one in each hand. When Lauren spread Leah's thighs, Leah impulsively turned and kissed the shiny wet tip of Ean's penis. Lauren tried again with Leah's oval, attempting to widen it. 'Push out,' she encouraged, stroking the flesh rhythmically and very firmly outwards with her thumbs, until Leah moaned and a deep drawing feeling came. Under such tenacious manipulation, though her sex did not truly open, the inner walls slowly erupted. 'Please . . .,' she begged, guiding Ean's penis closer.

'There . . . Teach him,' Lauren murmured approvingly, edging aside, steering her young groom by the hips.

Leah wanted to be penetrated deeply, properly. Ean was already close to gasping with excitement. She softened her grip on the shaft she was guiding but the barest touch seemed almost too much for him. She tried to hold that part of the stem where she knew there was less sensitivity. But in its tautly rigid state even the slightest movement triggered pulses that she could feel reverberating through the root. The buried seminal gland was already overflowing, for its oil was smearing against her out-turned inner lips. That feeling, of the trembling cock-tip painting its oil on her, was delicious. It could only be seconds before his climax. Steadily, gently, Leah tried to push just the glans inside her. 'Shh,' she murmured, deep and guttural, trying to calm this novice lover, trying to slow him. She groaned as the glans at last went in; her body held it, tried to burst it. None of the stem was in, yet the feeling was truly sublime. Leah stared up into his eyes, so drugged by this new pleasure she was giving him, so lost in longing. For a beautiful timeless moment Leah held the head of Ean's penis tightly captive in her flesh. Then, increasing the cruel pressure, she reached up and kissed him, very gently, and held that kiss, while her sex still squeezed just the head of his cock and she judged his come precisely – felt the hopeless spasm that immediately precedes ejaculation. Then she lay back very slowly and leisurely, took the exposed shaft in her fingers and made her sex gently expel the glans. A second later his fluid squirted like boiling milk over the out-turned bloated inner lips of her sex and up her belly. It seemed to keep coming, thrumming past her thumb-pad that was pressed against the underside of his stem.

Kapler swiftly lifted Leah's leg until her body twisted over on its side, and her fingers and thumb lost contact with Ean's penis. The last of his ejaculate sprayed over the horsehair encircling the top of her thigh and ran into the cleft of her buttocks. Her anus trembled, coated in warm semen. Kapler massaged it open with his fingers. 'See – it knows what to do,' he murmured. Leah dared not breathe now: the steady masturbation of her anus was stirring such lewd and pleasurable feelings. Suddenly the grossly distended head of Kapler's penis forced the semen-wetted opening wide. 'Tuck your knees up tight, girl.' She gasped as his penis pushed again and bulged against her tight vagina from behind. She tried to lift her leg to expose her pushed-out knob to toying. Lauren touched, deliberately too gently. Then Kapler's penis thrust inside Leah; its leather binding rimmed her anus; hot ejaculate burst inside her.

She reached again for Ean's glans. Lauren rubbed her between the legs, very steadily, extracting deep pleasure from Leah's womb. When Leah climaxed, Ean's ejaculate came again, hot upon her goose-fleshed breasts. When Lauren reached to smear it round her puffed-up nipples, Leah took Ean's weeping glans into her mouth and simply kept it there until it seemed a further climax overtook him. She put a hand against his belly and a hand beneath his sac, pressing the binding cord, taking deep sucks that drew his yield. He

82

shuddered and caressed her face as she continued to try to drink even when he was dry.

Neither of the two penises deflated fully, even after Leah had unwound their bindings. She licked and kissed the deep grooves that she had incised around their roots and under their sacs. While she was licking Ean's penis, Kapler fingered her anus open, and she felt his warm semen running out. Lauren brought Maria's moist knickers from where they lay on the floor; Leah thought she meant to put them on her. But Lauren carefully turned them inside out and bunched them up and very slowly pushed them up Leah's bottom. The pleasure came as the men looked on; Leah lay rigidly on her side, her knees tucked up, afraid to move, her fingers clutching the sheet, not wanting her pleasure to come in such a way, but come it did – very strongly and surely, with Lauren's fingers, sheathed in the half inserted knickers, rubbing their girl-soaked inner surface steadily through the tightening tender opening. Lauren then sighed and touched Leah between the legs very gently, extending the anal come to a beauteous soft and pervasive genital pleasure, such as only a woman's fingertips can bestow.

The men said that they would play with her overnight. Kapler lifted her into his lap, with Maria's knickers still half pushed inside her, and gently raised her ankles in the air. Then the door burst open. There was the briefest glimpse of an avenging Maria, before Merek – eyes wild, already crazed with jealousy – swept past the retreating chambermaid and crashed into the room, dragging his steersman, Asgal, by the ear.

For a few long seconds Lauren stared at the interloper, who appeared almost paralysed with rage as he glared back at her. Then she said calmly: 'Who are you, my lord? Though I suspect I can guess . . .'

Merek barked back: 'My lady, it is *he* ...!' – stabbing a finger at Asgal, cowering on his knees beside him – 'this despicable creature, my own steersman, who has guessed who *you* are!'

For the first time that evening Lauren paled, clearly thrown by the remark. Kapler looked distinctly uncomfortable as Merek went on: 'Your husband is a successful leather merchant, is he not? Well, he has his shipment aboard my boat. And this slime-bag ...' – he said, kicking Asgal – 'not content with prostituting my slave, now has it in mind to blackmail you with tales of what you get up to with your stable-hands while your husband is away!' He stared hard at Lauren. 'Madam – I care not that you cuckold your husband. But when my steersman seeks now to embroil me in his vile scheming, as a way of mitigation ... Tell her!' Again he kicked Asgal, who could only curl into a whimpering ball. Then Merek, temporarily drained, turned in hopeless disillusion to address the room. 'What price loyalty?' he asked resignedly. Lauren bit her lip. He had not looked at Leah even once but she burst into tears.

Merek turned sharply back to Asgal. 'Get out!' He manhandled him through the doorway and sent him crashing down the stairs. Then he came back for Leah.

Ean surged forward: 'Don't touch her!'

'Out of my way, boy ...' Merek raised his arm, threatening to strike the young groom.

'No!' Leah cried out. And this was the final betrayal for Merek, who immediately struck Ean down. Then he bundled his fickle possession under his arm and left.

# 6

# An Infusion of Pleasure

Ean stared dejectedly across the carriage at his mistress. In the lodge she had helped him up from the floor, though he had not needed assistance. He tried to return her smile now but could not. The unsteadiness that had caused him to trip was simply the shock at being attacked by Leah's master when all he had done was intervene to save her from his unwarranted and ill-directed wrath. On Lady Lauren's instruction Kapler had blocked the doorway to prevent Ean from going after them.

His heart still pounded. So many emotions in so short a time . . . He could not get Leah out of his mind. Until yesterday he had scarcely gone further than kissing a girl; then his mistress had beguiled him. And now he had met Leah. She was so beautiful – even those blemishes were like precious maculae on her soft white skin; she was angelic and warm and yet so sexual, inflaming him with a passion he had not guessed existed. He could not put aside that vision of the pleading in her tearful eyes as she had begged her master not to harm him – a slave-girl putting herself at cruel risk to come to his defence. He had never known such selfless kindness – not from any girl, not from anyone. When he thought of that, the emotion threatened to engulf him.

His mistress was staring at him with a concerned expression. 'Ean, come here and sit beside me.' Kapler tactfully turned to look out of the window into the night. Ean half-heartedly moved across. Her hand took his but she did not speak further. Perhaps she understood something of his inner turmoil.

He had earlier asked to be allowed to drive the carriage, saying the fresh air would clear his mind, but Lady Lauren had refused. She too was concerned about him. She drew his head lightly to her slender shoulder and, closing his eyes, he breathed the beautiful scent of her hair. He had never felt so warmly cocooned in female protection as he did tonight. He took the hand that had been holding his and quietly raised its fingertips to his lips: the soft musky scent and taste of Leah still lay deliciously upon them. His mistress shivered as he very gently sucked her fingertips. He wanted to search out ways of arousing women, in gratitude for the luscious feelings they aroused in him. His mistress was beautiful too. He felt his flesh stirring, then the warmth of her other hand upon his trousered thigh, moulding protectively around the growing bulge. It remained there until the carriage drew up outside the mansion.

Ean, self-conscious about his very obvious state of arousal, at first remained still. When he did attempt to move, his mistress knowingly held him back and nodded to Kapler, who got out and went in the direction of the stables.

'I don't want you going to your quarters in this state,' his mistress whispered. She put her hand across his brow. 'You seem feverish. You shall sleep in the house tonight. My husband is away, so you shall have his bedroom.' Her eyes met his and calmly held off his questioning gaze. 'Should your condition worsen in the night, the servants are to hand. My husband would wish it.' Still her gaze did not falter.

'Very well, mistress,' Ean whispered.

'Lauren ... You must call me that while we are in the house.'

The power of suggestion is strongest when the recipient conspires with the perpetrator. Ean did not want to rebuff the attentions of his handsome mistress. She directed the servants to prepare him a soothing bath. It lulled him almost to sleep and once the servants were gone his mistress returned. She sat by the bath, watching him through the wisps of steam until the water had turned tepid. 'Shall I ring for more hot water?' she asked.

'No, mistr ... No, Lauren – thank you,' he answered softly.

'Then you are ready?'

'Yes.' He felt his heartbeat quicken at the possible underlying meaning of her words.

'Ah, but not quite ready ...' She rolled her sleeves. 'Kneel up, Ean.' She poured perfumed oil into her palm and slowly and methodically spread it all over her fingers. His erection was building even before she clasped his penis and worked its foreskin back and forth with a slippery pressure that made the arousal almost unbearable. Her other hand caressed his buttocks; her fingers sought the crease; within a second, her oily thumb was inside, pressing against the wall of flesh behind the root of his penis. Ean shuddered and almost ejaculated as the thumb-pressure was maintained while his foreskin was stretched back, shinily tight, and simply held. He felt as if his glans would burst through it. He heard Lauren's breathing – deep but very slow and controlled – and she too was trembling. Then she raised her chin and murmured: 'Kiss me, Ean. But do not let the semen come. Control it. Learn to keep it in until I decide the time is ripe. Now, kiss slowly.'

Her lips were soft and small and brushed against his in little wisps of desire as her thumb pressed its delicious torture against his seminal gland, keeping it on the brink of convulsion. Ean gasped against her lips and then she drew back to look with pride and delight at what she was doing. 'When your coming threatens, I can feel the gland inside you start to pulse against my thumb,' she whispered. 'But it has not swelled enough as yet. We need to make it bigger – more swollen with delicious come. There – did you feel that little push against my thumb? Now kiss again.' The softness and pleasure of Lauren's renewed kissing almost tipped the gland into convulsion. Very slowly she eased the tight pressure on his foreskin before carefully withdrawing her thumb. Then she helped him from the bath and proceeded to dry him in fragrant towels. 'Good boy – it's staying hard. Turn sideways – put your hands behind you. Let Lauren look. Mmm ... It's quite lovely like that. Some say it's the test of a man – how long he can keep an erection. I prefer to think of it as the test of the woman.' She then led him by his penis to her husband's bedroom.

Lauren's slender fingers collared his aroused flesh with such a delicate squeezing rippling pressure that the feeling of wanting to come was ever-present. She kept hold until she had turned back the covers and made him sit on the side of the bed. Then she put her hand across his forehead again and said: 'There is still fever ... Do you feel faint?' Ean shook his head weakly. He felt drained of all ordinary strength yet brimming with desire and emotion. 'Open your knees.' She slid both hands around his sac, enclosing it very gently. 'You're hot here too.' The sides of her fingers, pressing into the sensitive angles of his groin, made him gasp softly as his erection stood harder than ever. Lauren bent forward, kissed his nipples, then gently took them in turn between her teeth. The finger pressure at the tops of his inner thighs continued; his sac tightened to a ball, which she clasped tightly as the nipple-nipping torture by her teeth continued. When Lauren finally drew back there was a globule of clear liquid at the tip of Ean's penis. 'Only a small escape – that's good,' she crooned. She sipped it swiftly and looked up at him with its glaze upon her lips. Then she kissed him through his murmured protests, smearing his own salty glaze over his lips – chiding him softly: 'Yes, you must have it, else how can you hope to know what a girl feels when she tastes you?' – while her fingers found the buried tubes feeding from his tightened ball sac and squeezed them expertly, cruelly, until his murmurs turned to gasps. She drew back again and admired his trembling, seeping erection. 'You must lie down, now, Ean. The strain has been great. I shall bring a preparation to quell the fever and to help you sleep.'

In the kitchens, Lauren took great care with the preparation of the infusion, selecting from her secret store only the fattest, firmest and greenest of the special seed cases, so remarkable in their properties – miraculous, some would have it, though Lauren, being more pragmatic, ascribed their ecstatic effects to hallucination rather than mystical intervention. Whatever the cause, the upshot was potent. She crushed the cases carefully with the opal pestle, tipped the precious debris into the little copper pot of boiled water and returned it very briefly to the fire. As soon as the bubbles appeared she removed it, stirred it with a stick of juniper and watched the pale blue colour appear and slowly deepen. The aromatic scent of juniper filled her nostrils. She then put the concoction aside to cool while she went to bathe.

Once there, she thought of her young groom – aroused, his sleep surely held at bay by his body's yearning – still lying in her husband's bed, awaiting her return. And she thought of that other yearning she had once induced, that long time past, within her first full

89

lover. He was a soldier, a captain, an acquaintance of her father's, though her father, a man of title, would certainly have prohibited the liaison had he ever found it out. Prior to that, Lauren's only experiences were of mutual discovery with her female cousin; but even that had swiftly taught her how to suffer pleasure and how to give it. And the girl-talk had nurtured her inquisitiveness about men.

Her captain was her elder by fifteen years. He knew enough not to attempt anything under her father's roof but in the event he knew little else, certainly nothing about girls beyond the basest attack, like a creature of the fields. Even so, for Lauren, there were aspects that were deeply thrilling – the clandestine meeting at the quiet inn, the first baring of her body before a man, the first fumbling fingerings, the primal sexuality of penetration by hot male flesh – her own nearness of pleasure when her captain had groaned and her body had felt his pumping start. After the swift withdrawal she had watched the white glutinous issue pulsing out – large quantities, as if he had been storing it up – coming hot against her naked sex, burning her taunted clitoris, scorching her soul.

For Lauren the experience was at once pleasurable yet acutely unfulfilling. Her soldier lover looked intensely pleased and replete. But Lauren knew there was much more to be undertaken by the sufficiently brave and willing. Though he was by far her senior and appeared knowledgeable and accomplished – organising the secret rendezvous, giving secure instructions to the servants at the inn, receiving deference from the landlord; in fact, seemingly controlling all that befell – nevertheless it was Lauren who had seduced her captain: she was here in this bed by her own design and now she would bend him to her bidding.

With the covers drawn back, the vision of her slim nudity held him fast. She lay sprawled just as he had

90

left her, her lips open, her breathing heavy, her small nipples erect, her thighs nakedly apart, a dense pool of his semen still warm upon her engorged sex, her clitoris still yearning. She kept her eyes fixed upon him as she sighed and moaned and dipped her fingertips into the pool and touched herself within and without, and all round the hard bud of her clitoris, inciting her arousal very slowly. The newness of this sensation of slippery warm semen coating her fingers made this means of arousal exquisite – the sliding against that shiny knot of flesh, the soft slither of her labia through her fingers. At her climax, her gaze slewed sideways, her belly cramped uncontrollably, she cried out loud and almost fainted under that beautiful feeling.

And then her captain was upon her once more, plunging in through the tightness of her inexperienced vagina now rendered so slippery, shoving up to the very hilt and spurting new semen deep inside her. Again he withdrew too swiftly, not knowing what she needed, perhaps not caring over-deeply. But her tightness as he pulled out kept the semen within her. A soft throbbing now taunted the entrance to her womb. All between her legs still felt swollen: that single climax was insufficient to her needs. But she kept her thighs firmly closed, kept that swollen feeling in. And as he lay abed, asleep, Lauren caressed him, kissed his back and snuggled close and – though much was missing from this liaison – felt powerful warmth for what this first experience with a man represented.

In the early hours, her desire was so compelling that she sat up. Her captain lay asleep on his front: she drew back the sheet and ran her fingers down his muscular back. He murmured but did not stir. One by one she traced the bumps of his spine; near the base was one more prominent than the rest – perhaps from an old injury in battle, she surmised. On an impulse, Lauren mounted him. She spread her thighs about him as if he were an animal she was riding and she rode his buttocks, rode his little bump with her own knot rubbing right against it. He woke but curiously did not resist: he simply raised his buttocks slightly to free his swelling erection. Lauren thrust all her weight against him, trapping his erection under his belly. And very soon she felt his shuddering come. It was as if she could feel his pulsing thrumming against her clitoris through the very knob of his spine. Her second orgasm came more powerfully than the first and kept coming until she felt the hot stored semen pouring out of her and soaking generously into the cleft of his buttocks. Slowly, studiously, Lauren worked it up his bottom, using her fingers, until, pressing inside against the root of his penis, she felt him shed another shuddering moan. Then she collapsed forwards against his back, satiated now, her teeth biting his shoulder and her nipples poking into him like little stones.

Such was Lauren's first experience with a man. By next day her captain was chastened. She did not renew their contract of secret meeting; there was no purpose to a reunion; he would remember her well enough from that single calling. Her husband, on their wedding night, had dubbed her playfully a 'nymph of desire' and she had answered, 'Yes my lord, you have it right – neither wife nor mistress.' He had taken her reply as jest but what she had spoken portended a truth: Lauren remained her own mistress, subservient to nobody.

After bathing, Lauren donned her bed-jacket and dressing-gown, returned to the kitchens, strained the infusion into a cup and carried it to her husband's bedroom, where her young groom had drawn the thin sheet over himself and now lay on his side, soundlessly asleep. Lauren placed the cup carefully on the bedside table and seated herself quietly beside and behind him on the bed. She sat for many minutes simply looking at him – his broad strong shoulders, his narrow waist, his youthful face – before she touched him, the tips of her fingers gently brushing the tousled hair from the side of his face. He murmured one word, 'Leah . . .', and turned on to his back, still asleep. Lauren bent over him and kissed him very softly on the lips. Her hand came to rest against his thigh, where the erection still burgeoned strongly. She closed her fingers round it through the sheet and when he murmured she put little kisses upon his lower lip until his eyes flickered open.

'Mistress . . .,' he gasped.

'Lauren . . .,' she whispered. Then she frowned. 'You were anxious, in your sleep, fretting, trying to cry out.'

'Was I? I cannot recollect . . .'

'No matter – it's the fever. Sit up and drink this. It will calm you.'

Ean drank the bitter contents thirstily and trustingly, oblivious of their potency. 'Drink it all,' Lauren whispered, 'every drop.' Her gown had fallen open and her jacket was unfastened. He was staring at her breasts. She wanted to bury his face against them and have his lips softly searching by blind feel for her nipples and for the soft undersides and for the musk she was making under her arms. When a man did that to her, the sensation was primordial, sublime.

'Lie down now, Ean – rest.' Again she laid her cupped palm against his erect penis through the thinness of the sheet. She wanted to leave it in that state of tauntedness, unable to deflate, while the potion spun its web and he became a living prisoner in its world of special dreaming.

A short while later he was breathing steadily in a deep, unmoving sleep. Lauren drew back the sheet, slid a supple, watertight sheath over his swollen penis and tied it off under his sac. He did not move – nor could he, through the efficacy of the potion – but the sheath would capture any emissions that enraptured dreaming might provoke. Lauren covered him again and left him.

# 7

# A Dream Shared

In the early hours Lauren returned to her husband's bedroom, where her young groom now lay in a state of semi-torpidity. This time she locked the door behind her, precluding any chance – however slight – of interruption. Sufficient time had elapsed for the drug to have infused its peculiar potency into his inexperienced body, and she knew that the first time always proved to be the most heady and compelling. Already her heart was thumping, her mind was racing – what pleasures lay in store? She removed her dressing-gown, leaving herself completely nude apart from her short bed-jacket.

Ean lay exactly as she had left him. He at first appeared serene, until she came closer. In fact his whole body was trembling, as if a bolt of lightning was passing through it, or as if he were a creature impaled alive. His lips were moving ever so slightly. Lauren leant across and touched her lips very lightly to his: there was no reaction other than the continued trembling. She kissed his brow and felt a genuine fever that had not existed before he had taken the drug. She drew back the sheet; his handsome erection stood harder than ever, proudly arching, swelling against the constriction of the thin sheath. Lauren untied the sheath very gently and began gently furling it back; the seal was gradually yielding; the shaft glistened with warm exudation; the scent of juniper filled her nostrils. She lowered her lips very softly to the freshly exposed base of the shaft and sucked the hot glistening undersurface, compressing the undertube in rhythmic sucks, pumping it like a slow heartbeat, tasting in the exuded moisture the slightly bitter suffusion from the drug, and feeling her own excitement quickening to an almost audible pulsing in her throat. She heard him murmur then moan: he was waking. When she sat up, he opened his eyes and tried to take in his surroundings. 'Where am I?' he mumbled. 'Where's Leah?' he suddenly shouted and sat bolt upright, shaking violently.

'Shh . . .' Lauren, her bed-jacket completely open, held him, breast to naked breast. 'Shh . . . my darling, you were dreaming – crying out, so I came to you.' She kissed his naked neck and felt the thudding pulse against her lips. Then she drew back and kissed him fully on the mouth.

'I . . . I don't understand, mistress.'

'*Lauren* . . . You must call me by my name.'

Looking down, Ean suddenly seemed to realise that Lauren wore nothing apart from her bed-jacket. He had never seen her so exposed. Lauren took his hand and pressed it softly to her naked belly. His erection pulsed in sustained arousal against the half-fitted sheath. He stared down in mystification at the sheath then back at her. 'If it were all a dream then how did this –'

'Was that in your dream, my darling?'

'Yes.'

'Then don't touch it. Leave it be.' Lauren pursed her lips, shook her head and took him gently by the shoulders. 'Dreams are sometimes augurs, Ean. Can you recall your dream? Then you must tell me – all that befell there, however painful or strange it might seem.' At that, his gaze faltered and Lauren's excitement mounted. She reached across and stroked his nipples very gently and nervously with just the tips of her fingers. She was in no hurry; she just kept cajoling him in this way, very softly until at last his belly tightened and the muscles rippled, like a shiver, and his sheathed erection bobbed and stood out from his body. Lauren vowed to keep him in sexual torment. She leant forward, brushed her cheek against his then softly sucked his ear lobe. She urged him again: 'Lie down, Ean. Tell me.' Ean sighed and succumbed.

'I saw Leah,' he whispered. Then his voice became stronger. 'So vividly . . . As if it were actually happening . . .'

'You were with her?'

'Not with her, but I saw and heard everything.' Lauren waited. Then Ean closed his eyes and whispered: 'She was being punished, Lauren, for what she had done with me.' Again Lauren said nothing but she slid her fingers gently into place against his belly, under the arch of his erect penis, reassuring him through gentle abdominal pressure with her palm whilst at the same time monitoring his erection, which, should it ever wane, would warn her by touching the back of her hand. As Ean's mind focused on the memory, his eyes remained closed but the words flooded from his lips and Lauren was pleased to note that his erection stayed strong.

'How could any master be so unforgiving? Even before he had made any move to discipline her, even before the gag was put between her lips, she was weeping abjectly. He took her below deck to a dingy cabin at the stern of his barge. I saw him fling her naked on the bed and make her open her legs. That boatman was watching them from the cabin doorway.'

'Asgal – the one who brought her to the lodge?'

'None other.'

'Her master allowed it?'

'Her master instructed him to remain there. He wanted a witness; I think he wanted to make her punishment that much worse.'

Lauren snuggled close, her pulse quickening at the mention of punishment. It seemed strange that Ean had so soon forgotten his role in Leah's whipping at the lodge; was it protectiveness or covetousness that fired his present rancour? Whichever, his passion was genuine and strong. Lauren laid her head against his chest and pictured Leah, afraid and wide-eyed, open in heart, open now in body, seeking some sign that the coldness in her master's soul might melt. 'Go on,' Lauren whispered, taking Ean's nipple into her mouth.

'He tethered her by her toes: he put separate cinctures round the big toe of each foot and drew the tethers over a beam above the bed. Then he drew the tethers wider until her body was wrenched open to its tender heart.'

With a shudder of pleasure Lauren pictured this submissive girl, her buttocks lifted from the bed, her toe joints stretched, her sex gaping – and with the hired hand's smirk to add piquancy to this beautiful exhibition. Lauren teased herself between the legs, pressing her labia open, wanting to feel the very pleasure that the slave-girl had suffered. She sucked Ean's nipple very fully until a deep ripple moved through his belly. Then she grasped the most swollen girth of his sheathed penis and squeezed, slowly increasing the pressure until she felt it kick in spasm and she held it at that point, gently tight. She knew that his pre-come would be slowly leaking its potent distillate into the head of the sheath.

She made him describe that scene again in intimate detail, all the while touching herself and holding his penis collared in that deeply sexual squeeze. His luscious pre-come flowed steadily into the sheath.

Then gently Lauren prised the sheath from his throbbing penis and carefully tipped its potent contents into her mouth.

When that heady liquid slid across her tongue, Lauren knew the rumours were true: the potency of the drug was doubled by passage through the male gland. The effect was immediate: she felt giddy; a shiver moved through her body; her vision seemed to shrink and she swooned across Ean's prostrate body. His naked penis swelled and pulsed above her lips. Again she clasped the glans, tightening her grip until the next clear droplet hung from the open tip. Then she urged him to tell what happened next. And now, as Ean spoke in broken phrases and Lauren closed her eyes and licked his droplets, it was as if the punishment in the cabin was unfolding under her own becharmed gaze.

She saw Leah's master, Merek, his expression freezing cold, standing between Leah's upraised thighs, putting delicious terror there, squeezing her puffy inner lips flat, smoothing them open and plastering them back with the sticky oil that she had exuded. Then he took hold of the twist of Maria's knickers that still protruded from her bottom and very slowly, against the tightness, began to withdraw it.

It made Lauren shiver and squirm. Her hand that had been collaring Ean's penis reached down beneath his ball sac and pressed two fingertips up against his anus. His penis bucked. Her lips sealed softly about its head and gently sucked the delicious intoxicating droplets that the gland was yielding while her fingertips kept taunting that defiant muscle in his cleft. She made him moan from the continual milking as, in her state of heightened vision, she seemed to see it all – the whipping of those tender inner lips, so deliciously plastered open; the narrow, searing lines criss-crossing each inner surface; and Leah's oil exuding like nectar through the very pores, her spray springing with each snap of the crop. Soon those inner lips would be swelling swiftly, grotesquely beautiful, like the petals of a lovely flower infested by galls.

Lauren, now beside herself with arousal, opened her eyes. Ean was breathing deeply, trying to delay his climax but almost on the verge of coming. Gently she withdrew her fingers from the cleft under his sac. Then she sat up. Still facing him, she manoeuvred herself across his chest and into the riding position astride his face. She took hold of his penis with one hand reaching behind her. Then she took her open sex and fed it through his lips – for it was important that it went all the way inside – and kept feeding it in, forcing his mouth yet wider to take it, while she clutched his penis ever tighter, choking it. She made him drink all the wetness that was coming out of her.

Suddenly his sucking became hard, urgent, almost as hard as she was squeezing him. Immediately she stopped squeezing and pressed her thumb where his penis rooted in his belly. He bucked and tried to thrust his tongue, like a cock, up inside her sex – far up – and she felt his bobbing penis seeking succour, thrusting at the air. She pressed harder and harder with her thumb until his hips rose from the bed and she felt the straining penis curving over and its mouth stabbing wetly up against her lower spine. And that contact, the wet stabbing in the small of her back, so rhythmically repeated and in so sensitive a place, stirred Lauren's arousal cruelly far. She had not wanted to allow her guard to drop, but now she could not stop herself. She grasped Ean's head and, in shudders of inescapable pleasure, deep inside his sucking mouth, impaled upon his swollen tongue, fucking it, she felt her captive cunt helplessly yielding its climax. Then she collapsed forwards over his face and lay panting, her burning cheek against the coolness of the pillow. Ean did not attempt to move; he was still acquiescent and that gave Lauren heart. She reached back, far back, in order to renew the contact with his penis and found it still erect and very hot indeed: the shaft was slippery with exuded juices and a new warm heavy droplet hung at the tip.

Lauren climbed off Ean's face and crouched beside him. Her tongue-tip gently sucked that droplet from his taunted glans. Then she immediately kissed him, poking that tongue-tip, soaked in his pre-come, far into his mouth until she again felt his erection buck. Withdrawing her tongue, she murmured: 'My darling . . . Ean . . . .' She leant over his penis and pressed her moist lips against the sensitive upturned underside, softly sucking the pleasure centre near the crown, until she heard his first gasp. Then she immediately drew back, holding the penis very still, her finger and thumb collared round its base. She raised her head and whispered: 'You have not finished your story.'

As Lauren continued to stimulate his leaking penis, Ean spoke with his eyes tightly shut. 'After the whipping, the master threw his boatman from the cabin and then came back to Leah.'

'And what did he do to her?'

'He unfastened her gag and he . . .' Ean's voice hesitated as the emotion welled inside him.

'What?' Lauren maintained the gentle rhythm of that finger-collar round the base of his soaking penis. When Ean did not go on she whispered: 'He kissed her, didn't he?' Again she felt his penis jerk, so she repeated: 'He kissed her – wouldn't you, Ean?' And she felt it jerk once more and she clasped its head with her other hand and kissed his lips and he moaned into her mouth. 'No, not yet, my darling . . .' With this other hand, she made a second finger-collar – very wet – and held the widest girth of his penis lightly encircled, as if by a little wet rubbery vagina that every

101

so often would go into a soft moist spasm. She maintained this singular simulation while she taunted him gently by taking up the story.

'I see her now: the little slave, fully naked in her proud master's arms, returning his kisses – wanting them, even with her legs wrenched open in the air, even with her wanton knob so buried in the swollen scarlet petals of her punished girlish folds . . . And – see – he tries to touch it and she gasps into his mouth. Even through the pain she experiences pleasure as he bursts aside her burning petals to taunt arousal into that sensitive little tip.'

Lauren pressed her thumb-pad into the underside of Ean's penis an inch below the cap and slowly rotated it back and forth as she continued to ply him with her vision of the story.

'The master tries to unsheath her lovely clitoris but it will not come out properly, though he kisses her gently and her legs are still open and her little cunt is burning, scarlet from the whipping. But all her pleasure is being channelled through that buried erection that he tries to extract. Our little slave groans and twists in her tethers; her master holds her clitoris nipped, pursuing each surge of her twisting, preventing slippage. And for that long beautiful time of writhing, the master watches her face. And he smiles with satisfaction when her pleasure does not come.'

Lauren smiled now, for she had kept Ean's erection strong. She took her thumb away and replaced it with her pouted lips, whose sucking then quick withdrawal extracted another heavy droplet from the tip of his penis, to fall into the clear pool that was steadily accumulating on his belly.

'Do you see the parallels, Ean? The master stimulates her clitoris till it subsides into acquiescence; her arousal is ever-present yet her pleasure does not come. How beautiful . . . All the turmoil in her lovely belly is expressed in oil – just as you are making now, Ean. Her burning petals glisten with it. If you close your eyes you will see her now. Tiny, delicious beads of musk mist the creases of her thighs. See – her master's tongue-tip licks them but does not venture up against her knob. He tortures her this way. And now he unties her toes, massages them, kisses the aching muscles of her inner thighs, then says he will possess her in a very special way.'

'What way . . . ?' Ean murmured.

'The way the monks used to use her . . . that is what he tells her. He brings a length of hessian sacking. He asks her to turn over.' Lauren sat up, whispering: 'Turn over, Ean, on to your front. Let me help. Lie on the pillow. Double it up. Do not trap this . . .' She carefully directed his erection down and then, against the tension, back between his open thighs, so that she retained access. It curved down like a buttress into the mattress. Its balls were clinging to the stem with the tightness of acute excitement. She spread his knees to expose the cleft of his buttocks to touching. Then she stroked her trembling fingertips gently down the crease from the base of his spine; when they reached the puckered mouth she let them rest there very lightly. And while she spoke, her fingertips made little nervous strokes and teasing gestures up against that fleshy rim.

'Our slave-girl lies open-thighed – just as you now lie – but she is open-bellied and stiff-nippled, with her girl-parts now against the roughness of the sacking. She closes her eyes when her master spreads her cheeks.' Gently Lauren slipped her other hand under the head of Ean's penis and milked his oily overflow on to her fingers. 'Then the master sinks his glans.'

Ean gasped out loud as Lauren's oiled fingers slowly opened his anus and slid inside him. Lauren experienced deep satisfaction from this sexual act, a penetration at once depraved and sweet, bunched female fingers stretching male inner skin. It kindled memories of that night with her first lover – her first move to possession, her first true pleasure. In her mind Lauren now saw that other scene, one of monastic quiet, the monks gathered round the lovely girl-slave on the path to training.

'The monks taught Leah anal pleasure, Ean. Even as her hymen remained unbroken, they taught her bottom all the skills of squeezing; they taught the pleasure how to come that way. And in that cabin on the boat, her master seeks only to advance her from where her tutors left off. Now I shall do the same with you. There is a place inside you, up behind the base of your cock – a swelling and ah, yes . . . it is deliciously enlarged.' Ean moaned as Lauren stroked the special gland. 'Now squeeze my fingers with your bottom, squeeze like Leah's bottom does in cleaving to her master's penis so tightly she can feel every detail of its shape' – Lauren's other hand now demonstrated on Ean's penis – 'this thick vein all the way up its undersurface, and this rim around its cap. She feels the thrum of fluid rising up his tube, tickling that pulse just inside her bottom where the muscle grips it. Then the spray of long-held semen bursts inside her; even the tightness of her muscle spasm cannot choke its flow.' Lauren broke off. 'Turn over, Ean. No – I want to keep my fingers in you, for Leah has not come.' He had to lift his leg over her arm and he gasped as he felt her fingers twisting inside him. As his penis bobbed up, Lauren captured the cap in her mouth and just held it, her lips a tight ring around it, simulating the grip of the slave-girl's spasm round her master's penis. Finally her lips released their grip and she sat up and watched the trembling penis dribble seepage from its tip. She kept her fingers inside as she continued.

'The slave-girl dare not move; her arousal is so intense that she is weeping. Her master, seeking a second pleasure, heedlessly thrusts anew, through the pools of jism still inside her. And suddenly her own climax is triggered. Do you know what it feels like to a girl, Ean? It's like a red-hot needle pushing up the shaft of her clitoris, up the deep part, and all the way inside her – a burning, sizzling pleasure that impales her like a squirming thing.'

She felt a shudder through the root of Ean's penis, then hot semen began to spill into her cupped hand, which carried it to his mouth and forced him to drink it. 'There ... Good boy ... You are learning,' she whispered, licking her palm then kissing him deeply, licking salty glutinous circles round his tongue. Deep inside him, the fingers of her other hand proved how generously swollen the gland remained. The more she tongued inside his mouth, the more that gland inside him tightened and hardened until the inner skin felt as if it were stretched around a buried ebony ball. And while she tongued and toyed with him she murmured: 'Do you see now, Ean, why Leah has chosen slavery? Unbridled possession is surely sexuality at its rawest and most beautifully extreme. See how she lies there, her arms outstretched in sweet submission, breast-naked, breathing deeply, awaiting her master's next command. And she is still aroused – for that inner passion never goes away. When he moves to lift her, she murmurs softly, for the sacking draped between her thighs remains, adhering. When he frees her from its cruel embrace, the pattern of its warp and weft remains imprinted into those inner lips and into the delicate smoothness of her beautifully swollen knob.'

Lauren slid her fingers out of Ean's body. She stared at his pulsing erection. 'I am pleased that you have held yourself strong all this while.' Then she lay down beside him and directed him to lie upon her and to go inside her with his penis. She took him very far, for she was very ready; she took him to the balls. But she would not let him move. Instead she wrapped her legs around his, drawing them open and she held him tightly, one arm around his shoulders, the other reaching down his back, her fingers slipping inside him, seeking again that place, the swollen buried ball, and simply pressing and tapping it, pressing then flicking, protractedly, at a pace of her choosing, smothering his anguished gasps with her lips, then grasping his head and whispering, 'Wait ...' until – again at her choosing – the paroxysms of deliverance took him and the powerful, deeply satisfying squirts of thick semen came against her womb.

Afterwards, when it had liquefied inside her, she knelt astride his mouth and made him drink it and found she did not have to force him. And as she suckled him this way, she reached back and felt his erection stiffening for more. It was with his penis rising through her fingers and with her flesh inside his mouth – all the way in again – and with his lips drawing sexual sustenance from her body that Lauren's climax came again, like a freezing electric needle this time, sparking pleasure-jolts inside her. It came twice more that night and she kept him in bed till noon next day. Her new groom was handsome, strong and acutely responsive to the effects of the potion. He was ideally suited to her current needs. She laid plans to enjoy his submissive flesh whenever the opportunity afforded.

But by nightfall he had gone from the house.

'Where is he?' she demanded of Kapler.

'He looked drugged – in a daze.'

'Drugged? Where is he?'

'He said he had to go after that girl, the one from the boat.'

# 8

# Breast Training

While Ean, still abed in his mistress's mansion, was
beginning to awaken from the potion that Lauren had
administered to him, far away aboard Merek's boat all
had fallen quiet and calm. Leah's punishment had
lasted a long time but her unwavering submission had
earned her absolution of a kind and Merek at last
became gentle with her.

'I've dismissed Asgal,' he whispered. 'I blame him
more than you.' He wiped her tears with the tip of the
sheet. Leah tried to reach up to kiss him but she could
move only her head: after the whipping, Merek had
trussed her like a bundle on the bed, with her knees
drawn up and each wrist bound to the corresponding
ankle. 'There . . . like meat for public sale . . .,' he had
sneered; such contempt had lashed her far more cruelly
than the whipping.

Then, shuddering and gasping, she had felt the
freezing clyster nosing into her body at the front,
where she was already so swollen from the sexual
punishment. He said that he would not have her
becoming pregnant by those stable-hands; Leah
pleaded that no seed had got inside there but Merek
did not believe her. Her virgin's chains tinkled against
the barrel of the clyster. Her back hollowed deeply
when she felt the pressure of the fluid in her womb. He

made her come like that. He pulled her nipples as if he were milking her, 'like a heifer,' he said. The distension from the instrument made her clitoris protrude. When he nipped and kiss-taunted its tip, her pleasure came – so strongly that a small pulse of ejaculate squirted and it almost felt to her as if the fluid from the clyster was extruding through her pee-hole. But it was her own come, and Merek became very excited and fell to playing with her like that. Only a little more fluid came. He left her in that state and must have gone to deal with Asgal, for when he returned there was a calmness in his expression and it seemed that Leah was forgiven.

He took hold of the instrument and started to withdraw it from her sex. 'Let the muscle relax,' he chided gently. 'It acts too swiftly and too strongly; it is too ardent in its clinging. And though I love it, it must learn to obey.' Leah whimpered through the kiss he gave her; she too felt full of love, full of giving, but after the horsehair and the whipping she could not help the tightness. Merek persisted, gently increasing the traction. Her bottom lifted from the bed. His lips gently stifled her gasps until the instrument slid free. The stretched, tortured walls of Leah's inner flesh collapsed, and she felt the warm unguent gushing from inside her, flooding the bed, wetting her back. Merek shook his head. 'Don't mind the mess – look at me, Leah – kiss . . . There . . . It is for your preservation that I do these things to you. No babies . . .' Still trussed, she could barely move, so he lay close against her. She managed to kiss his neck and felt warm inside; the ache of that dreadful stretching was now a throbbing pleasure; her nipples still tingled from the pulling they had suffered. Gently he forced her bent knees outwards, pinning her tethered arms, exposing her sex. 'There – like a beautiful butterfly now . . .,' he whispered.

Merek had said from the outset that he would stretch Leah's body open at the front because, being newly broken, she was so narrow there. At first she had been frightened because it meant she would be different from the girl she once was, and that would feel strange; but now it felt nice: her inner flesh was acutely sensitised to being touched up there, far up past the broken membrane. Merek examined her again by touch. As his fingertips explored the broken membrane, caressed its ragged edges, probed deeper, Merek kissed her. As the kiss continued he stretched her open and held her thus. He told her that she was his oyster and that her clitoris was the pearl. Then he kissed her pearl until it protruded from its fleshy surround. He brought salve, which he applied very gently to each of the most prominent of the livid streaks that the horsehair had put on her belly and groin and breasts.

Then very carefully he turned his butterfly over on her front, splayed wide, against the warm wetness of the sheet and, putting his thumb up inside her, pushed her pearl out from behind. 'Don't tighten your bottom when I do this,' he reproved her gently. Then, with his thumb still inside her sex, pushing down and forwards, he leant across and penetrated her bottom with his penis, his burning rigid flesh going deeper, up and back, stirring soft sucking sounds in the semen trapped inside her from before.

In laboured whispers in her ear he asked her again what the other men had done with her. As she tried to tell him as truthfully as she was able, she felt her bottom opening out inside, accommodating the beautiful pleasure of that bedded glans, rocking back and forth, moistly kissing the tender walls of flesh inside her. His thumb kept probing inside her sex, pressing her pearl of pleasure into the slippery wet sheet. When his fingers tried to join the thumb, her sex went into spasm around them. Her climax triggered his. She felt his hot semen squirting deep inside her, stimulating her where the cap of his penis could not reach; she felt the pearl of her clitoris jerking, drowning, pressed into the little foaming pool of her issue.

Afterwards Merek unfastened her, stretched her legs, turned her on to her back and rubbed the tender, punished muscles of her inner thighs. Then he made her spread while he opened her sex with his thumbs. He asked her whether the men had administered something to her to make her come so wetly. Leah shook her head, anxious that her making fluid this way might be considered wrong. Gently, inquiringly, Merek's fingers returned to touch the foamy flecks of issue. Though she enjoyed the touching, she was tense about his wariness. His penis was half swollen and she wanted to caress it but was afraid to make a move. He asked again about what exactly the two men had done – what touchings, penetrations and the like. He asked if she had enjoyed what they did.

'I thought I was there by my master's will – by your will, master.'

'That was not my question.' His expression was unforgiving.

Leah was now so torn by emotion that she could not answer.

Then he said: 'Did you have them both inside you at once?'

'No! It was not like that . . .' Yet it was almost like that – the raw desire that she had experienced with the two men – one of whom had at least shown some kindness. Leah reached up to try to caress Merek. The hard edge of his gaze seemed to soften as he looked at her. Then he said:

'The merchant that I put you to the other night – he said something about your breasts, the way that they are swelling more in the middle, puffy round the nipples. He told me that training could enhance that particular shaping.'

'Training . . . ?' Leah whispered anxiously.

'Don't look so frightened. Here . . . Let me hold you.'

Next morning, Merek had a special leather halter cut for his slave's breasts, with holes wide enough only for her nipples and their velvet surrounds. At the final stage of fitting, Leah stood bare-bottomed in the saddler's workshop while Merek removed her shirt completely and the saddler fitted the halter. 'Hold your arms up,' Merek instructed her. Leah's nipples came erect as the saddler's fingers trembled; she murmured when the halter was tightened. The middle part of each breast was free to extrude through the narrow circular gap while the rest of the breast was constrained and flattened. Merek then stood in front of Leah and made her spread her legs. He lifted her chin. Then quite deliberately, in the saddler's presence, he masturbated her gently. 'Tighter,' he told the man and kept playing with her between the legs. The saddler nervously tightened the halter. Leah murmured with the constriction and the sexual touching; her nipples protruded a little more. 'Tighter,' Merek said again. He had got her clitoris standing hard.

'They won't come any more,' the saddler protested shakily.

'They must. Please do as I say.' Merek stopped touching Leah.

Shaking his head, the saddler tremblingly oiled the surrounds of her nipples to help them squeeze through the gap. Then, as the straps bit in to her ribcage, she felt her nipples slowly extruding more. And suddenly she closed her eyes: that was the moment she needed to be touched, for she could feel their trembling projecting weight swelling against

111

the delicious tightness of the nipple-skin; so distended were they that the slightest movement made them shake. When no touch came, Leah opened her eyes and beheld Merek, now strangely agitated, just staring at her transformation in aroused awe. Then gently he reached for those fleshy engorgements, clutching their puffiness with timid fingertips. 'They're truly heifer's teats now,' he murmured in fascination.

He took her there and then, bent forward across the work-table, clutching her newly sculpted teats, even as the saddler was watching. Merek's thrusts, deep within Leah's belly, kept lifting her heels from the floor. He made her come by thrusting: the masturbation had prepared her; then her teats' brushing the leather-topped table was the trigger. Leah gasped out loud, her liquid pleasure sprinkling its silver beads across the leather tracery of the saddler's table.

During subsequent days Merek kept this training halter on Leah almost all of the time, except while she was sleeping. Gradually her breasts developed their new, elongated shape. Their erect fleshy columns, extending almost a hand's-breadth from her ribcage, felt alien to Leah and bestowed unfamiliar sensations and strange pleasures wherever they were touched or sucked. Merek liked to watch the way she lay in bed, doubly self-conscious with the halter gone, not knowing where to put these breasts, unable to get used to their shape. But the removal of the device became an interlude of deep sensuality for Leah.

The unfastening would be so slow and gentle that every soft tiny skin-hair came erect. Her cheek lay on the pillow; her eyes stayed closed. She would feel her master's breath against her cheek; his lips would kiss her eyelids; her shoulders would feel deliciously naked as the freed straps were lifted away. And he would kiss there too – with small tickles of his tongue-tip in the

112

furrows transecting her shoulders. The strap would fall
forward; the kiss would progress under her arm; the
halter would be gently prised away from her breast and
the first tubule of captive flesh unthreaded. The tight
constraining ring of leather, sliding up this narrow
tubule, would cause a deep sucking pleasure, gently
propelling the swell to the teat, and the feeling would
come, as if fluid were being expressed through her
nipple, and she would look down at herself in trembling awe in case that should happen. Then her eyes
would close again as the leather ring came free and
Merek gently grasped her naked tubule in his hand and
squeezed it. But the only fluid that came out of Leah
was that expressed by arousal between her legs. Merek
would paint this about her labia and sometimes he
would taste it. His tasting of her moistened sex would
always make his penis very hard and Leah would try
to touch it.

Merek would remove her halter completely, freeing
the other breast, and make her lie naked on her back
across the bed with her head and arms overhanging.
Her breasts would stand like fat pink fleshy columns
which he would then take individually into his mouth
and suck upon, while Leah sucked his penis. The
deeper she tried to take his shaft, the deeper he would
take her breast. When she felt his lips against her chest
and the tip of her nipple touching the back of his
throat and her other nipple brushing his ear lobe, and
his swollen penis filling her throat, with her lips pressed
up against his sac – reaching, craving even deeper oral
penetration – the weight of pleasure between her legs
was delicious.

Merek liked to ejaculate on her breasts and coat
them with his semen. 'They look like twin cocks that
have come,' he once whispered to her. Leah, her chin
tucked in, watched the white oily warmth trickling
down them. His fingers would chase the dribbles back

to the tips of her nipples and rub the length of each breast as if it were a shaft that he was masturbating. He made her come that way, with one hand gently frotting the slippery breast and the other between her legs, by turns slowly milking her clitoris then rotating the slippery tips of his fingers very firmly against it. At the point of climax, the end of Leah's stimulated breast swelled like a glans, and when he sucked it – just the tip – her clitoris simply bucked against the slow steady screwing pressure of those finger tips.

During the day, Merek kept the halter on her with her breasts poking through. When she was on deck, there would always be men looking at her, either from the wharfs or from other boats. Merek seemed to want her to be the centre of attention. In part Leah enjoyed it too. Sometimes she would look with secret longing at one or another of these men; occasionally her heart would leap. If Merek sensed this he would take her below deck and use her, meanwhile asking her what she felt about the man who had caught her attention. The questioning inevitably led him back to the details of what she had done with the two men in the bedroom of the lodge; then dark jealousy would again hold sway.

It came to a head one fateful and beautiful day after Leah had returned an admirer's gaze. Merek ominously docked the boat. 'Go below. Make ready,' he growled, his eyes shining with cruel fervour. Leah glanced back with a dread heart-surge when she saw that Merek had called the stranger over and was inviting him on board. Her belly quaked with fear-taut arousal as she crept down the stairs.

She could not stop her limbs trembling. A helpless giddiness gripped her; her breathing was quick, shallow and strained; already the tingling sensations kissed her lips, her ear lobes, the tips of her fingers, her constrained nipples, the flesh between her legs and the undersides of her toes. She turned round, stood against the table and watched the stairs in expectant, silent, sinking, frantic fear.

The new master had kind eyes; he was strong but looked gentle, which was what had attracted Leah. He was a little younger than Merek. His dark eyes scanned the room then returned to Leah.

'She looks frightened,' he said quietly.

Merek was still on the stairs. 'Take off your halter, Leah,' he said.

Her nervous fingers fumbled with the fastening, high between her shoulder-blades. The new master was already looking at the naked place between her legs. He whispered to Merek, who nodded, then he came to Leah. He stood in front of her and reached round behind, taking hold of her struggling fingers and caressing them. The way he touched them forced shivers down her spine. Her nipples were erect against his gown. He drew her close and simply held her, supporting her warmly and gently. Leah closed her eyes and pressed her cheek against his chest. When she opened her eyes, Merek was still staring from the stairs.

'Look at me,' the new master whispered. His fingers deftly freed the fastening of her halter. He stood back a little and withdrew it from her breasts – gently where it was tightest. When the looped restraints came free, her breasts shook, and he sighed and looked at her nudity with gentle longing. He put the halter on the table, then picked her up. She hung limply across his arms. 'Where shall I take her?' he asked Merek.

'Use my cabin.'

Merek left the lovers undisturbed until sundown. His schedule, already put out by having Leah on board, was now in complete disarray. Asgal had gone and, without a deckhand, arrival would be delayed by more than three days. Girls should always be left on the wharf – that was what the boatmen used to say. Perhaps they were right. But once Leah had been carried across his gangway on that first day, Merek's fate was sealed. No slave – no girl of any kind – could compare to Leah in responsiveness and loving sensuality and limitless desire, and Merek could never let her go. The more he put her to these other men, the more her craving for love deepened. One day, one of these interlopers would surely wrench her away from him, and yet, were he to cloister her now, the beautiful flame of her desire would surely gutter and might die.

He had watched the way her new lover had carried her – her arms hanging down, her shoulders back, her breasts beautifully erect and shaking. Then Merek had spent time on deck, with jealousy gnawing at him – at the thought of this younger man, abed with his slave – until he had finally found some excuse for going back down.

The door to his cabin remained ajar; standing back in the shadows, Merek, now a tormented voyeur, peered inside and saw his young slave on tiptoes at the side of the bed, leaning across her lover's prone body, her breasts pendant, her lips locked about his erection, her fingers between her legs. She was playing with herself as she was holding him in her mouth and he was coming and she was drinking his fluid as fast as it came and her legs were trembling from the pleasure of the sucking and from the fingering that she was giving herself. Merek crept back on deck and sat in tortured silence. He could have curtailed this tryst and the visitor could have had no cause for complaint – in fact he would have had cause only for thanks for the generous privilege he had been granted – but none of this was about the visitor.

An hour at least must have passed before Merek heard a sound. At first he thought it was the stranger coming up from below deck but when no one appeared he went round to the port side. The wharf was devoid of people; the only voices came from the tavern that lay at a distance. Then a noise came from near the rear of the boat. Merek quietly moved aft then crept below to check the steersman's quarters: perhaps Asgal was attempting a return after his precipitate eviction. But he found no sign of anyone. Once Merek had satisfied himself that nothing seemed out of place, he returned to the deck and to his sombre musing, but kept a watchful eye. Another hour passed before the stranger appeared on deck, alone and a little dishevelled in his gown.

'She's asking for you,' the man offered shyly.

Merek nodded. 'A drink before you go . . . ?'

'Thank you, but no.' The man hesitated, showing no sign of wanting to go. Then he ventured: 'She is very beautiful. Are you staying here long? No? Then would you consider . . . ?'

'Consider what?'

'Selling . . . For a solid offer . . . ? She would be well looked after, I promise you that.'

'No – but I shall tell her of your kindness.'

The man now looked shifty.

Merek uttered what he had guessed: 'You have already told her of your aspiration?'

The man nodded anxiously.

'I understand. No umbrage taken . . .' Merek offered his hand, not curtly, but clearly wishing to bring the interchange to a close. When the man was gone Merek spent another few minutes in quiet consideration then went below.

Leah was propped against the pillow. She looked dreamy-eyed, her pupils dilated. Her skin was flushed; the red rash from the horsehair had flared again on her lip and breast, as if it had now become her body's reaction to pleasure. Merek took her lovely small body

117

in his arms; she put her soft warm lips against his neck and Merek felt his erection stirring. A girl who has just experienced fulfilling pleasure is beautiful, just to hold in your arms and kiss. He took her lovely stiff breasts in his fingers.

'Did he kiss them?'

Leah nodded and closed her languid eyes. Merek opened his shirt and clasped her in his arms, her naked breasts against his bared chest. His fingertips explored every bump in her narrow backbone. Leah reached up and kissed him on the mouth, taunting him gently, slipping her little tongue inside. He could taste the residual sweet-salt aromatic savour of her lover's issue, yet he could not pull away from Leah's kiss, which was so loving and sensual and knowing. She knew she had made him erect: her fingers sought the proof. 'Lie down,' he told her. He put his fingers gently between her legs and watched her eyes. Touching a girl so intimately while you study her eyes is a unique pleasure; your eyes make love to her; your fingers worship her precious places – the swollenness, the soft warmth, the feather edges, the little punctures with their tiny raised edges, the moist fragments of her chain, its links sealed by her lover's fluid. His fingertips found the open end of her prepuce; her breathing faltered as he rucked that limp thin softness gently back, exposing the clitoris through a film of slippery semen. He slid a fingertip inside her vagina – through the lover's liquid issue, kept warm by her body – and Leah gasped and reached again to kiss him, her arms round his neck. His finger was inside her, against the soft, frilled, visceral, pulsing flesh, slippery with her lover's come; the hard pearl of her clitoris was under his thumb. He laid her gently down on the bed. She had not climaxed through this touching. Arousal was still burning her lovely body. He slid his finger out and Leah immediately reached down to suck it.

'Bring my pleasure, master,' she pleaded. She spread her legs. 'Kiss it, please?'

'It is not done, for a master to kiss a girl in the place where another man has been.' The aroma on her tongue was one thing; her sex was thick with issue.

'Some masters do,' Leah whispered wistfully. She closed her lovely eyes and drew her arms above her head, exposing her underarms. She knew he loved to kiss them and she shuddered when his lips touched there. When the tip of his tongue drew liquid lines up the complex saltiness, her belly shivered and her legs spread wider.

Then the wanton weight of Leah's last words bore down remorselessly on Merek's possessive heart. 'You say that other masters do it? Then let us seek a volunteer – perhaps from the tavern.' Leah paled and her gaze fell away. He stared at her in silence. But all the while his wrath was mounting. Finally it burst – not hotly but in calculated coldness. 'Stretch your arms back.' He tied her wrists to the head of the bed then got up and said quietly, resentfully: 'I ought to whip you first.' And with the poisoned barb of that comment embedded in Leah's heart, Merek swiftly left the cabin.

In his haste he stumbled headlong into a figure concealed by the shadow at the top of the stairway, knocking the man sideways. For an instant Merek took him for the stranger, returning to bargain for Leah, then recognition struck home. He summarily grasped the intruder by the arm and neck, then kicked his feet from under him.

# 9

# Two Masters

Merek manhandled the intruder down the stairway and back into the cabin where his frightened slave lay tethered on the bed.

'Ean!' Leah gasped as the young groom was thrown down at her feet.

Merek was intent solely upon his slave's reaction. Her astonishment was unmistakably laced with concern for the young man. Had her arms been free her instinct would have been to reach for him; Merek could see this quite plainly.

'What are you doing here?' Merek demanded of him. 'Was our last encounter not a sufficient lesson?' He took a step closer to the crouching interloper; the desire to kick him was compelling.

'No! No, master, please.'

It came like a slap across Merek's face. Leah had intervened again, exactly as in the lodge. With his anger threatening to choke him he screamed at the interloper: 'Answer me, damn you!'

'I had a dream about her . . .,' came the tremulous reply. 'And I had to know that she was not harmed – that her master had not punished her too severely for my transgression.' The younger man turned to look at Leah and she looked back with tears in her eyes. Merek's heart sank like a stone, for he saw in this young man's actions a misguided bravery that might once have been his own.

'As you see, she is not harmed,' he answered defensively.

'I see cords binding her wrists, my lord.'

'She is not harmed in the way you insinuate,' Merek whispered weakly. Yet he felt compelled to sit on the bed beside his slave, sliding his arm under her shoulders to raise her closer. To her supreme credit Leah turned to her master and offered her lips, which he took in a soft prolonged kiss, into which her tears now trickled their tender loving blessing.

'Don't send him away, master,' Leah whispered.

'I love her,' Ean broke in.

'No – don't say that,' Leah chastised him – but far too gently. Merek was watching her eyes, which now lay upon the younger man. Eyes cannot pretend to lie as bluntly as words. 'I am my master's slave,' she added faintly, turning to look pleadingly at Merek. He had no choice.

'I am short of a steersman. Perhaps the young man could assist . . .,' he offered without enthusiasm.

'Yes – oh, yes!' Leah cried and tried to snuggle against him. Then Merek saw the sparkle of victory in the younger man's eyes and knew he had been trapped. Even as his slave lay beside him, warm and loving, the coldness of jealousy gnawed at Merek, deep inside. He kept picturing the scene of debauchery he had interrupted at the lodge. He kept mulling over Leah's latest spiteful jibe: 'Some masters do . . .' Well, perhaps he now had the kind of volunteer he had thought to find in the tavern. What better test of putative love could there be?

'Then that's settled,' said Merek, standing up. 'And your first duty, master steersman, lies in this very cabin. I want my slave sucked clean; if she comes, you will be rewarded in kind.'

121

Leah shook her head and kept shaking it. 'No – don't ask him to do that, not when –'

'Not after your own master has refused the savour of a stranger's issue? Surely a true lover would not deny her, however perverse her craving?'

The young man interrupted softly: 'My lord, do not press the point. With one so beautiful and precious I should look upon it as a supreme privilege.' With that he took Leah's tethered wrist and kissed it. As if oblivious of Merek's presence he then kissed her fully on the mouth and Leah shared the enthusiasm of that kiss.

Merek, reduced by his own obstinacy to being the voyeur again, was rewarded only with excruciating torture. Still, his final pronouncement, though softly spoken, remained laced with venom: 'Take as long as you like but get her clean.'

Yet he felt compelled to remain in the cabin throughout. His jealous desire had robbed him of choice; he had to be there, in readiness to take her tethered torso in his arms and put his lips to hers at the moment of her climax – in order not to lose her.

Her burgeoning arousal made her look repeatedly at her master, searching his eyes for approval. How could he rebuff her? Merek quietly returned to the bed and Leah reached to kiss him, even as her young lover's head lay cradled between her thighs, tonguing her, probing her, teasingly kissing.

Merek reclined alongside Leah, bestowing small brushing kisses upon her arms and face – especially her lovely eyebrows and her nose and those luscious lips, which stayed parted. His kissing returned repeatedly to the beautiful swelling on her upper lip, which darkened and thickened as her climax neared. He could feel her tremulous breathing upon his cheek; then those breaths turned to gasps, and her head began twisting from side to side, as if trying to throw off the pleasure, or perhaps to delay it. Merek slid his arms under her shoulders and lifted her head and torso from the bed, stretching her tethered arms even as she was being sucked so deeply and earnestly between the legs. And all the while she was coming in beautiful, wrenching throes, such as only a love-slave can experience.

The instrument of Leah's deliverance having earned his promised reward, Merek watched him take it with gusto, his knees about her tethered arms, her head raised upon the pillow, his turgid flesh seeking her throat. All Ean's former tenderness seemed swept aside by desirous passion and base instinct. Therefore Merek now took responsibility for Leah's pleasure. He crouched between her legs, holding that bulging slippery pearl of arousal through its thin prepuce of skin. When Ean's climax came, Merek felt the pearl of Leah's erection tugging at his fingertips – her body's lewd empathy with her lover's pumping. The pumping continued yet no semen issued from her lips; she swallowed it all and still sucked. Above her tethers, her fingers clutched the air, and between her legs, the pearl of her clitoris kept tugging Merek's fingertips as if her whole body craved to milk every last drop of her lover's semen.

Afterwards, with Ean despatched to the steersman's quarters, came the chance that the bond between master and slave might yet be mended. Leah's mouth was redolent with the scent of his rival's semen yet Merek kissed it. He ran his fingers slowly up her belly and sucked her teats. He did not think her pleasure had actually come a second time, during his holding of her knob, and he ached with desire for her. But all he did was unfasten her and begin to put her to bed. Then she asked about protection.

'You mean, regarding what that stranger did to you earlier? But surely it was you who gave him the glad eye on the wharf? It was you who chose to let him

123

come inside you.' Again, the gratuitous, spiteful tirade had spilled out uncontrolled. Merek shut his eyes, despising himself.

'I know this, my lord,' Leah answered quietly. 'I needed the pleasure of proper penetration – face to face, in love, as my lord was once wont to do. Something inside me yearned for this pleasure again.' She fell silent for a moment. 'And when it came, it felt good,' she murmured looking at him with those lovely eyes. 'And you are my master and my lord; so now I seek your help to make me safe.' She opened her hands in supplication. Merek, reproached and chastened, bowed and kissed her fingertips.

She watched him preparing the clyster. He put her on her side, as much from his desire to hold her as from any prophylactic requirement; she needed only to have the unguent left inside a little while for any traces of the male emission to be rendered harmless. He first anointed her vagina with a small quantity of the liquid. She murmured when the metal barrel went inside; she was so small between the legs that the nose of the instrument was discernable as a bump in her lower belly. He made her hold her prepuce back on the pretext of working the protective liquor beneath it, which he did very gently with the tip of his finger while he stroked her nipple-tips until her breathing changed and her belly seemed to strain or tremble, with the instrument half protruding. Then he pushed the plunger a little and watched her anus tighten. He stopped fingertipping her clitoris. 'No – keep holding your hood back for me, Leah.' Then he pushed the plunger firmly home and her anus remained in spasm and every part of her body shook. He left the spent instrument in her, lying upon her thigh, while he ran his fingers over each shaking, lovely part, returning again and again to that round belly and those quaking breasts, but not touching the clitoris, which quivered

124

in stabbing pulses that reverberated through her taut belly to his stroking fingers.

Merek undressed and lay with Leah. His flesh ached; all the trapped seminal fluid was swelling the inner gland to bursting. His erection leaked silk wherever it touched Leah. She took pleasure from the contact, evidently well aware of what he was feeling. She touched him gently, the brushings seemingly accidental but intensely stimulating. Merek took her in his arms, her head to his chest, his balls against her naked belly, with the clyster still inside her. She fell asleep with her fingers lightly clasped about the head of his penis. He was still burning with desire. But that contact – her breasts against his torso, her delicate fingers clasping the tip of his penis – was without equal. He dozed and dreamt of penetrating her bottom while the clyster was flooding her sex and when he awoke, her softly pulsing fingers were sticky with his come.

She tried to feed it to him, then when he refused she fed it to herself. His tongue followed because he so needed to kiss her, this beautiful sexual creature, with her swollen upper lip and her constricted, puffy-nippled breasts, and that delicious pubic nudity that rendered her unique.

The next few days were the happiest of times for Leah. She took pleasure in being the female of the household to her two men; she was pleased to cook and care for them in their separate places; and she liked to talk with Ean, who listened with a quiet compassion and seemed to want to understand her point of view. She remained contentedly deferential to Merek in ways of the flesh, aware that his jealousy was never far at bay. She might kiss Ean tenderly at each meeting and parting but there was no repetition of that night in the cabin; Merek never mentioned it again. Yet it was plain that his desire for her was spurred on by the presence of the younger man, for throughout this time, Leah never suffered the want of satiation and her master always proved himself a considerate lover. She did not realise, until it was too late, the effect of this arrangement on Ean.

On the fifth day she happened to be sitting with Ean in their usual place at the stern and noticed that he seemed quieter and more thoughtful than normal. She got up and looked at the passing landscape. The waterway was curling its way through greenery and wooded hills.

'We seem to move so slowly, yet the scenery changes by the minute,' Leah said, trying to draw Ean into conversation.

'Like the clouds,' he mused. 'When you look at them on a calm day, they seem fixed, but a few minutes later their pattern is entirely changed.'

Leah glanced at him but could read nothing in his gaze. Then she saw ahead a blemish in the landscape, like a jagged diagonal notch cutting into the hillside from the valley floor to the skyline. 'Ean – what is it?' she whispered, pointing.

Ean locked the tiller and stood by her side. The lush green of the hill appeared sliced through to bare brown rock and deeper, where the brown turned to bright red. 'It's as if a giant sword has cut a wound and the hill is bleeding,' Leah murmured. 'What is it?' She put her arm around Ean's waist and felt him shiver, and at first she thought it was in awe at that remarkable scene. So when he didn't return the gesture or respond she moved closer, snuggling against him. Finally she had to ask again.

'It's iron,' he murmured distantly. 'They dig it from the ground here and all about for many miles. And beyond these hills are the furnaces where they melt it down – grim places. I came through there once. We shall pass them in a day or two.' Then he said abruptly: 'Leah, do you love me?'

The question stunned her. Surely he knew? Or perhaps he meant another kind of love – exclusive and possessive, a love that could exist only between a master and his slave. A master might cast his slave aside as failed and worthless but a loyal slave could never put aside her master.

'Merek is my master,' Leah whispered. 'I obey him and I love him.'

'That was not my question.' Ean gazed directly at her.

'Your question is weighted with a deeper meaning.'

'What deeper meaning can there be but love – a man and a woman, an equal bond?'

'Love between equals is forbidden.'

'If it is forbidden, then so be it.' Ean took her gently by the shoulders and enfolded her very lightly in his arms. He did not attempt to kiss her. The embrace lasted but a few seconds but Leah was left distraught inside. She stood immobile and silent – what words could she utter? Then she hurried away. A dreadful nausea gripped her, and she could hardly breathe.

'You're pale,' Merek later told her. 'Here.' He released the halter from her breasts and pressed his hand against her brow and her neck. 'Your skin feels cold.' He put her to bed in a separate cabin and brought her warm drinks throughout the afternoon. In the evening, once the boat was docked, he bathed her then returned her to her bed. He said he had to go out on business. 'I'll get Ean to look in on you,' he said rather awkwardly.

'No,' Leah whispered. 'I shan't need it. I have water and warmth. I shall sleep. Take Ean with you.'

Merek hesitated then nodded. 'Yes, why not?'

She heard the two of them leaving together and the relief surged through her like a wave. But it was

127

short-lived: she lay in bed in the terrible silence, interrupted only by the occasional creaking of timbers, all the time thinking of the two men that she loved and did not want to drive a wedge between. Eventually she dozed and dreamt of Ean – his touching her, arousing her like on that first night, at the lodge, when he was learning the fervour of passion.

When Leah woke she was wet between the legs; her desire throbbed sweetly cruelly inside her. She lay bared from the waist, gently touching herself, taunting her clitoris, but denying deliverance, keeping her flesh on edge, punishing it with arousal without the prospect of completion. Such was the true Tormunite way; so the monks had taught her. Eventually the merest touching with a fingertip made her moan: she hung, balanced on that edge of provocation, her whole body dissolving in desire. Then she heard footsteps and voices – the men had returned. She waited with bated breath for her door to be opened; she vowed to remain exactly as she lay, her belly aroused and exposed. She wanted both men to see her like this and, with one mind, to desire her. The footsteps approached; Leah closed her eyes, held her breath and held it long, but nothing happened. The door did not open. She heard muffled sounds, more steps, then quietness. Surely her master at least would come in to see how she fared? But no one came. Leah waited an age then quietly slipped out of bed, wrapped the sheet around her, picked up the candle and crept to her door.

She opened it silently: the corridor was empty, so she crept further, to Merek's cabin. She would speak with him – spill forth her heart and all her turmoil concerning her feelings for Ean. Her master would surely see her crisis of emotion and some arrangement would be devised; she had love and compassion enough in her heart for both men, though Merek would always be her foremost master. The door was agape. Merek lay abed, snoring softly, oblivious of her tormented world.

Deflated, thwarted, disconsolate, Leah hung on the edge of tears. Then she turned to go back to her bed – and found Ean standing, quietly waiting, at the door to her cabin. He took the candle from her and put it on the little table. Then his arms enfolded her, sheet and all. Her face was wet with tears as he nuzzled her and kissed her. 'Salty hot,' he murmured.

'I love you,' Leah whispered.

'I know it,' he replied. She put her finger to his lips; her sheet slid to the floor. Their love was consummated, standing, just inside the threshold of her cabin but deep inside her belly, hard against her womb. She was forced on to tiptoes by his height. Her climax was all-enveloping, all warming and liquefying; her thighs would not stop trembling. Still locked to her, he carried her to her bed, laid her down, stretched out upon her and, rolling on to his side, lay still locked inside her. She fell asleep. When she awoke she wriggled off his penis, which was still erect. He seemed not to have slept. She wiped him gently with the sheet then kissed his lips and, in a concerned whisper, told him he must go before they were discovered. He did not protest but softly gripped her hand in a parting gesture before quietly closing the door behind him. Leah felt warm and beautifully sated. She pulled the sheet around her, closed her eyes and slept.

She awoke in the greyness before true dawn. She lay on her side, her knees drawn up, and felt warm stickiness on the back of her thighs. She felt good about last night but now there were practicalities to consider. She wiped herself then got out of bed with the sheet draped round her. In the galley she filled the clyster, then felt its coolness and girth and the steady, reassuring pressure of the salve going up inside her. She balanced with one foot on the stool. Gently she withdrew the instrument and the pulling reminded her of the way Ean's erection had so reluctantly withdrawn from her body as she had wriggled free. Carefully she put the instrument on the table.

'What are you doing?' The voice came like a freezing rapier pushed between her legs, on and up inside her, through her vitals.

'Master?'

'Where is he?' Merek screamed.

'No!'

Breast-naked, the sheet wrapped round her thighs, Leah ran after him, up the stairway, tripping headlong across the deck, gathering herself up, half-falling down the aft stairway, then running for the steersman's quarters and the grunts and cries of that dreadful fight.

Merek was on his knees and bleeding from the lip and nose with Ean, still naked, standing over him, threatening another punch. Leah wrenched the sheet off herself, fell to her knees between the two men and began ministering to Merek. Shaken, crestfallen, he tried to push her hands away. 'Move back, Ean, give me room,' Leah shouted, trying to hold back her own tears even as she tried to clean the blood from her stubborn master's face.

'I want him off my boat – now!' Merek growled.

'No,' Leah begged weakly, but the situation was hopeless.

She felt Ean's firm hand on her shoulder. 'Come with me, Leah?' he whispered.

'No – how can I? How can I, Ean?' But when she tried to look at him she found she could not.

'You told me you loved me,' he muttered mournfully.

'I do love you – very deeply . . .' She turned to Merek. 'And I love my master even more.' She put her arms round Merek and kissed his bloodstained face and this time he did not try to push her away. When

130

she turned back again, Ean had already gone to get his things. When she caught up with him, he was poised at the foot of the stairway, ready to leave.

'Where will you go?'

'Why would you care?'

'I told you – because I love you, Ean.'

'Like you loved your previous steersman, Asgal? Merek told me.'

'Told you what? There was nothing to tell. I hated Asgal – truly; as truly as I love you. I never wanted it to come to this.' Then her tears flooded as he took her in his arms one last time and kissed her with tenderness and warmth. Leah clung to him, not wanting this precious moment to pass.

'Shall you go back to your mistress's house?' She felt a gnawing in her belly as she waited for his answer.

'I cannot – I stole her husband's horse and sold it at the wharf.'

'And you took the horse to get to me? – Oh, Ean . . .' She held him closer as her tears flowed freer than ever.

'I'll get work here – at the foundries or the diggings – somewhere I can work with horses.'

'Then one day you can steal another one and ride back to me?' Leah tried to smile through her tears.

'That would be nice,' Ean whispered, 'so nice.' And that was how they said goodbye.

All the love and emotion that dwelt inside her Leah now bequeathed to her master. She never denied her love for Ean; rather she wore it like a badge of pride, and the desire it stirred within her she assuaged on Merek. She now craved penetration more than any other form of love – locked about her master's body, locked with him inside her. She would remain like that for as long as he could sustain. Sometimes, even while he was at the tiller, she would ride him in daylight and

131

in public: the added arousal would keep him hard and make the seal tighter and the penetration more protracted. In the dusk she would watch the smoky, raucous furnaces drifting by, but she would be thinking of Ean, out there somewhere. In the day she would look out upon the scarred, reddened hillsides and hope that she might see him.

After three days, the wounded landscape was left behind. Leah was on deck, looking back. Turning, she saw ahead that the waterway was emerging from a valley that seemed to hang over a precipice. Suddenly the channel swung round to the right into a notch cut into the rock face. Leah ran to the outside edge of the boat, near where Merek was at the tiller, and stared out in awe. The ground plummeted down and down; the boat was moving like a bead on a thread, round the front of a mountain. On the inner edge the horse moved quietly forward on the narrow towpath, oblivious of the dread drop across the way. Leah peered over the edge. Far below and ahead, the dry landscape suddenly halted against a vastness of blue. This must be the ocean that Merek had promised. There were tiny dots upon it that must be ships and, at the edge, a great cluster of tiny buildings. Leah could not see how the boat could ever get down there.

Suddenly, she was grasped round her waist and lifted high against the side. 'No, Merek. No!' she screamed. He had locked the tiller and crept up behind her. He turned her around and sat her on the side. 'No, master, please,' she whispered as he slowly pulled her shirt off.

'Give me your hands.' They were clinging to the side. 'Both hands.' Only when they were round his neck and her legs were round his waist did Leah stop shivering. 'I want to feel these lovely breasts against me,' Merek whispered. The moment he touched her, all the unfinished feelings of utter dependence came

132

flooding back as if they had never left her. She clung to him, naked, balanced on the edge while he reached between her legs and masturbated her clitoris very gently and expertly through the skin of her hood. And while he was between her legs and in her arms, her lips were softly kissing his neck.

A long way ahead, at the end of the crag, was a portal buttressed against the rock. The boat in front disappeared through it and Leah watched with increasing curiosity as their boat neared the dark entrance. Merek had stopped playing with her to take control of the tiller again and seemed strangely uneasy.

'Go and get some trousers,' he said. 'And put your shirt on.'

'Why?'

'Just do it – quickly.'

Anxiously she obeyed, then ran back to him. He put one arm around her. She reached up and kissed his neck.

'Is it a tunnel?' she whispered, hoping that her clothes were simply needed against the cold.

'It's a toll-house.'

Something very grave about his manner made her cling closer to him. But he feigned attention to the steering and stared ahead at the looming entrance. Leah took his hand but he did not hold hers properly. She tightened her grip and looked up at him with mounting concern. He called to the horse, which slowed its pace. The boat drifted forwards through the entrance.

'I'm cold, master,' Leah whispered, her voice echoing from the cavernous ceiling.

On the left, daylight spilled through a row of arches. On each side, the waterway split into a series of parallel wharves, each wide enough to take a single vessel. Overhead, a heavy rope moved slowly on an endless loop, drawing boats in each direction along the centre section of waterway, where no towpath existed. But the first bay on the right was empty, so when the horse halted, Merek simply steered the boat slowly past him then jumped off and brought it to dock.

There were two other boats nearby. Men from the wharf were boarding them and going below deck, as if checking their cargoes. Some barrels had been taken from one of them. She saw a girl being taken off the nearer boat. Now she was frightened. Two men were approaching along the wharf. Merek was busy watering the horse. Leah clambered over the side of the boat, quickly lowered herself and ran in panic to Merek's side.

'Shh . . .,' he murmured, lifting her. He sat her on the side of the cold stone trough and stroked her hair and cheek.

'What do they want?' she whispered.

He stroked her body through her clothes. 'All the boats passing through must pay a tariff – a portion of their cargo.'

'You must give them some of the hides?'

He bit his lip. 'This cargo is bonded to the leather merchant; he remains the owner. The hides are not mine to give.'

'Then what shall you give them for passage?'

Then she saw all in his pained expression; she twisted round and saw the girl from the next boat being led away. Suddenly the cavernous ceiling closed in upon Leah, threatening to crush her; she could not breathe. Merek's hands closed about her waist, gripping her belt, holding her in place as the men came nearer.

'It is only for a little while, Leah – a few days at most, until I get back from the port . . .' His other words were lost in her rising panic as he ceded his place to the strangers, who took her by the arms. They put a token on a chain about her neck and gave a

134

matching token to Merek. Then they began leading her away.

'Wait!' Merek cried. The men stopped. Leah tried to break free; she wanted to run to him. 'Carry her . . . and treat her gently,' Merek said. As they lifted her up and took her away, she looked back despairingly at her master who had abandoned her and now stood simply watching her, his face paler than when Ean had knocked him to the floor.

# 10

# Into the Fire

Leah's mind raced. Merek's boat would soon be under
way again; she had to get back on board without his
knowing, but she knew she could never escape from
her captors while she was being carried. She had been
taken up a ramp inside the cavernous building, then
down a series of intersecting stone-lined corridors. This
place was very busy. There were porters arguing with
merchants, barrows and alcoves heaped with cargo,
and several small pens of slaves, mostly girls. The
guard carrying Leah was tall and agile; his companion
was old and portly and his breathing was laboured.
Leah had to act swiftly.

'I'm going to be *sick*!' she cried and started choking.

The guard immediately put her down. She fell to her
knees, coughing, spilling long gobbets of saliva on to
the paving. People were starting to gather. 'Get the
nurse,' the older guard said, and the tall one hurried
off. By the time he was out of sight Leah had been sick.
The remaining guard crouched beside her. 'We're
getting help.' As he reached to stroke her head, Leah
suddenly sprang up and ran deliberately in the direction the other guard had taken. Once round the next
corner she slowed her pace and kept turning randomly
to left or right. As she had guessed, the place was laid
out as a series of corridors that intersected at right

angles. It was like a busy underground warehouse, with porters constantly moving in and out of the many portals and separate stores. Leah picked up a porter's hat from a pile of boxes and put it on, tucking her hair under it.

One area opened out into a kind of market. As she drifted past the stalls she watched out for something to carry, to distract attention, but there was nothing unattended and she was afraid of being spotted as a thief. She pulled down the visor of her cap and kept moving purposefully forward, even though she was now unsure of the direction. She decided to try to circle round in a wide sweep and keep moving downhill wherever possible, reckoning that that would take her back to the level of the waterway. Eventually she found herself in a narrow corridor sloping downwards, with water dripping from the ceiling, and she hurried on, hopeful that this was a tunnel and the waterway was above her. Sure enough the floor began to slope upwards. She took the next corner and after a few seconds she was back on the wharf – but on the wrong side. Once she got her bearings she saw that the berth was now empty – Merek's boat had gone.

Her heart was thudding. What now? She could not give up; she would never go back to those guards. She looked around. There were other boats – every minute or so, another would come through the portal whilst others would be leaving at the far side. She could stow away on one and follow Merek, all the way down the port if needs be.

Her plan gave her courage. She studied her surroundings. The side she was on was set out like the other side, with individual berths cut into the wharf at an angle; but this side was for traffic returning from the port, while the other was for outbound traffic. There were two footbridges. As she watched, a boat drifted in, heading the same way as Merek's, in fact docking in the same berth. Leah quietly sat on some packing cases and observed it. A crewman unfastened the horse, led him to a trough and gave him some feed. Then two porters appeared and started to unload the tariff, which seemed to be planks of wood. The two crewmen talked with the porters, then all four wandered off in the direction that the guards had taken with Leah. This was her chance: she moved swiftly on to the nearer bridge. There were people on the wharf but, sure enough, this boat was now deserted. Two hatches were open, one at the back and a larger one in the middle. She reckoned that the middle one would give her more options for concealment below deck. She moved swiftly across the bridge and, almost without stopping, shouldered one of the shorter planks off the pile then ran up the gangway and down the main hatch.

Once below deck, she stowed the plank under the stairway and looked around. She was in a medium-sized hold, nearly empty but for some sacks and barrels; it had corridors leading fore and aft. She crept forward. In a cabin she found a loaf and a flagon of beer. She tore off a chunk of bread and took a large quaff from the flagon. Then she quickly moved on, past two more rooms. Suddenly, ahead, she heard snoring. Very quietly and cautiously she crept all the way back to the rear of the boat, where she hid in a small storeroom, pulling some canvas over a gap between packing cases and waiting warily for departure.

After a few minutes she heard rapid footfalls and shouts followed by banging noises that made her retreat further under the canvas, fearful that the guards were searching the boats. But no one approached the storeroom. The banging sounds continued and she decided that the crew must be loading goods. The activity went on for a long while, then abruptly stopped, and she heard footsteps and muffled shouts coming from the deck above. The boat started backing out of its mooring, began rocking, then banged against the side and stopped. Leah guessed it was being attached to the moving rope, to be hauled to the far side of the toll-house before the tow-horse took over again. Soon the forward movement began and, after a short pause, she felt the familiar slow, gentle surging as the horse settled into its steady rhythm. Her plan was to wait until dusk before creeping on deck. Now, for the first time, she could relax a little. She settled back against some sacking and kept slipping into slumber. In between she thought of Merek – the hurt of separation, the feeling of rejection when he left her. She needed to confront him with the defiance of her love and dare him ever to put her aside again.

She finally woke in total darkness, thinking she had heard shouting from outside the boat but fairly sure that it was still moving. She groped her way to the grey light of the doorway and started creeping up the rear stairway but was forced to retreat: the dark shape of a man was at the tiller. She retraced her steps, past the storeroom to the hold, now full of sacks and barrels. As she crept up the central stairway, she saw reflected from the casks and boxes on the deck a flickering orange glow as if from a bonfire. But when she emerged, her belly sank as if into a pit – a dread pit of despair.

Strung out along the foot of the dark hillside, belching flames of orange and showers of white, were furnaces, the very furnaces she had passed the day before, on her journey with Merek. The boat on which she had stowed away had not gone onwards. It must have loaded at the toll-house then turned back. And now it was docking in this awful place. She was further than ever away from her master. She now had to make her way back through the toll-house and past the guards and find an outbound boat; and then she had to try and find Merek at the port. Leah sank to the decking. She felt sick inside, truly sick this time, sick to her belly and sick to her soul.

Then, in the coldness of the night air, she thought of Ean. He had mentioned this place and had spoken of seeking work with horses. He might be here, or near here. Once off this boat she could ask; someone might know. She would try to find Ean and ask for his help.

She was apprehended on the wharf, after less than twenty paces. Her hopes of finding succour here plummeted.

'We don't see many girls here on their own, Gangmaster. Creeping off that boat like that, I took her straightaway for a "runner".'

'You did well, boatman,' the Gangmaster answered, examining the metal token round Leah's neck whilst keeping a firm grip on her belt. Then a more dread prospect opened when he added: 'The men will be over the moon at this one. They get little enough amusement. Here.' He pressed a silver coin into the boatman's hand and the gratified man thanked him profusely then retreated.

Leah had been taken into a large but very humble room of a wharf-side building. There was a long table set with at least a dozen metal plates and knives, a desk in the nearer corner and a fireplace with a well-filled grate. At the far end was a doorway to a kitchen, to judge by the smells and sounds. Leah was afraid to look directly at the man who had taken charge of her. His gaze was evil, his expression cold. Once the door was closed, he released his grip on her belt.

'Not what you're used to, up at the merchants' grand retreat, is it? You'll find our ways – my ways – a little different, girl. More direct.' Leah knew nothing

140

of any 'grand retreat' but was afraid to admit it in case that brought deeper trouble. But the man took her anxious silence for insolence.

*Smack!* The blow – swift, harsh and unexpected – knocked her to the floor.

'Get up!'

She struggled to her feet, the side of her face stinging cruelly, shedding tears of shock and distress. Automatically her hand went to her punished cheek.

'Put your hands down. Now, Miss Priggery – answer.'

'I don't –'

The smack – harder still – knocked her down again. 'That word is not in our language. Now, missy – on your knees. Get your hands down – I shan't tell you again. Put them behind you. Straighten up. Head back. There, nose up in the air; that's just how you like it, isn't it? But we'll fix all that. Now say after me: "Master – how shall I please?"'

Her tongue clung in fear to the roof of her mouth. Through her tears, she tried to repeat those words. Then she screwed her eyes closed, trembling, waiting for the next cruel blow. It didn't come.

She heard the door open and glimpsed a workman coming in. Then she saw that the Gangmaster seemed less interested in her. She wanted to wipe her tears but remembered his warning. She could only remain kneeling on the bare boards with her hands behind her and await his next instruction. He spoke to the workman, asking about the firing and the supply of coals, but though they talked of these things, both men kept looking back at Leah. Then the workman said quietly: 'I notice she wears a token – shall you be sending her back?'

'In time, if she's learnt some manners. But a runaway is free booty, as far as I am concerned. If they want her, they'll come after her. Don't doubt it.'

The man nodded, still studying her keenly.

Two other men came in, acknowledged the Gang-master, stared briefly at Leah, then went to the doorway of the kitchen. The face of a girl, pretty and dark-haired, appeared at the doorway, but when the Gangmaster turned that way she disappeared. Leah took comfort from the possibility that she might have a female companion in this fearful place.

Over the next few minutes the men were joined by a steady trickle of other workmen who stood chatting before seating themselves at the table. Leah, left kneeling near the door, considered making a run for escape in the dark, but she was scared to the core by the prospect of the Gangmaster's reprisal, should her attempt fail. She remained still but her eyes followed his every move. Dinner was eventually brought out on platters and in pots by the girl, who kept looking at Leah while the men fell noisily to eating, crying: 'Where's the beer?' and 'Get some drink in, sharpish, Denni.'

The Gangmaster returned to deal with Leah. His tone was calmly calculating. 'Now for your first lesson in manners, girl. Stand up. See that chair by the desk?' Leah nodded apprehensively. It was an open-backed wooden chair. 'Bring it here.' She hurried to comply. 'Now set it facing away from this end of the table. Just there.' He pointed to a spot about five paces from the head of the table. Most of the men had turned to watch; some began to smirk. The girl Denni, casting an anxious backward glance, retreated to the kitchen door. 'Good. Now get on the chair.' In trepidation, Leah prepared to sit down. 'No.' The Gangmaster shook his head. 'How shall my men see you if you sit?' She got up. 'No. Stand on the chair.'

'Yes, master. If it please . . .,' she whispered uncertainly. Carefully, fearful of the coldness in the master's expression, Leah climbed on to the chair, steadying herself with her hands behind her on the back of the chair. The master was standing a little to one side. Apart from a few muted sniggers from the men, the room was now alarmingly subdued: they were waiting for some spectacle to unfold. She glanced sidelong for approval from the Gangmaster but he was still shaking his head.

'Please, master?' Leah begged him, then, remembering his warning, added softly: 'How shall I please?'

The first glimmer of approval crossed that almost unreadable face. He nodded, then said: 'You shall please by standing facing my men.'

'Yes, master.' The chair rocked as she turned unsteadily towards that sea of expectant faces. The door opened and two latecomers sneaked in and found vantage points against the walls.

'Now, one more thing . . . what is it?'

Leah bit her lip, wondering what he wanted. Then very nervously she took her hands off the back of the chair and put them behind her, immediately casting a sideways look seeking approval from her master. But there were still sniggers from the table and the master was again shaking his head.

'Just one more thing, young missy – now, what could it be?'

Lost, Leah was about to shake her head then suddenly remembered not to risk so negative a gesture. And again the Gangmaster had noticed and seemed pleased.

'Master – how shall I please?' she whispered.

'Excellent. You shall please by dropping your trousers.'

Eyes shut, Leah trembled, trying to keep her balance as she fumbled with the belt. She felt the cool rush of air as her trousers dropped to her ankles. A collective gasp filled the room then ebbed to silence, pierced only by the Gangmaster's next instruction: 'Lift your shirt, if you please.' A gasp now greeted her tubular teats.

143

Exposed, on public view before so many strangers, she had never felt so tremblingly naked. Cool wisps of air licked up her belly and curled like icy tongues around her teats. Then she heard the Gangmaster unbuckling his heavy belt.

'Now the lesson ... six strokes, for a first time. Provided you stand still and stay straight and keep that shirt up ... Should you topple from your perch then I fear we must begin anew.' She glimpsed his arm sweeping back very far.

The force of that first lash – searing across her buttocks – knocked her off the chair and sent her reeling into the table, with the chair skidding after her. The workmen caught her and put her back. The second lash did the same. With her trousers now twisted round her ankles, she could not steady herself. So she kicked them off, and the men cheered. Before anyone could steal them, the girl Denni ran forward and retrieved them, then retreated to a safe distance.

The next lash struck Leah like a broadsword, still glowing from the forge, being laid across her bottom, the burning pain was so excruciating and prolonged. The chair rocked, not quite toppling. Through her tears, the pain kept coming, burning pain upon shivering pain, then waves of fiery needles, then the next lash and her toes cramped from trying to keep her balance and her arms trembled from trying to hold up her shirt. But Leah knew she must do it, and, although her skin felt as if it were being flayed from her bottom with a burning wire, she somehow managed to keep her balance through six consecutive lashes. Whereupon the master, true to his word, immediately stopped and buckled on his belt. Now the only sounds in that room were Leah's sobs, and the only movements her tremblings from breast to belly to buttocks and thighs. Still she held her shirt up. Her buttocks felt as if they had been scalded.

'Turn around and show them. Quickly.'

'Y-yes, M-m-master,' Leah sobbed. She tried to do so unaided, but the Gangmaster helped her. Her buttocks shone livid red, without a single strip of white. They wouldn't stop shivering.

'Keep your shirt up. Good.' He spread his large hand across her belly to steady her. The hand was hot from his exertions. 'Well, men?' They clapped and cheered and whistled and, though Leah could not stop the waves of violent trembling in her legs and buttocks, she felt glad of this acknowledgement that she had suffered her punishment bravely. But the pain would not lessen. A lump formed in her throat and suddenly she could not repress the choking sobs and could hardly see through the veil of tears.

'Denni – come here,' the Gangmaster shouted. Leah heard the girl hurrying across. She seemed more confident now that the Gangmaster's belt had been safely buckled. He took her aside. While he whispered to her, she looked at Leah, then at the table, then nodded.

A few seconds later, Denni was crouched in front of Leah and was smearing her hand back and forth in a platter bearing the broken carcass of a large roast bird. The Gangmaster pinned Leah's elbows behind her, thrusting her naked belly towards Denni's reaching fingers, now shinily sheathed in grease: the counterpoint to all that pain was about to be administered.

Once those female fingers had opened Leah and toyed and slipped, and pulled and shaped her outer lips, and squeezed her inner lips and chain, and one by one slipped up inside her sex, then expertly unsheathed its knob and rubbed its shaft as if it were a tiny penis, trying carefully to thin the sensitive root, trying to draw its erection outwards so as to make the tip engorge – with Leah scarcely breathing and all the movements kept slippery and not stopping and the grease now running thinly under Leah's body heat and the girl working attentively by feel alone, for she was watching Leah's face – then, sure enough, Leah felt that first beautiful deep drawing sensation, the signal that her body was yielding all control, and the only thing that mattered now was that the pleasure should continue and deepen, plumbing the depths of her sexual wanting, slaking the craven need.

All the while, the master kept her elbows pinned back with one hand, his other hand kneading her hot burned buttocks, working them, bruising. When his thumb, dry and rough and harsh, thrust up Leah's tightly squeezed bottom, her climax triggered – delicious and merciless and deep – and she swooned against the master, his thumb still reaming her bottom, her belly thrust out for Denni's cruel sweet slippery fingertips, plucking persistent beats of excruciating pleasure from the distended head of her clitoral knob.

Then the Gangmaster calmly lowered Leah's limp body from the chair. 'She can share with you, Denni. Show her the ropes; she can attend to the night shift with the firemen.'

'Denni – what did the Gangmaster mean?' Leah was lying in only her shirt on the little bed in Denni's quarters.

'About what?' Denni's countenance was bright; she was young – about Leah's age; her eyes were a beautiful shade of green and her hair was almost black.

'The ropes and the firemen,' said Leah.

' "Showing the ropes" means I have to show you how things work around here and what you have to do.' Denni was slender but not tall; with almost no breasts and her short-cropped hair, she might be taken for an underfed boy. But her scent was that of a girl.

'And the firemen?' Leah whispered.

146

'They stoke and tend the furnaces. But they are just men – they think they know what they want – though they're stronger and blunter than most.'

Denni wore a sleeveless shirt and her neck was bare. 'You don't wear a token, like I do?' Leah said.

'That's because I'm a freeman, like the others.'

Leah smiled inwardly at Denni's choice of words. 'Yet you still take their orders?'

'Only the Gangmaster's.' She looked away, then added faintly: 'I can leave or stay, as I wish.'

'But I cannot?' Leah ventured.

'You said yourself: you wear the token. You've already been punished for stowing away. How can you leave without getting into more trouble?'

'You could help me.'

'Why would I want to?'

'Because you like me.'

Denni did not smile, as Leah had meant her to do; she went quiet and her bright gaze slipped self-consciously away. 'I liked it when you touched me,' Leah continued in a whisper, touching Denni's slender naked arm. She raised herself on one arm and kissed the girl on the lips. Then she winced because, through stretching, the skin of her bottom burned from the effects of the Gangmaster's lashing.

'Let me look at you,' Denni whispered, her self-confidence returning and strengthening as Leah embraced the role of the timid submissive.

Denni bathed Leah's stinging buttocks gently with a soft cloth soaked in freezing perfumed water. 'It's cold,' Leah murmured. 'Where do you get water so cold?'

'There is a spring inside the hill; it's supposed to be a secret. The firemen showed me. I've perfumed the water with flowers.' She made gentle arcs with the moistened cloth, working outwards and downwards from the small of Leah's back, in alternating sweeps across each cheek.

'He has not cut you; the bruising will go in a few days,' Denni whispered.

The cloth kept returning to the sensitive hollow at the base of Leah's spine, causing feelings both reassuring and deeply pleasurable.

'There – is that relaxing?' Denni whispered. The cloth was now replaced by Denni's cool, manipulating fingers.

'Mmm . . .,' Leah answered.

'Has the Gangmaster cut girls before?' Leah asked.

'I don't know. You're the first runner I've seen. I've only been here a week.'

'What? But then how do you know so much?'

'There's not that much to know. I have my duties and I don't need to worry about much else. But lie still, now. He has been harsh with you.' Then her voice went quieter. 'Though the harshness did not seem to stem the pleasure . . .'

Leah twisted round. 'That came through you,' she said, caressing Denni's hand, 'these beautiful fingertips – so expert and knowing.'

'Then I must have retrieved something from the ashes of my former employment,' Denni murmured wistfully.

Leah stared at her anxiously. 'Was there a fire there?' Denni shook her head. 'Then what?' Leah asked.

'I was dismissed because my mistress thought me her rival for the attentions of a boy I had not even kissed. I was chambermaid; she hired him because he was young and handsome and she planned to seduce him. She was already bedding her equerry. What she didn't know was that he was also bedding me. I wanted to learn and he was more than happy to teach me in the time that she left him spare.'

'So you weren't interested in the boy?'

'Oh, yes,' Denni whispered. 'I used to talk with him sometimes; in fact he was the one who told me about

148

this place. I really liked him; I still do.' Denni stared wistfully into space.

'But what about the other one – the one who –'

'The one who was fucking me? That's what it was, Leah – that's all it was. He used me but I invited it and I enjoyed it.' Seeing Leah's frown, she added: 'Have you never sought pleasure with a person you don't really care for?'

Leah remained silent.

'Well?'

'I've never sought it, no.' Then she knew she had lied on that count. 'Yes, I have . . .,' she finally whispered.

Denni nodded. 'And my equerry was good to me in ways that matter. After the first time I became frightened that I would be pregnant. So he set off in the night, through the rain, to the apothecary and brought me a preparation that saw me right again.'

Leah nodded in approval. She saw parallels, for Merek did the same sort of thing for her.

'After that, the fear was taken away but there was still the pleasure and the secrecy,' Denni continued. 'I used to practise on him in the kitchen with goose-grease on my fingers. I was seeking the pleasure, not the man, but he was experienced and took care of me. Then Ean appeared on the scene.'

Leah's jaw dropped; her mind raced. 'What was your lover's name?' she whispered in dread anticipation.

'Kapler.' The reply came like a rapier of ice pushed through Leah's vitals. She didn't hear any more of what Denni said, so Denni repeated: 'What was your lover called? The one you didn't love but simply wanted?'

Gradually Leah's attention refocused. 'He was called Asgal,' she finally whispered miserably and felt physically sick. She laid herself down on the bed.

149

'Come on – tell me. I want to hear it,' Denni said, stroking Leah's back.

Leah had never confessed this to Merek; in fact she had never told anybody and the guilty secret was gnawing into her. She now had the opportunity to unburden her guilt to this sympathetic girl, who knew neither of the other parties. So she told her.

'Asgal was the steersman aboard my master's boat,' Leah began. 'In the early days I did not take to him: I found him too inquisitive about my master's comings and goings, and with me his manner always seemed aloof. How I wish it had remained so.'

'You mean, he made unwelcome advances?'

'No. When I told Merek – my master – about my concerns he suggested I just pass Asgal a friendly word, now and then, to break the ice. I think he spoke to Asgal too, because after that Asgal's manner changed. He became helpful and interested in my concerns. It got to the point where I felt I could confide in him, and I would sometimes sit with him at the back of the boat and we would talk. There was never any impropriety; he always behaved properly.'

'But your master became jealous?'

Leah turned round. 'Oh, no. Merek can be a very jealous master but he trusted Asgal. It was his trust in me that was misplaced. It all started with a stupid row over my chain – my virgin's chain that was put there by the monks and nuns in the Abbey. My master had always resented that, when I came to him, my chain was already broken. One day in temper he suggested that I had connived with the cruel men who broke it – who callously broke me open. I was stung by such heartless insinuations from the man who was supposed to be my protector and my lover. Then he just went off on some errand of business for three days, leaving Asgal and me in charge of the boat.

150

'Nothing happened that first day, but Asgal knew I was upset and in the end I confided in him about the row. He said: "I wish I could have known you first; I might have fixed your chain for you." It was a kind sentiment. I may have held his hand, but only briefly. It's true, I had the desire to be loved, to be held, but I could wait and hope that all of that would come from my master on his return. I hardly slept that night. Then next morning there was a strange incident. An unusual boat passed while we were still tied at the wharf. It had an unfamiliar design: it was longer and broader-bellied than normal and the prow carried a carving of a young woman with long flowing hair.' Leah looked at Denni, who simply shrugged, so she carried on: 'All the crew were women: they looked like soldiers or guards. The hold of the boat was open to the air and there were perhaps twenty slaves standing in it, all naked, all of them young men. They had some kind of thin harness round their waists and between their legs; it must have been put there to keep them permanently erect, for that was the effect.'

Leah was now sitting up. Denni's eyes glittered with excitement. Her fingertips, which had been very lightly stroking Leah's knee, moved up and began tracing a pretend harness-line round Leah's belly. 'Go on,' Denni whispered.

'Two of the guards were moving among the young men; I don't know what they were doing but I kept imagining, all the while that boat was passing.'

Then Denni started to do to Leah what Leah had been imagining: her fingertips found the firm female counterpart of those male erections and began mauling it pleasurably, sliding Leah's oily leakage up and down its stubby shaft, trying to make it more prominent. Leah felt the muscles of her thighs beginning to tighten and her legs involuntarily beginning to straighten open to permit those beautiful fingers free exploration. 'Tell

151

your story,' Denni said with a wickedly cruel smile, her fingertips never ceasing their restless manoeuvres. Then she whispered: 'I like to make a girl stand out in here, more than any good girl really should. And with a cock so lovely, why not?' Now Leah wanted to come, but Denni made her keep talking.

'I watched the boat,' Leah began again unsteadily, 'until it had disappeared. Then I saw Asgal standing quietly a little way along the deck. Neither of us spoke and I hurried off in the other direction. But I was unable to dispel the images of those naked young men in that state of –'

'In the state you are in now, Leah. Your cock does you proud. Stand up – let's get it harder. Stand on the floor – hands behind you, legs open – and I shall play the guard.' Denni sat on the edge of the bed and sucked Leah's erection until Leah thought her knob would burst in Denni's mouth. Then Denni pulled away and pushed her fingertips in a closely fitting sheath around Leah's knob, pushing back the soft surround, as if searching for a root buried inside her. 'Oh – it's come out very far now, Leah – like a little curved shaft. Can we keep it so? We can but try. Now, what happened with your Asgal?'

Leah closed her eyes against the delicious pleasure of the touching. She felt as if she were sinking into Denni's hands, as if those fingertips had somehow thinned to blunt needles that had pierced the flesh all round the base of her knob and were slowly sliding inside her. 'I went back to Asgal under the pretext of asking what he knew. He must have guessed my true purpose. He said he'd heard rumours of colonies where women took men to be trained as submissives. I foolishly asked him if he'd like that to happen to him. "Only if you were my trainer, Leah," he said. Then I kissed him.'

'How?'

Leah pulled back from the touching. She needed to tell this, confess it, try to expiate the guilt. 'The kiss was not given in the manner of friends, but desirously, wantonly. Then I couldn't stop shaking, the desire was so strong. He said I was getting cold. Before I knew it he had swept me into his arms and carried me below deck. Then he laid me on the big table in the galley and said he would fix my broken chain. I didn't understand what he meant but I was excited and I let him remove my trousers and examine me. As soon as he started touching there, my pleasure came so quickly that I couldn't conceal what was happening. He unbuttoned my shirt and looked at me in my nakedness as I lay stretched across the table. Then he loaded the clyster. "Just a precaution," he said. I told him "No," meaning that we shouldn't, we mustn't. He said: "You don't want any precaution?" and I just said: "Hold me." Then he did it to me – put his penis all the way in and up, and the pleasure and intimacy when he was so aroused was delicious – you know, when they come inside you. Though it is all so dreadfully risky and wrong, still your contractions continue to pull every last drop of wickedness out. Why is it that it feels so good?'

'Perhaps because you had at hand the precaution – that's what it was like for me.'

'Yes . . . Then he sat me up while he joined the two ends of my chain. He dripped wax on them and sealed them with his signet. His cock remained hard and glistened with leaked come all the time he was touching me and I kept trying to get the end of it in my mouth. But the touching was the best part. "There – all precious and new," he said. Then he stood me on the floor and turned me round and when I felt that chain, complete again after so long being broken, and saw the clyster loaded and ready on the table, all the memories of the Abbey flooded back and the arousal was so

153

strong I started trembling. I reached behind and ran my hands over his chest and belly, and he felt very warm but my hands seemed very cold – the desire in me had made all the blood drain away. I was covered in goose-pimples. Have you had this happen to you, Denni? They talk of desire being hot but my desire that day was cold.

'I took hold of his cock and directed it between the cheeks of my buttocks, against the mouth of my bottom – because I wanted it there, like the monks used to do it – and the slippery head just went straight in and up. I took it deeper and deeper, until I could feel his balls dangling hot between my legs. I took hold of them from the front, trying to force his flesh ever deeper into me. Then he lifted me up and grabbed the clyster and with my knees tucked up he carried me on his cock to the big mirror. Then with my feet on the frame – climbing it – and me looking at myself with the cock up my bottom and the chained lips of my sex gaping, his come trickling out, he started to slide the clyster in between them. Up and back it nuzzled, slowly expanding my insides until the chain pulled tight across the barrel. Then he pressed me until the plunger touched the glass and he just kept on pressing until the beautiful spasms started between my legs and I fell forwards with my nipples squashed against the glass, shuddering with the issue from the clyster coming inside my front and the issue from his penis coming up my bottom.

'We did it together three more times during that day and the next. I didn't let him come inside my sex again. I liked it best standing against the mirror, with his penis in my bottom. He would masturbate me and, when he sensed my pleasure was coming, I would feel the skin of my hood being drawn back and held ready. I would be moaning and shaking, and feel my anus tightening around the root of his cock. Then he would press my knob up against the cold glass and my pleasure would spill.' Leah had been very gradually backing away from Denni. She knew the girl would pleasure her very soon but she had to finish her story.

'When Merek was due back I became very anxious. Asgal was annoyed to discover that I had broken his seal; he saw it as treachery. I don't know what he had expected of me; he knew Merek was my master and his employer. I told him I treasured what we had briefly shared but I could not continue to betray my master. He said he would tell Merek what we had done. "Do it – if you value me at naught," I said, "and then, for your part, he will probably kill you." But Asgal didn't tell. Instead he continued to taunt me about it and bided his time until one night when he finally tricked me into cheating on Merek with strangers. When Merek discovered the deceit he threw Asgal out and punished me.'

'How?'

'He tied my legs open and whipped between them.'

'And you still love him?'

'Yes.'

'Come here, Leah. Let me look at it. Would you love me if I whipped it – if I whipped this little cock and made it come?'

Leah shivered. 'I love when you touch.'

'Then touch I must. Get on the bed and lie on your belly.'

Leah did as she had been told. Every nerve in her skin was a-tingle as those fingertips began their magic. Soon, the simple stroking at the base of her spine was causing beautiful reverberations of arousal through her bottom and belly. She sighed softly. Her thighs moved open, waiting for the more focused touch. She could hear Denni's breathing. Then the touch came: slender, cool, soft fingertips gently touching her anus, which responded, tightening at first then pouting as the touching turned yet softer and more teasingly gentle. Then the fingers parted her cheeks and Leah's heart stopped as she felt Denni's breathing coming ever closer to that place. The tongue-tip touched her anus and she moaned. It felt like a lubricated, arched penis opening that sensitive ring, pushing up inside it and touching the back wall, pressing there, causing peculiar, deeply pleasurable feelings. Then the tongue seemed to expand against the pressure of the fleshy ring, like a swelling penis becoming more excited still. Leah spread her legs apart so Denni's fingers did not have to hold her buttocks open and instead were free to slip beneath to torture Leah's labia, gently pulling them, nipping the feather edges of flesh, pressing gently upwards under her protrusive knob, peeling the hood back with gentle fingernail pressure, making Leah's sex stand open, exuding warm honeydew from its inner walls. The segments of her chain hung down, trailing curves of liquid arousal on to the bed.

All the while Denni's tongue was gently thrusting through the fleshy ring of Leah's anus, forcing it open, then allowing it to contract a little, forcing a rhythm that she could neither ignore nor escape. As her moans became deeper and her breathing more shallow, that cruel delicious tongue pressed on and up, stretching her bottom open, touching the back wall again, even as the fingertips pressed upwards at the front, forcing her knob to extend itself for taunting, gentle wet scratching, a delicious inescapable itch that wanted to cry out against the gasping moans of the climax that burst her heart and soul like a beautiful death. Now all she wanted was to lie there torpid with that tongue inside her bottom and those fingers gently clawing her open at the front.

When she found the strength she reached back and down and gently kneaded Denni's hair and stroked her neck. The collar of Denni's shirt was wet with sweat.

Denni's tongue was still inside her. Leah eased herself off its luscious impalement and twisted round. As Denni moved up the bed, Leah clasped her round the head and shoulders and kissed her, drawing Denni's tongue deep inside her mouth, caressing it with her lips, squeezing it just as lewdly and sexually as her bottom had squeezed it. Simultaneously she pulled Denni's shirt up, exposing the small firm breasts, and her fingertips found the broad velvet areola and the nipple as hard as a bead. Then she slid her hand down Denni's trousers, through the dense bristly hairs that were softened by moist excitement. She found the clitoris fully engorged and milked it swiftly, and immediately Denni's pleasure came, with Leah's other arm locked round her waist and Denni's tongue still captive in Leah's mouth.

Leah then stripped Denni naked but the girl seemed shy of nudity. 'Let me touch you, and look at you properly,' Leah whispered. 'What's the matter?'

'It's just that I'm not that used to girls.'

Leah could not believe her ears. She cajoled Denni into allowing her to kiss her and to bring her to pleasure with her mouth. Afterwards they lay intertwined. In the simple intimacy of this contact, Leah slept contentedly.

It was still dark when Denni woke her. 'We need to bathe quickly and get something to eat, then get you up to the furnaces. You mustn't keep the firemen waiting.'

# 11

# Primal Thirst

The furnaces stood in two parallel rows at the foot of the excavated hillside above the wharf and the stables. Staggered burnings took place day and night; by night the lower hill-slope seemed festooned with glowing broken teeth. While one furnace was alight another was being emptied and yet another was being filled with charcoal from the wharf-side heaps and ironstone and limestone from the hillside. Below the end of the lower row of furnaces stood a small brew-house, and at the door to the brew-house stood the two girls. Denni opened the door and urged Leah inside.

A warm aromatic shroud of humidity enveloped Leah. Even the glazed brick floor was damp and warm to her naked feet. Denni drew her by the arm, past large wooden vats and barrels and pipework then barrows and buckets of sprouting grain.

'Can you smell the malt?' Denni asked, scooping up a handful and offering it to Leah, who picked a grain and tasted it suspiciously. 'Good?' Denni asked.

Suddenly there was a noise from above and a white-bearded, enquiring face appeared over the balcony. 'Beccanay!' Denni cried and the old man immediately dropped the wooden paddle he was holding and hurried open-armed down the rickety stairs. Denni ran to greet him, flinging her arms about him and kissing him with such intimate familiarity that Leah felt embarrassed. Finally the old man chided Denni softly: 'Enough now – my new assistant is hoisting grain.' He pointed up the stairs. 'You wouldn't want to make a young man jealous.' Then his pale blue gaze turned to Leah. 'And who is this gentle friend?'

'I am Leah, my lord.'

'Please – call me Beccanay.' He extended his hand; the skin felt warm and soft, the grip reassuring. 'I see you wear the token. Mind it not: in here, Leah, we have neither lords nor slaves; we are all honest workers, who treat as we find. I assume our gracious Gangmaster has sent you to assist?' He turned to Denni, who simply nodded. 'Good,' he said. 'We have a job for you. Wheel this barrel of beer up to the firemen on the terraces. Deneca will show you. And Deneca – no dallying up there. We don't want to incur our good Gangmaster's displeasure.'

The barrel pivoted upright in a two-wheeled frame resembling a handcart. The girls each took a handle and Beccanay opened the double doors. Leah waited until they were out in the open before asking Denni: 'What did he mean, no dallying?'

Denni looked back at Leah in silence. Then she turned and set off pulling the cart before finally whispering: 'The Gangmaster caught me with them once. He gets jealous.'

'Does he . . . does he use you?' Denni didn't answer but her expression told that he did. But then there was the forward way she behaved towards Beccanay. Again, Leah wondered at this girl, here such a short time yet already appearing to court dalliance with one and all.

They continued up the gently sloping track towards the furnaces. Then Leah risked an oblique remark about Beccanay.

Denni was irked. 'Have you never done it with an old man, Leah?' Leah was obliged to admit that she

159

had. Denni continued: 'Beccanay is a good man. I get pleasure with him and he makes no demands – he is nothing like the Gangmaster. I am a free girl and I go with Beccanay as and when I choose.'

'But if you are a free girl, why put up with the Gangmaster?' Once again, Denni didn't answer but her expression was forlorn. Leah stopped and put her hand on Denni's.

'No – it's all right,' Denni whispered. 'Come on.' They pressed on steadily up the track. Denni seemed to brighten as the clamour increased, but now Leah was growing anxious. She could see swiftly moving figures starkly silhouetted against the fiery glow, rods or shovels in their hands. Everyone was shouting. There were men working giant bellows that drove the heat. Every few seconds there was a roar and sheets of flame rose into the blackness. The air was filled with the smell of burning charcoal and hot metal. A figure was poking a rod into the mouth of the furnace at the far end; sparks were flying; then a fountain of molten metal erupted into a pit on the ground.

'Here – put these on!' Denni shouted, handing Leah a pair of wooden clogs. 'Hot cinders. Be careful.' Once shod, the two girls continued their advance, Denni leading and Leah pushing the barrel from behind. They came to a standstill in the middle of the terrace. 'We can't go any closer – not on this level,' Denni shouted. Leah was thankful for this at least. The heat from the furnaces was like the burning sun on a cloudless day: she could feel it through the front of her shirt and her trousers; her face felt as if it was scorching. Yet her back felt cold. Most of the workers wore long aprons, with gloves and hats; some wore only loincloths and clogs. Denni's gaze was upon one particular group of these semi-naked men. Leah edged away as, in twos and threes, they started drifting over to the beer station and Denni began smoothing her hair.

Leah stood back and watched the men chatting, filling their mugs and quaffing their beer. She thought she remembered one or two of them from the occasion of her punishment at the meal hall. Denni seemed to know several by name; she was laughing and talking freely with them. They kept looking over at Leah, then asking Denni something. Leah heard only fragments of what Denni answered – 'She's shy,' then later, 'Oh, yes – very much so,' and 'I'm sure she would if we . . .'

Ears burning, Leah had no alternative but to approach and appear sociable, if only to curtail such talk. But first she drew Denni aside to admonish her. 'What were you saying about me?'

'They've heard you're a runaway slave. They want to know what a slave girl does, and what rights they, as free men, might hold over you – whether you can be held in common or whether you're like the paid girls that visit here each month. See, Leah – they are very polite. They ask first.'

Denni's complicitous tone was making Leah very anxious. 'What did you tell them?' Leah whispered.

'I told them to treat you as a free girl, with the right of choice and refusal.'

'A free girl – like you?'

'Just so, though far more attractive and loving.' Denni took Leah gently in her arms and kissed her in front of all the men, provoking some jeering but mostly sighs of approval. When Leah, with Denni's arms still round her, found the courage to look properly at the men, they did not seem quite so hostile as she had feared. One of them proffered his mug of beer, which she took with a smile of thanks and sipped.

'She's a good one,' someone said. Then another: 'Did you see how she took that belting from the Gangmaster? That bastard!' And then: 'She's a tough one. She'd make a fire-girl, I'm betting.'

161

Leah felt the emotion welling. She couldn't speak, beyond thanking them and smiling; she was content to listen and to let Denni do the talking. The men spoke of workaday things – problems with the firings and poor charcoal; they joked and complimented Denni on the drink. As Leah relaxed a little, she began to see what Denni found attractive in these men – some, at least. With the fire-glow reflecting from their sweat-glistened figures, they resembled the perfectly proportioned bronze statues she had once admired in the Abbey, except that these figures were living, breathing, warm and sentient. When she glanced across, Denni's eyes met hers with a knowing gaze.

After a while, Leah became aware of shouting from the terrace above. Denni said: 'Come on, Leah. We're late for the boys at the top.' But before departure, Denni had a brief whispered conversation with two of the younger men. Leah felt sure it had been to arrange an assignation.

The late arrival of the beer station on the upper terrace was greeted with some good-natured jeering but, once again, Leah was impressed by the warmth and kindness of these men. Denni introduced her and again there were scathing comments about the Gangmaster. It gave Leah increasing concern as to what might happen if they were late getting back.

'There's plenty of time,' Denni said with a laugh. 'Besides, Beccanay would never tell on us. And there's something I want you to see.'

She took Leah by the hand, leading her away from the beer station to a small alcove in the rock face at the end of the terrace. The men had extended the natural roofing with canvas sheeting in order to fashion a shelter. It had a brightly lit brazier at each end and with the radiant heat from the adjacent furnace it was very warm indeed. There were tables, a few chairs and a hollowed-out area at the rear with several mattresses, all unoccupied. Denni picked up a torch from a heap and made Leah do the same. Then Denni lit her torch at the brazier. 'No – don't light yours yet,' she said, 'Come on,' and led her to the back of the shelter. There, in the broken shadows of the rough rock face, was a narrow defile. 'It's a cave they broke into when sinking footings for a furnace. It goes right into the hill and down under our feet. It's beautiful – magical,' Denni murmured, her eyes glittering.

Apprehensively, Leah allowed her friend to lead her down the uneven sloping floor, into a narrow blackness licked by the tongues of torchlight. The air was cool and still; the only sounds were the spitting of the torch, the scrape of clogs on rock, and Leah's tense breathing. The walls were smooth but the floor was broken. Then ahead Leah heard the hollow drip of water into pools, then a faint bubbling and trickling before the floor levelled and felt sandy and the cavern widened and the roof lifted high. 'Here – light your torch with mine,' Denni whispered, and when she did, Leah was filled with awe at the vision that opened out before her.

Beautiful curtains of smoothly sculpted coloured stone adorned the walls; shapes like icicles hung from the roof and dripped into a glass-clear pool of water. Everywhere were streaks of colour, from the blackest blue through azure to orange and blood-red. The rippling sheen of water on the walls made them appear soft and gelatinous; Leah touched them but they too were stone.

'Over here,' Denni said. On the banks of the far end of the pool stood a group of flagons, and a stone-encrusted metal cup on a chain bolted to the floor. A stream of tiny bubbles was rising from the bottom of the pool, causing an upwelling of the still surface.

'Is it hot?' asked Leah.

'No – it's the spring. The bubbles are air or something. Feel it.'

'You first.'

Denni slotted her torch into one of several rings high in the wall then, crouching, scooped up a handful of the bubbling water and drank. 'Taste it, Leah. It's lovely.'

Leah had to agree: it was cold and deliciously fresh, slightly sweet yet with a very faint but pleasant bitterness, and the tiny bubbles seemed to keep forming around her tongue, as if the air was still escaping from the liquid. Leah cupped her palm and took another drink. 'Refreshing. Nice. It makes you want more.'

'Exactly. So, hang your torch up and get some.' Denni picked up the chained cup. 'When they broke into the cave, this was already here. The place must once have been a shrine.'

'To what?'

'To love and beauty,' Denni mused, gazing around her, then laughing at Leah's frown. Soon the two girls were drinking freely. Then Denni said: 'I keep a flagon of it hidden in the brew-house and another, disguised with perfume, under my bed.'

'Why hidden and disguised?'

'The Gangmaster forbids it – says it's bad water. But if it makes you feel good, how can that be bad?'

Leah was becoming apprehensive. 'What does Beccanay say?'

'He tried the water once and it certainly worked on him. I think he might use it in secret, now.'

'What do you mean – "worked"?'

'You know – with a man . . . It makes him fitter and stronger. I know some of the firemen use it.'

'The ones you were whispering to?'

'Why shouldn't a girl banter with a good-looking boy?' But Leah suspected there was more involved than talk. 'Didn't you think them handsome, Leah?' Leah admitted she did. 'Then you should see what the water does to them – especially Finn.' She then described him intimately.

'Have you ... you know – with the firemen, with Finn ... ?' Leah asked.

Denni took another sip of the water and smiled decadently. 'It works on girls too.'

'On you?'

'You too, I'll wager. Let me look.'

'No!'

But Denni smothered her protests with gently insistent kisses. 'Let me look, I say,' she whispered softly in Leah's ear. The gentle kissing – in her neck, now – and the soft, seductive breathing against her ear melted the little resistance that Leah felt. In truth, Leah found it acutely arousing to have the girl unfasten her trousers in the hush of this secret place. All her senses were on tiptoe as the naked coolness touched her belly in the flickering torchlight. The anticipation of those delicate, slender, expert fingers stirred feelings of lewdness far more than all the talk of potent waters. Yet even as those fingers touched, seeking gently to open her at the front, and her trembling legs bowed wide to oblige, the faintly bitter aftertaste of that water lingered as a pleasant dryness that fuelled the desire to continue to drink.

'It's here and it's coming on hard, poking its little head up,' Denni whispered. She pulled the trousers from Leah's ankles and carefully replaced her clogs. Then she reached back, filled the chained cup with water and placed it on the floor between Leah's feet. Leah heard her dipping her fingers in.

'Oh, no,' she whispered but she wanted it and the anticipation was delicious.

'Oh, yes,' Denni crooned as Leah gasped and the icy cold fingers touched and pushed the fleshy hood back and the icy wet drips drenched Leah's knob. 'Oh, yes – see, it's not even shrinking from the cold, it's coming harder.' Leah could feel it, swelling, drawing all the blood from its surround until the thinned skin of her hood had retreated and tightened to a noose that only caused the knob to swell harder. Even when Denni withdrew her fingers, Leah could feel it still standing proud. 'Here, crouch and let it drink.' She filled the cup to the brim.

'Oh, no . . . please . . .,' Leah whispered weakly but again, even as Denni made her crouch to take it, Leah wanted it this way. She wanted to be made to do these sexual things while she was so aroused. Very slowly Denni offered up the brimming cup between Leah's legs. The jewelled chain tinkled, then Leah shuddered as her knob and labia were suddenly plunged into the freezing prickling water and the involuntary contraction drew the rush of tiny bubbles up inside. Denni kept lifting the cup until it overflowed and all of Leah's sex was submerged, the rim of the cup pressing into the sensitive place at the very top of each thigh. Denni kissed Leah again while Leah crouched with knees akimbo and Denni kept the cup tightly in place as Leah's sex slowly drowned in the icy water. Then Denni slipped her fingers over the front lip of the cup to massage Leah's knob very gently. She started to milk it. 'Pee,' she murmured lewdly. 'Pee into the water; make the cup overflow and I shall drink it.' Leah shook her head, gasping while Denni's depraved fingertips pried a little further within to stimulate the secret aperture where the pee comes out. She tried to push the tip of her little finger into it and the peculiar pleasure-pressure made Leah moan.

Denni made her stand. 'Turn round.' Leah faced the smoothly fluted cavern wall with its sheen of running water. She felt Denni's fingers slipping up between her legs from behind, slipping up into her sex and pushing her swollen knob out until it touched the freezing wall. The water drizzled over it, tickling, making fizzy bubbles where it touched the skin, stirring the need to come. Gently Denni pressed and Leah's knees locked. Gasping, she collapsed, arms outstretched against the wall. Then Denni's other hand came round to the front, gently cleaving the labia open, carefully feeling for the pee-hole, pressing the tiny mouth. 'Do it,' she whispered into Leah's ear. Leah tried but, though she wanted to be lewd, it would not come. 'I can feel the little mouth pushing out,' Denni murmured. 'It has a tiny rim, nice to touch, nice to tap – can you feel the tapping; is it good?' Then Leah moaned and a kind of pleasure came – stiltedly, not deeply, for she was frightened of losing control and peeing while the pleasure was coming; yet the feeling of being touched exactly there was deeply sexual. It felt as if a narrow stiff rod of flesh had been inserted up her pee-hole, for the finger-tapping at its tip reverberated all the way up inside her. The tapping gently diminished and Denni's fingers slid away. She turned Leah round. Leah's saturated shirt-front clung against her nipples, which Denni fingered through the cloth. 'Keep your legs open for me. You need to drink some more, so you won't be able to hold it from me. Then I need to watch and feel while it comes out. Understood?'

Leah closed her eyes in abdication. The profound need to embrace submission welled in her throat; a knot of deliciously sexual nausea tightened within her belly. She felt Denni undoing the buttons of her shirt and drawing the flaps open. Then Denni reached and touched, not the breasts, but the knot of Leah's belly, standing out as if a fist were thrusting from inside it. Again, a feeling like an orgasm came, though Denni was not touching her knob or even her pee-hole. 'The water's working,' Denni whispered. 'Now, some more

'– as much as you can drink. And keep your legs open so I can see and feel.'

The water dripped from the cup and ran in trickles between Leah's breasts. Denni encouraged the trickles by tipping the cup too far; when the flow reached Leah's sex, Denni's fingers intercepted it and wetly, gently kept her open, touching, pressing there, keeping the feelings lewd and strong.

Then Leah heard a noise quite different from the cavern sounds of running water – the echo of footsteps. 'What's that?' She turned her head in terror towards the approaching light.

'No – stay still. Don't try to cover up. They won't hurt you. I asked them to meet us.'

'Who?'

'Those two boys – Finn and Arno. See.' And, clad only in their loincloths, they emerged from the passageway.

As Denni went forward to greet them with kisses, Leah drew back against the wall, buttoning her shirt quickly. The shock of discovery had killed all arousal and now all she felt was embarrassed fear. Denni was very forthright, especially with Finn, the taller of the two. Already, while she was whispering to him, her fingers that had just now been inside Leah were stroking his face and lips. And he was looking at Leah, who suddenly realised that Denni was deliberately planting Leah's musk on the young man's lips. Neither man had approached Leah, though Arno too was looking at her. She kept still against the wall, her thighs tightly together to conceal her naked sex – more yet, to conceal her swollen clitoris, that beacon of lewdness which, despite the shock, had not gone down even a little. But the grip of her thighs only made the pulse in her groin more distinct: she felt it throbbing in her erection.

Denni was feeding the men water from the spring; concentrating her attention on Finn, the more handsome of the two. Arno hung his torch close to Leah. She turned her head half away but she could still see Denni with Finn. Denni's hand was under his loincloth while he was drinking. Then, smiling wickedly at Leah, she drew it aside. Leah looked away but too late, for the image of Finn's thick erection burgeoning in the girl's hand was already locked in her mind. That mind, in its present state of disarray, in those few brief moments, did unwanted, dread and beautiful things with that erection to keep it coming on. Then she felt Arno's hand tentatively touching her clenched fist.

He made no other advance than to seek to hold her hand until Leah, her gaze involuntarily drawn back to the scene of the other two, finally acquiesced. She found reassurance and warmth in the strength of that unassuming hand. She secretly glanced at the man she had deemed the less attractive of the two, and found him the more attractive in manner. With a shiver, she saw a deep scar, like a burn, down his side, as if he had been branded with a hot iron bar. Then she realised that the hand she was holding was damaged; all the fingers except the index had lost the first joint. Automatically Leah closed both her hands about this damaged one, squeezing it protectively. Arno smiled at her and she drew closer.

Denni, on her knees, had Finn standing at the edge of the pool, where she was alternately bathing then sucking his erection. He was reaching down, touching her between the legs. Then Denni gasped and shuddered with the head of his penis still in her mouth. Leah felt that shudder too and the sensation communicated through to Arno's hand. 'Do you want to drink?' he whispered gently to her and Leah nodded, though she had already drunk aplenty. But desire was returning and desire dispels caution. When she drank from the cup he held, she kept kissing those damaged fingers; she wanted to kiss his scar.

'You drink too,' she said, openly touching his scar. And when he finished his cupful, she said: 'More. Keep drinking.' She wanted him filled with desire, a desire to be expended on her – perhaps within her. She shivered at that thought and, bowing forward, gently kissed his scar and felt the beautiful tension of arousal in his belly.

'If you're ready . . . ?' Denni said. Leah frowned.

Finn, holding a brimming flagon, said: 'Let's go up to the bath-oven.'

Arno put his arm round Leah's waist. 'Come on – I'll fill a flagon for us too.'

Finn took up a torch and led the way. He took them deeper into the cavern then, turning, entered a narrow gallery whose steepening floor gave way to steps cut into the rock, before becoming a spiral stairway cut into the sides of a near-vertical water-worn shaft. They emerged through a trapdoor into a furnace room, half sunk into the rock, partly roofed with timbers. It was open on one side to the night but still the radiant heat was intense. There was a heavy door on the other side, which Finn bolted. Then he ran back and bolted the trapdoor. 'Set the damper on the oven,' he cried.

Arno hurried from Leah's side, collected a long iron bar and slotted it into a giant lever on the side of the 'oven' – which was more like a furnace than any oven Leah had ever seen. Then he began dragging its doors shut with a hook. Denni explained that the oven warmed the bath-house on the hillside above. She set the torches into low slots in the rock wall. Then she lifted the flagons on to a rough-hewn table that had cups and other small implements, along with a small cache of bread, dried apples and cheese. Fleeces and straw lay on the floor.

It was obvious that Denni was well acquainted with this place, and the men had moved swiftly to seal the entrances and prevent disturbance. Clearly it had all

170

been planned, yet Leah felt deeply excited by this prospect of a tryst. Denni was looking at her, her eyes glittering with lewd anticipation, her nostrils dilated by her deep breathing. Finn was peering out of the open side of the chamber, doubtless checking that the coast was clear. Leah looked again at Arno, still wrestling with the controls of the giant oven, his muscular body bathed in the red light. The air felt hot and dry, like the desert. Leah went to the table, poured a cup of water from one of the flagons and drank it off in one swift movement. Then, even as the bubbles were still tickling in her throat, she poured another. She felt giddy with elation.

Arno came back and quietly slipped his arms around her waist, under her shirt; they were hot and she could smell the musky scent from his exertions. She put the cup down and let her fingertips search out his scar. She shivered as they slid along the furrow, lined with the softest, smoothest skin but bounded by hard lumpy ridges at each side. Touching that damaged place gave a strange pleasure to her – an arousal that was as powerful as it was wrong. Her knob was swelling with blood and she opened her thighs to relieve the sexual pressure but as she continued to stroke that deep furrow in Arno's skin, her arousal simply deepened. She felt him tense and catch his breath and, suddenly self-conscious about what she was doing, she withdrew her fingers.

'No, don't stop – that was nice,' he whispered. Leah knew that if she were to turn to face him now, her erection would be obvious. She picked up the cup and tried to carry on drinking, only to spill water down her shirt, which he slowly unbuttoned even as she was drinking. And so she was laid bare: her broken chain, which intrigued him, and her lack of pubic hair, which aroused him, and most of all her erection, which he said was beautiful. But it was her swollen-nippled breasts, wet and tight, upon which he concentrated first. While he sucked them gently, her fingertips returned to the perverse sensuality of that deep furrow in his side, until the finger-touching was not enough, and her lips and tongue yearned to kiss it. Head bowed, her lips touched the hard outer ridges and her tongue-tip slid along the smooth heart of the furrow. He was already holding her knob – 'like a little hard cherry,' he murmured – and her climax came immediately he squeezed it while trying to get his damaged fingertips all the way round it, as if to pluck it from her body or to burst it from its stone. That was what the pleasure felt like, but her knob was not burst at all; under the spell of the potent waters, it just kept on swelling.

She had tried to conceal her climax, holding her breath, trying to defer the swoon, taking his hands in hers, interlacing their fingers to prevent his continuing to touch between her legs. She was uncertain whether he had realised what he had brought about; she tried to distract him by kissing; her legs were trembling from the act of concealment. But the delicious swelling continued. She could feel the pressure now in the buried part inside her, still distending, and the tiny pores inside the inner lips of her sex secreting their oil, the gentle oil that helps the penis slip inside.

Arno drew aside his loincloth and she felt his naked erection, burning hot against her belly. As he lifted her bottom on to the edge of the table and her clogs clattered to the floor, she reached to capture the head of his penis between her fingertips just as he had captured her knob. Gently her fingers squeezed it under the rim and held it, while he shivered and she removed his loincloth with her other hand. Then she realised that both Denni and Finn were watching her. Still holding the trembling glans, Leah calmly turned and poured more water into her cup. Denni smiled and whispered something to Finn, who approached Leah more closely. He too was completely nude and Leah saw that, of the two men's erections, his was the larger. Denni came closer. 'Touch her clit,' Denni urged Finn, who sought a nod of agreement from Arno, whose erection had grown larger and more upstanding under Leah's grasp.

When Finn's fingers touched her erection, Leah's lost their grip on Arno's glans and she collapsed on to her side on the table. One hand was still clutching the cup. She heard Arno move behind Denni. Finn made Leah put the cup down. 'Lift your leg. Hold it up for me,' he ordered her very softly. She used her hand to support it from the knee, in effect offering all between her legs for his unbridled attentions, while the others watched. Finn's head bowed down between Leah's legs in readiness to suck and Leah tightened and the feeling came – the feeling of falling, a deep drawing sensation between her legs, the beautiful pressure of that inner erection against the tube of her pee-hole, and the dread, lewd expectation that if the pleasure came then she might pee.

Finn's lips closed around her knob and started sucking very gently, as if it were a delicately swollen fruit that he sucked in the sweet anticipation of its bursting in his mouth. Leah's free hand reached out for Denni, clawing softly upwards between her legs, through those moist black hairs, and slipping inside her sex. She heard Denni's moan, then felt the bulging head of Arno's penis trying to enter Denni's sex from behind, vying with Leah's knuckles – poking repeatedly, trying to push in, while Denni gasped under the distension. His ejaculation came too soon, with Leah's knuckles pressed against the underside of his penis, and the semen squirted over her fingers, which moved up the furrow of Denni's slit to bathe her knob in the warm liquid, triggering Denni's climax. The feeling of

173

that hard, slippery female knob jumping uncontrollably against her fingers made Leah pull her knee up so tightly that most of her sex pushed inside Finn's mouth, and the urgent tightness of his sucking made the pleasure burst so strongly that she thought she had peed. She rolled, gasping, on to her back.

'She's peeing,' Finn whispered. 'See – it's coming.'

'Oh no!' She shivered.

'Shhh . . .' He ran his hand over her belly. 'It's good. It's what we wanted, isn't it, Denni?'

Leah's distraught gaze turned to her friend, who was nodding enthusiastically, her eyes glistening with excitement. She crouched over Leah's face and kissed her, dipping her fingers between Leah's legs, tip-touching the tiny hole, gently pressing, stemming the last of the flow.

'Let me touch her,' Arno said.

'First – taste her.' Denni put her wet fingers into his mouth, murmured, 'Good,' and watched his erection burgeon.

Arno's touching was the gentlest of the three. Leah reached across for his penis, still wet with semen and Denni's oil. Then he kissed her inner thighs and her hairless sex, saturated with the wetness sprayed by Denni's fingertipping. He whispered: 'Your scent here – it's like the broom-flower on the hill – so soft, so sweetly musky.' His lips slid once more over the soft wet skin. She touched his penis again and found it fully hard and hot, the blood pulsing in steady thumps. Then he kissed her, transferring her own scent to her mouth, and she found such kissing to be deeply, shamelessly, lewdly arousing. She kept hold of Arno's penis, locking her fingertips round the head, caging it, gently squeezing. She knew this gentle, slow squeezing would make the gland inside him overfill. A man's second spill was often more liquid. She wanted to force that gland to expel all its fragrant semen at a time of her bidding.

'Let's put her in front of the fire, where it's warm and we can dry her,' Finn said. He spread fleeces on the floor; Arno lifted and laid her on the soft cool fleeces before the heat of the oven. She tried to keep finger contact with the head of his penis. 'More water,' she begged. She felt his glans jerk with excitement against her fingertips. Denni brought the flagons. Finn opened the oven doors a little and raised the damper. Leah's nude, relaxed body was bathed in the ruby glow.

Finn started kissing Denni. She had hold of his erection near the base, not moving her hand, just squeezing to the point of throbbing. Arno cradled Leah's head and fed her water from the cup; she drank the cupful swiftly. 'More,' she said and felt the arousal pulsing through her body, buzzing in her head. When he raised the second cupful to her lips, she said: 'Hold me between the legs.' And she directed the hand with the damaged fingers to her naked wet sex and shuddered when they touched.

Denni now began administering water to Finn. She kept fingering his erection at the root, stimulating it while he was drinking. Then she started sucking his balls. Leah had an urgent longing to have the bobbing head of that penis pushed in her mouth while Denni was sucking the balls. At that thought, a feeling came between her legs, a feeling so intense, where the stunted fingers were touching, that she moaned. Arno smothered her moans with his mouth while his hand, still cupped between her nude wet thighs, gripped her flesh ever tighter, ever more intimately, the outer fingers pressed into the sensitive join of each thigh, the palm against her knob, the heel above it, steadily pressing. A delicious hot numbness came between her legs and then, through the numbness, a piercing thrill of freezing pleasure, as if a melting icicle were being pushed up her pee-hole, pushed slowly, remorselessly, deliciously far inside her. Then he tried to lift her with that hand that still clutched the naked flesh between her legs, and suddenly the icicle seemed to burst into a hundred shimmering needles, showering their prickling, freezing tiny stabs of pleasure up inside her.

'There ... do it,' he crooned. He took his hand away, glistening wet, and the spray started coming in full. Then his fingers came back to hold her inner lips spread wide to expose her pee-hole. 'It's like the mouth of a tiny fish,' he whispered. And that little fish kept squirting with a steady and strong rhythm and Leah, watching his fascination with it, felt her nipples tighten with wantonness. She reached for his penis, and held the glans in the jet of liquid. 'Oh – hot,' he gasped, 'Lovely ...' He started to shudder and his fingertip grip upon her labia faltered as she bathed the glans, drenched it, before the flow finally stemmed. Then she reached to kiss that dread, tender furrow of injured flesh running down his side. She dragged him down beside her on to the fleece, with the furrow exposed. Then she mounted it, putting her thighs astride his ribcage as he lay on his side, feeding her labia up against the furrow, bedding her clitoris in the soft smooth flesh inside. Exquisite pleasure came when she tightened her thighs and the sides of the furrow compressed her clitoris, bit it, it seemed, and she hunched forward, gasping, so near to coming, but the pleasure stayed on and she felt herself wetting again and the furrow flooding and overflowing down his side.

She reached back, smoothing the tight head of his cock with the slippery wet she was exuding. Then she felt the cockhead jump and jerk against her fingers and she climbed off him and twisted round. 'Quickly – in my mouth,' she told him, hunching down to meet it, so as not to miss a drop. The head – bitter, aromatic, dripping wet – she took into her mouth and a second later her mouth was flooded with semen, salty but sweet too, and lusciously fluid, not glutinous. She kept it in her mouth and savoured every last drop. His hand was on her nipples, helplessly moving from one to the other, clawing at their tightness. Her hand was between her legs, caressing the minute erectile tissue at the mouth of her pee-hole, pressing a fingertip against it, putting lewd pressure there, in the way Denni had shown her.

And so it continued through the night. The little group slept a little and took sustenance from the cache of bread and cheese, but mostly they took water. When Arno was sent to refill the flagons, Leah watched Denni with Finn, saw his heavily swollen erection going into Denni's body, slipping smoothly, lubricated by the oil from Denni's sex. Leah felt emboldened to play with him while he penetrated Denni. Denni's oil dripped warmly on to Leah's fingers as she drew the skin of the swollen penis tightly back and held it. Then she squeezed the heavy ball sac until the deep contraction came and the sac gathered and tightened hard and, in the next second, Denni's sex overflowed with semen.

Afterwards, Leah held Finn's penis while he peed. She controlled the flow with finger-pressure under the base, whilst her other hand directed the tip. Denni got wet – very wet; that was Leah's lewd intention. It bounced off her breasts and sex and spilled all over the fleeces; it wetted her lips and eyebrows. Her body looked beautifully, shinily wet; her nipples were as tight as Leah's; her lips were full and glistening. Leah gently sucked the strong male wet from between Denni's legs and felt Denni's climax coming. While it was still pulsing, she held her open and Denni peed and Leah tried to control the flow with her fingers but the flesh was too slippery. She played mistress to Denni, pushing the tip of her little finger into the tiny mouth that was still streaming, applying firm pressure to stem the flow. While she pressed, and Denni gently squirmed under the sexuality of that fingertip restraint, Leah sealed her lips about Denni's in a mistress's gently suffocating kiss. She felt Denni's whole body tremble, as if she was drowning in all the pleasure sealed up inside.

When Arno returned with the recharged flagons the men took Leah in their charge, plying her with water, kissing her, touching her between the legs, sucking her. Finn bundled her into his arms and slid his penis effortlessly into her sex from behind. Arno came to her from the front and started to masturbate her with just the tip of his erect penis until she was on the verge of coming and the tightness spilt her first droplets. 'Not yet, Leah,' Finn whispered. 'Hold it in. Give her some more water, Arno.' Leah took it and the probing with the tip of the penis started again until she moaned and pleaded. Then Arno suddenly gasped and drew back, the head of his penis leaking pre-come.

Naked, impaled on Finn's shaft, with her knees tightly tucked up, Leah was carried to the open side of the dugout. He stood on the edge so her bundled body jutted into the night and through the giddiness she could see far below the glitter of furnaces and the glint of moonlight on the waterway. Then, in an instant, Denni was beside Finn, reaching under and between Leah's legs, telling Finn to get her knees more open. This spreading of her knees made the bulging glans inside her press against her swollen bladder. Then Denni began masturbating her, focusing on her knob – the flat of two fingers rubbing round it, under it, lifting it like a stubby penis. Leah groaned in delicious resignation. Denni did not slow the finger-torture. Firmer and deeper came the pressure, through the root of the clitoris, drawing profound and uncontrollable pleasure, intensely protracted, as if many climaxes had run together, like knots of pleasure on a long, oiled necklace being drawn from her pee-hole. The glittering beads of liquid arced in long wrenching spurts into the night and splashed on the rock face far below. Then she felt Finn coming inside her but all the fear of male ejaculation in her body was as nothing; the only object was pleasure, this deep, drowning pleasure and the primordial urge that rendered her deliciously powerless to want to expel the penis, let alone to try.

Afterwards, they laid her on the fleeces, which were warm, damp and aromatic with the musky scent of wanton abandon. It drugged her; her inner body cared not that she already harboured a copious yield of male emission, but welcomed more, and she climaxed when it was Arno's turn to come inside her. She clung to him and felt deliciously drowsy, beautifully sated, and fell asleep, the skin of her breasts, belly and legs tight with all the dried fluid, her nipple pressed into the furrow of his wound, her sex lips still sealed snugly round the root of his penis. His every movement, however slight, she felt deep inside her, where it counted most, feeding desire and depravity into all her dreaming.

She woke with a start in full daylight. The boys were gone. Denni was shaking her. 'Come on,' said Denni. 'We can bathe in the spring. Then we'd better get back. Beccanay will be wondering about us.'

'But what if the Gangmaster finds out?' Leah asked belatedly.

'He's away – not back for another two days, according to Finn. And besides – how would he find out? Who's going to tell him?'

# 12

# A Reward for Promiscuity

The girls quietly trundled their empty barrel back into
the brew-house. There was no sign of old Beccanay so
Denni said: 'Come on. Let's have a look at where they
malt the grain.' She took Leah by the hand and led her
up the wooden staircase to an upper floor where the
bare boards were strewn with sprouting grain. Leah
was startled to see a young man, stripped to the waist,
hunched over in the gloom at the far end, scooping the
grain back and forth with a wooden paddle. Denni
showed no surprise; in fact she was unashamedly
staring at him until Leah tugged her arm. Denni
breathed the warm, scented humid air. 'I love the smell
of malt,' she said.

'Mmm . . . Sweet . . .' Leah nodded.

'Isn't he just?' Denni was again staring at the
semi-naked young man.

'You know what I meant.' Leah was mortified.

'But he's nice – just look at him.'

Leah risked a fleeting look then turned away in
embarrassment, afraid he might have overheard them.
He had stopped working and was watching them from
the shadows. Then she heard his footsteps slewing
towards them through the grain and in a panic she
turned for the stairs.

'Leah!' he cried.

She froze. How did he know her name?

'Leah!' the voice came again. And this time, recognition struck home and Leah, in shock, felt giddy and joyous and sickly faint all at the same time. Denni watched open-mouthed as Ean pushed past her, catching hold of Leah just in time to prevent her sliding sidelong down the stairs. He crushed her limp swooning body in his arms, as if he would never let her go.

Denni, with a look of stunned consternation, quietly negotiated her way around the pair and crept down to the foot of the stairs, where she waited, casting perplexed upward glances as if to reassure herself of what she was witnessing.

Tears of joyous deliverance streamed down Leah's face.

'Don't cry,' Ean chided her gently. But she did not stop: she cried from guilt that she had so swiftly forgotten him and from joy that he was found. And he was safe.

'I thought I had lost you for ever.' She covered his face with tear-wet kisses. She clung to his breast and kissed that too.

He held her at arm's length to look at her. 'So beautiful,' he murmured. 'I should never have left without you. But how did you find me? I waited and watched the boat until it disappeared, hoping all the time that you would change your mind and follow. And you did.'

Leah's gaze dropped away, as the wave of guilt struck: she had not tried to follow. Then she gasped in horror: 'They've shackled you!' He was chained between the ankles to a leash-chain snaking across the floor. Leah turned on Denni, demanding: 'Why?' until Denni's bleak, accusing expression silenced her.

Ean laid his hands gently on Leah's shoulders. 'I tried to take another horse from the stables here – to borrow it, really.'

181

'To steal it,' Denni pronounced solemnly.

'To get back to me, like I told you to?' Leah whispered, staring up at him.

'Yes,' he said softly. 'But you beat me to it.'

A delicious exhilaration, intoxicating and overwhelming, swept up through Leah's soul. She clung to Ean so tightly that she was oblivious to the sounds around her until he anxiously eased her away and cast a furtive glance down the stairs.

'No mixing between prisoners!' the voice boomed out. Leah gripped the handrail in fear. Ean, his chain trailing, edged back to his work. The Gangmaster stood at the door. His displeasure now turned upon Denni, who, shocked by his unexpected arrival, began proffering frightened excuses to try to fend off his growls. 'You – a free girl – ought to know better than to let this happen!'

Denni never said anything to implicate Leah or Ean; she took all the blame upon herself. So, free girl or not, Denni paid the price. The Gangmaster made her drop her trousers there and then. He whipped her bare bottom mercilessly with his crop and, with every cruel blow that he laid upon it, Leah's conscience was flayed by barbs of self-reproach.

'Come down, girl,' the Gangmaster ordered Leah. Her frightened gaze turned to Ean. Defiantly, he strode back towards her but she shook her head, knowing full well that no good could come if he attempted intervention. Meekly she crept down the stairs. With her arms behind her back she fell to her knees, remembering to murmur those special words: 'Master – how shall I please?' Miraculously the Gangmaster did not touch her. He continued to glower at the weeping Denni. Then, turning to Leah, slowly weighing her up, he pursed his lips and finally nodded approval. Then he pointed to Denni. 'See to her. Get her pants up. And don't mess with the prisoner again. Understood?'

Leah nodded. 'Yes, master.'

He struck a final vicious lash across Denni's buttocks and Leah hurried to pull up Denni's trousers to protect her cruelly punished flesh.

Suddenly a door under the stairs opened to reveal Beccanay, hunched under a sack of grain, which in his surprise he immediately dropped. His pale-blue eyes swiftly took in the scene. He glanced up the stairs then said: 'Some problem, Gangmaster?'

'Not now, Beccanay. All quiet and calm.'

The old man tilted his head enquiringly at Denni. 'And my chief assistant – what ails her?' His gaze set hard upon the Gangmaster.

'She forgot the rules. But she recalls them now, is that not so, Denni?' He turned the tear-stricken girl to face him.

'Yes, m-master,' Denni blubbered. 'P-please forgive me.' Leah watched in horror as Denni offered up her lips and the Gangmaster kissed her like a lover: Denni was acting like a slave. The kiss was finally interrupted by an irritated cough from the old man. The expression on Beccanay's face was one of utter disdain for the Gangmaster but it softened when it fell upon Denni. Denni's eyes looked hunted. Beccanay shook his head in almost imperceptible admonishment for what she had just allowed them all to witness. 'If you will forgive me, Gangmaster, I must be about my work – with the help of both of my assistants.'

The Gangmaster released his grip upon Denni's waist. He quickly whispered something to her and her look of oppression deepened. Then he pressed the crop against her breasts in one final gesture of ownership before turning on his heels and leaving.

In the recriminatory silence, Leah pondered why the love-life of a free girl seemed more tortured than a slave's. But in sacrificing herself to protect Leah and Ean, Denni had shown a generosity of spirit that shone through it all. Leah put her arms around the tear-stricken girl and kissed her. Ean looked on guiltily from the balcony. It fell to Beccanay to break the strained silence: 'Ean – return to your duties, if you will. Under my charge, no further danger will befall them.' Leah thanked the old man with her eyes. 'Now you two can stay in my quarters tonight. I'll sleep on the landing.'

'No,' Denni whispered. 'I'd better go back or he will miss me: there's the meal to help with. Let Leah stay.'

'I'm going with you, Denni,' Leah said protectively, ignoring Ean's forlorn expression.

'Then that's settled.' Beccanay sighed wistfully, shaking his head.

On the way down to their quarters they were silent until Denni said: 'You never told me you knew Ean.'

'No – I'm sorry. I ought to have said. But you never told me he was here.'

'Why would I? I had no idea you even knew him.' Then she said in a low voice: 'He seems to like you very much. How did you come to meet him? I never saw you up at the house.'

'No – I was never at the house.' Leah was forced to confess in outline, at least, whilst omitting many details, the gist of that first meeting with Ean.

'Do you love him?' Denni's tone was forlorn. It was clear she still held him in regard.

Leah felt trapped between the honest question and her own confused misgivings. 'I don't know. I think I might,' she finally admitted weakly. Then she put her hand on Denni's.

'No – it's all right,' Denni whispered. 'Come on.'

That night, after her ablutions, Leah was sitting on Denni's bed, watching the meticulousness with which she was washing. Leah's thoughts returned to anxieties about what had been allowed to happen with the firemen – their coming inside her sex. She knew that washing would not help. When Denni came to bed, Leah broached the matter. Denni asked about the timing of Leah's last issue of blood.

'Many days since,' Leah answered.

'How many?'

'I'm not sure.'

'The seed has to get all the way up into the womb, through a tiny hole; there are not many days when that can happen; the opening is mainly sealed. But sometimes you can feel it. The surround is swollen – like a flower bud ready to burst. It leaks nectar from the opening.' Denni's words, her expression, intent and knowing, hungry almost, caused a peculiar feeling in Leah's belly, as if the words laid her belly open to Denni's scrutiny. Her pupils were dilated to utter blackness as she stared at Leah. Leah felt her nipples stiffening and made to cover herself with her arms but Denni stopped her. 'Lie down. Let me feel inside,' Denni murmured.

Her middle finger slid without resistance into Leah's sex, far up inside until the pad pressed accurately against the small protuberant entrance to her womb, pushing against the tiny hole. 'It's open – I can feel it. Can you feel my finger?'

Leah nodded. Denni gazed at her almost hypnotically. The arousal from the pressure of the finger-pad was growing stronger, from a dull throbbing to a deep dark wanting up inside her. When Denni kissed her, with the finger still there, it felt as if a squeezing hand was tightening about her womb. Then she felt her sex being held open so the finger might be withdrawn without smearing what was on the tip – a gluey exudation, slightly opalescent. 'Nectar,' Denni whispered, gently licking it from the tip.

'What can I do?' Leah begged.

Denni put her finger across her lips, then leant across the bed and opened a bedside drawer. 'Here,' she said. In her hand lay three small bulbous discs of resin. 'It's an emetic for your womb.'

'Where did you get them?'

'The Gangmaster has a stock. I took them when he wasn't looking.'

'Does he use them on you?' Leah ventured. Denni nodded. 'Do you like it, with him?' Leah whispered. She desperately wanted to know whether Denni was coerced into doing it.

'Stop asking so many questions.' Denni looked away until Leah put her hand in gentle apology on Denni's arm. 'Lie down again,' said Denni. Leah lay there while her friend carefully administered the emetic. Denni's fingers were so gentle and expert that Leah experienced arousal from the implanting of the disc – the sexuality of that pressure against the entrance to her womb. Denni said the disc would dissolve but Leah felt its presence for a long time as a coolness drawing the heat from her womb.

As she lay in bed she thought about what had happened with the two firemen. She felt remorse because she had done it all while Ean was a prisoner, chained up because he had been trying to get back to her. And none of what she had done was from slavish duty; she had gone willingly with both men and had knowingly used them for her own pleasure just as much as they had used her. She had already determined to sneak back to the brew-house to see Ean, just as soon as Denni was asleep. Leah waited and listened; then, the next thing she knew, her eyes opened with a start – she had dozed off, for how long she could not tell, but Denni wasn't in the room. Leah's plan had been foiled but she could at least get away without being followed. She collected some provisions in a cloth then crept out into the night.

Silently, she opened the door to the brew-house and stepped inside. There was a light in Beccanay's room and the door was ajar; stealthily she crept past, hoping he would be asleep. But she heard soft groans coming from inside. Keeping back from the door, Leah peeped through the gap and her heart missed a beat: a lithe nude figure balanced astride him on the bed; even from the back, the figure was unmistakably Denni. An overturned flagon of spring-water lay on the floor. Leah was shocked at first then quietly retreated, leaving the lovers their privacy. She turned for the stairs. And there on the stairs stood Beccanay.

Leah turned back in disbelief to the lighted doorway, and immediately saw what she had missed before – the chain, Ean's chain, no longer pinned, snaking across from the bed to a heap on the floor. She was felled as if by a hammer. Collapsing against the door-frame, she screamed: 'No! No!!' at the pitiless betrayal – by Denni, by Ean, even by Beccanay in his conniving.

She heard the outer door being closed, then a gasp from Beccanay. When she opened her eyes and looked up, the Gangmaster was towering over her, sweeping open the bedroom door and transfixing the terrified lovers with a sinister and calculating gaze.

He dealt with Ean first. In Beccanay's little room he took off his broad leather belt and lashed him exactly as he would a girl, across his naked buttocks while he lay prostrate on the bed. Then he dragged him, chain and all, out into the night, declaring that he would be back directly for the other two miscreants. For the next few minutes the girls waited petrified, Leah propped against the door-frame, Denni slumped naked against the wall, neither looking at the other. Beccanay paced up and down, helplessly wringing his hands; he didn't even speak to the girls to offer a thread of hope;

there wasn't any. Finally the outer door burst open again and the Gangmaster was back. Denni ran to the far corner of the little room and slumped down, pleading. Beccanay tried to intercede but the Gangmaster knocked him out of the way and started slapping Denni into deeper submission. Leah stood up, shaking, sobbing. The Gangmaster bundled Denni under one arm and came for Leah. She winced, waiting for the hand to strike. Then a voice shouted through the doorway.

'Shardlan's here, asking after the slave-girl.'

'Show his lordship to my quarters.'

'I have done.'

Leah was jerked off her feet and carried away with Denni, down the track and into a large hut. It had ironmongery, buckets and all manner of ropes at one end and a bed, table, cupboards and fireplace at the other. In the corner, a tall secretive figure stood motionless in the shadows. Beside the fireplace was an enormous full-length mirror with an ornate gilded frame. In the middle of the room, staked out between hooks on the ceiling and rings on the floor, was Ean, facing the bed, naked, gasping through the gag and shuddering, his limbs drawn out to the four corners of a cross, his buttocks striped with bright, fresh weals.

'I had to gag him to stop his caterwauling, my lord,' the Gangmaster snorted. 'I've had girls take their punishment better.' The tall figure in the corner didn't answer.

Leah wrenched herself free of the Gangmaster's grip and ran to Ean, throwing her arms round him, reaching to caress his anguished face, racked by humiliation and pain. With her fingertips wetted by his tears of shame, all thought of what she had witnessed with Denni was banished from her mind. Her own tears burst forth uncontrollably and she blurted out: 'I love you. It is all my fault that this ill befalls you.'

'I take it she is the slave?' A soft voice resonated from the corner.

'Aye, my lord. Shall you take her away directly?'

'Not directly.' The tall man stepped forward: he was mature in years and very calm. 'We are grateful for your reporting her, Gangmaster.' His eyes were knowing but his expression seemed not unkind. 'We have three other runaways in the boat; my assistant is presently dealing with them. She may require a little time, though they will all come right in the end. And I confess I am interested simply to watch and learn a little more of this one here.' He nodded towards Leah. 'Pray continue, Gangmaster.'

'I aim to find where the fault lies and where the ill is owing,' the Gangmaster proclaimed, dragging Leah off Ean and across to a chair by the bed. 'Now strip, girl – everything off. Now sit. Legs open – wider! Move once more without my say-so and I'll whip him till he bleeds.' He turned round. 'Denni – on the bed . . . run!' he growled and Denni tripped and dragged herself up again in the panic of compliance.

The Gangmaster collected his crop from the table and the interrogation began. The visitor simply folded his arms and watched.

'Denni – prepare yourself,' the Gangmaster barked and immediately Denni tucked up her knees to expose herself to scrutiny. The speed and precision of the manoeuvre clearly showed he had trained her like a slave. Her knees were almost touching her chin; her sex and bottom were raised in offering. She was straining to push her inner flesh out – like a slave girl being assessed for service. Leah stole a glimpse at the visitor but could discern nothing from his expression.

'You too,' the Gangmaster barked and Leah flinched. 'Don't make me tell you twice.' Leah struggled to achieve the pose without overbalancing. She raised her knees, then clasped her ankles and finally wriggled forward to expose her sex and bottom. When she pushed, she felt her sex opening to the inner pink and staying open. Still the visitor looked on inscrutably.

The Gangmaster sat on the bed. His weight made Denni's curled-up body roll towards him. He extended a finger until the coarse nail touched the edge of the lip of her open sex, making her shiver. 'I cannot trust you one iota – can I? Can I?' Though the tone was measured, still the flame of jealousy burned within him. Before Denni could answer, the crop whipped down between her legs. Denni gasped and her knees shook. 'Keep still! And keep it pushed out.' The crop whipped down again and Denni moaned. The tall visitor moved to the end of the bed. But he was watching Leah more than Denni. The Gangmaster now turned on Leah. 'You! Start at the beginning. Well?'

'We ... we went to the spring in the hill,' she stammered, her belly tense, waiting for the crop to fall. Through the dread sinking feeling, her gaze crept across to the visitor – the lord. She prayed he would intervene. He did nothing but his eyes stayed on her as the crop edged into the nakedness between her tucked-up legs, sliding under her chain, its thin shaft pressing into the sensitive crease between outer and inner lips, pressing firmly, so the inner lip, chain and all, curled over it and the responsive inner flesh erupted, creating a sensation of something being slid inside her body at the front, all the way upwards, like a smooth impalement, up through her belly to her throat.

'We?' the Gangmaster repeated, still pressing on the crop.

'Denni and I,' she whispered. Again she felt compelled to glance at the visitor, seeking some reaction, but none came.

'And who else?' the Gangmaster urged, glancing disdainfully at Ean before his free hand moved in to scavenge her inner flesh. She felt the rough fingernail scraping up the out-turned inner lip, then under the sheath of her clitoris. The sensation made her squirm.

'The boys,' she confessed in hopelessness and again looked past him to the visitor, who now spoke to her across her interrogator:

'Don't heed me.' He mouthed the words almost in a whisper. 'Pay attention to your present master.' The words implied that he would become her new master, and that gave her heart, for his reproof seemed measured and gentle, not harsh.

'Boys?' the Gangmaster repeated.

'Firemen,' Leah whispered. The Gangmaster said nothing at first and didn't even look at Denni, who was hardly daring to breathe. Instead he concentrated on completing the minute fingernail examination of Leah, stimulating little pulses of swelling in the head of her knob while the crop pressed deep into the crease to the side of her sex and the skin of her hood thinned and tightened over the swelling.

'Which firemen?' he asked.

To her shame, Leah gave the names. In reward he exposed her erect knob in all its fullness, touching it very gently with a moistened fingertip – now rubbing it, side to side, then pressing. 'You see – she's an honest girl, my lord. I like that. And such a beautiful cut – so smooth and naked.'

'Delicately put, Gangmaster. But she is altogether beautiful,' the visitor replied, moving closer. 'No – pray continue. Don't let my interjections stop you.'

'Now tell his lordship all that you did to your firemen and all that they did to you. And spare no details – or Denni's wanton little cut shall pay the price!' He turned to the bed and knelt heavily between Denni's ankles.

'Oh, no, master, please ... *please!*' The crop descended swiftly three times between the lips of Denni's slit. He waited for the stinging to bite before whipping three times more. But the visitor was still watching Leah. Denni was sobbing, gasping, trying to keep her shaking knees high up beside her chin while her master spread her swelling inner flesh wider with his thumbs. 'I must shave you and make you pretty here, like Leah,' he mused. 'And expose you that much better for your whippings. Would you like that, Denni?'

'Yes, m-master,' she blurted through her sobs. But Leah noticed that he was now touching Denni quite tenderly between the legs. In fact he remained there, touching her sex, sometimes reaching for her nipples and pinching them gently, while Leah told all that had happened with the firemen. He had only to use the crop on Denni once or twice, when Leah was discovered to have omitted some detail, either forgotten or suppressed. Everything that had befallen was laid bare before the master and the visitor. Even Ean in his anguish could not help overhear from her own lips what Leah had done in seeking gratification with those other men. Her heart sank to the pit of her belly when she glimpsed his pained expression. And the Gangmaster had all his suspicions about Denni's promiscuity vividly confirmed. He called her his little harlot but did not punish her further on that account; in fact he seemed to grow almost tender with her, twirling her nipples up to points.

When Leah first mentioned the peeing, the visitor advanced from the end of the bed and stood by Leah's chair, listening with great interest, examining the token round her neck, then venturing to stroke her hair. In the end, he sought the Gangmaster's permission to touch her more intimately. He sought Leah's permission too, first introducing himself as Lord Shardlan before asking: 'May I touch it while you tell your tale?'

It was a strange request, coming from a powerful master: in the acceding, Leah looked into Lord Shard-

Ian's grey-blue eyes only very briefly but saw steadfastness and gentleness there. Control had now shifted from the Gangmaster to Lord Shardlan. He kept stroking her hair while he touched her, seeking quite directly and unashamedly the naked place of which she was speaking. He asked about the pleasure that the drinking had induced there. He made her push out hard for him to examine the tiny mouth where the liquid had come out. His touch was as confident as a physician's but far more tender; it caused sexual shivers. He asked Denni and she confirmed the depth of Leah's response. He touched again, repeatedly pinching the minute rim until she gasped under the peculiar, deeply sexual feeling. He asked her if she knew what a wet-slave was and, when she nodded, asked if she would like to learn to become one. She was unsure how to answer. He did not press her but said: 'We have many wet-slaves at the Retreat, young men as well as girls.' And he detected another little shiver in the flesh that he was pinching.

Leah glimpsed Ean's erection, bobbing hard, for he had once touched her there, exploring those feelings. She felt the inner walls of her sex becoming slippery and swollen as Lord Shardlan continued to touch and probe the entrance to her pee-hole, making its tiny rim erect. The act of pushing her inner self out to meet that pressure drew a delicious sinking feeling through the pit of her belly, as if a thickly oiled cord were being slowly drawn out through her pee-hole. She wanted him to touch her knob now, to squeeze it while the fingertip continued to stroke that tiny erect circular rim.

He had noticed the way she kept glancing at Ean, and asked if Ean had ever touched her there. 'And you liked it from him?' Suddenly he got up and went to Ean and she turned her head away in shame but her heart surged when she heard Ean's sensual murmur.

Then the lord came back, his fingers glistening with Ean's pre-come. 'See – he sheds it even now for you.' She gasped as the pre-come was smeared gently all about her trembling clitoris and the rim of her pee-hole and she shuddered as he tried to push a clear droplet up inside it. 'There – take him within you.' Then he said: 'Now I would like to take the inner measure of this lovely narrow place. I have something I can test it with but I want you to consent.'

'What is it?' Leah whispered.

For the first time, a frown clouded Lord Shardlan's brow. A cold shiver rippled over Leah's belly. With one hand he took gentle hold of her tightening nipple. With a single finger of the other hand he continued to tickle-stroke the tiny entrance to her pee-hole and he waited patiently until she whispered: 'I . . . I agree.'

As the master nodded very slowly, Leah felt the sublime shudder of inner submission being shed between her legs, then the soft after-beats coming through the sensitive, pushed-out inner flesh, now gently stabbing itself upon his fingertip. Behind the firm enquiry of his blue-grey gaze Leah detected the reassurance that she needed, that all would come well, whatever the treatment. Lord Shardlan then sealed the bargain with a slow gentle kiss upon her lips; meanwhile, high up between her legs, that fingertip continued to press pure pleasure up through her.

He left Leah's side, stepped briefly outside then returned, apologising for the delay. 'My instruments are in the boat. My assistant will bring them.' In the meantime, he asked that water be administered to Leah.

'It is not from the spring,' the Gangmaster told him.

'No matter.' Lord Shardlan watched as Denni was put in charge of helping Leah drink. He seemed to be weighing Denni up. Then he looked at Ean. Finally he went over to him, removed his gag and asked him something. When Ean was slow in replying, the

Gangmaster threatened him with the belt but Lord Shardlan said: 'No – let him be,' then immediately looked for Leah's reaction. Leah thanked him with her eyes and took more water from Denni, in acquiescence to the new master's wishes.

The assistant then appeared and handed her master a small casket. She wore the cap and tunic of a guard but appeared fresh-faced and youthful. She treated his lordship with familiarity rather than deference and kept stealing glances at Ean as she stood casually by the door. Lord Shardlan now returned to the matter of Leah's testing. The casket had a lid inlaid with polished flat gemstones, mainly green and red, and was lined with green velvet. The objects inside it were shiny black, perhaps the length of two finger-joints, and shaped like tapered rods in progressively increasing girths. Each one had a neck crowned by a ball-shape at the wide end, with the greatest girth coming at the shoulder just below the neck. 'They're worked from smoothest ironstone – quill-stone, I believe the diggers call it,' said his lordship. 'I had them made up by the jeweller at the Retreat. They're copies of gold originals. I'll need you on the bed.'

He waited until Leah had complied. 'Turn over. On your knees. Spread them open. Lift your bottom. Belly down, hard down – hanging.' She quickly became keenly aware of the quantity of water she had drunk. Very gently he felt for the opening. 'Ah – don't tighten. Keep pushing open.' The tip of the first instrument touched, chill as ice. She shuddered sexually as it started to invade so private and lewd a place. The minute mouth opened and the fleshy tube began to swallow and distend. 'There – keep pushing. Come here, Denni, and watch. Does she not look beautiful with this going in?'

'Mmmm.' Denni crouched and kissed Leah's back and touched her labia while his lordship selected quill-stone rods of steadily increasing gauge. Applying each one individually and gently, using spittle as a lubricant, he slipped them up the narrow barrel of Leah's pee-hole until the shoulder was swallowed and the ball was cupped against the minute erect rim. The smoothness of sliding, the coldness, the precise pressure of the smooth ball against that rim – when Leah was already so aroused – induced a sexual feeling both unnatural and exquisite. All the while, Denni was toying with her labia, gently pulling, softly trying to spread them back.

After each insertion, with the rod in place, his lordship would cradle Leah's taut belly with his hand and ask her to bear down. Her sex would stay open like a swollen-petalled flower. Then his fingertip would press the ball of the instrument against the mouth of her pee-hole, transmitting feelings of acute strangeness and pleasure through the cold, rigid smoothness of the rod into the warm tube within. Before one instrument was fully withdrawn, her flesh already craved the next girth of distension. Finally a tightness came that made her gasp. 'There,' his lordship said with a sigh, withdrawing the quill-stone. 'We have your measure.'

He got up quickly, taking the instrument over to Ean. Leah heard a groan and glimpsed his lordship shamelessly squeezing the root of Ean's erect penis. When he came back, the quill-stone was soaked in pre-come. 'See – he salutes you. Now relax; let the insertion accomplish to the hilt.' Trembling, Leah felt the delicious sliding penetration start again. She shuddered at the sensation of Ean's pre-come being pushed up her pee-hole. 'Just a little more – take the shoulder – and the quill shall lodge without slippage. Bear down. Kiss her, Denni. There . . . Done!' Leah gasped; she felt her sex contract, drawing the ball securely against her, locking it in place, expelling Ean's excess pre-come in a globule which his lordship gently spread about her clitoris.

'Close your legs,' his lordship whispered, and he picked her up in a bundle and took her to the big mirror to show her. The only visible sign – the ball – between her legs was tiny, yet the feeling was so strong, like having a second clitoris. 'Touch it,' he told her. Nervously, her fingertips tried and the first tiny self-touch made her gasp, for it felt as if she were touching the head of a sexual bolt screwed all the way inside her to the tip of her spine, so deeply rooted was the pleasurable feeling.

He took her back to the bed and made her lie on her side with her thighs closed around her sex while he confirmed with the Gangmaster the arrangements of transfer. Every pulsebeat Leah could feel vibrating through that little quill of arousal pushed up her pee-hole.

Her heart leapt when she heard the Gangmaster offering his lordship Ean too, declaring: 'He's been nothing but trouble; he's a thief.'

His lordship was unwilling. Then Leah spoke out of turn: 'My lord, please take him.' He stared his disapproval at her defiance. 'Master, please?' she begged very softly, one last time, before lowering her gaze.

Then the girl-guard at the door interjected: 'My lord, perhaps the boatwomen's barracks might use him.'

He glanced back in mild annoyance then shrugged. 'Very well.'

Then Denni blurted out: 'I want to go too.'

'Take no heed of her,' said the Gangmaster.

'Surely, Gangmaster, as a free girl, she may at least ask, if she pleases?' Lord Shardlan retorted.

'Let me speak with her,' said the Gangmaster. He took her outside. A few seconds later came the harsh sounds of the crop then sobs of desperation. Then Denni was brought back in tears.

'Tell him,' said the Gangmaster.

'I w-w-want to . . . stay here,' Denni sobbed.

'Very well,' said Lord Shardlan curtly. 'Then all is settled. We take these two.'

Leah wanted to plead for Denni but his lordship's eyes narrowed upon her to silence her. Denni was bundled out before she could even say goodbye. Lord Shardlan came to Leah. 'Know your place – lie still. Raise your leg. Let me touch in there.' She murmured under the feeling as his fingertip pressed the little ball of the insert up against the mouth of her pee-hole. Then he whispered: 'Denni is not a slave like you; in the end, she does as she chooses. Would you have me do to her what the Gangmaster just did, to attempt to induce her to leave?'

'Not that, but –'

'Enough. Had she spoken up or even shown a sign, I might have intervened. Neither you nor I know what drives her. Her resolve will surely find its level in the end.' Then he turned to the girl-guard. 'Get our own shackles for the male.'

Ean was hobbled and tagged. His wrists were fastened behind him to a chain around his waist. Finally a cruel clamp was applied to his ball sac – two flat pieces of wood fastened round it with wooden screws that could be tightened. 'It secures swift compliance,' Lord Shardlan explained. 'Even the slightest girl can handle several men.'

'What about her?' the girl-guard asked. 'All runaways need restraining.'

'Her restraint is well inserted; I shall monitor her,' he replied coolly.

He carried Leah to the small boat. The girl led Ean. 'Don't hurt him,' Leah pleaded. 'She will take appropriate care,' the master answered.

There were three other runaways aboard but the master avoided them. He laid Leah on a little bed, on her side with one leg stretched out and the other tucked high and his fingers in between them, at her core, gently squeezing the flesh around the quill-stone insert, gently pressing the protruding ball, gently loosening it when the pressure became too strict to bear, allowing a little warm fluid to escape, sometimes on to the bed but mainly by dispersal over the skin of her thighs or, if there was a lot, upwards towards the nipples, keeping them in erection, then licking them clean. He asked if her breasts had lately been put in constraints to shape them, then said: 'For now, we shall let nature take its course. What your master does with them when he gets you back will be his affair.' He made no move to penetrate her. Several times Leah touched and squeezed his penis and made him leak but not come completely.

For her, the keenest pleasure came when the bedded insert was very slowly twirled – it brought a feeling at once intense and uncontrollable, deeply sexual, deeply wrong, deeply sweet. It made her reach up to kiss the master's mouth, suck his tongue, hold it captive, just as her pee-tube held that twirling quill-stone up inside her, clinging to the uniqueness of that pleasure until she groaned into his mouth. Her nipples felt as if needles had been put through them; her belly cramped and yet through her sex the climax was exquisite and would not cease. His hand was becoming saturated, for she could not stop herself, nor did she want to. 'We shall have a wet-slave of you yet,' Lord Shardlan whispered, slowly kissing the dangling musky droplets from his fingers then kissing Leah's lips, imparting her own wetness to them, nuzzling them gently, and all the while keeping the pressure of an obsessive finger up against the tiny ball at the tip of the insert that was bedded so precisely to engender such restive feelings in that special place.

While his lordship's finger nurtured his budding wet-slave, a nurture of a different sort was happening to Ean, who was chained in a separate compartment from the runaways and whose penis was already very erect after the earlier touching. The young girl-guard had now re-entered the compartment and put down her whip. Silently she removed her tunic top, revealing breasts that were beautifully sculpted, markedly swollen, with the burden of plumpness drawn to the tips, which were very dark brown, almost black, as if she might be pregnant. Her small belly bulged in beautifully tight roundness against her low-slung belt. Without a word she approached him and knelt before him as he stood chained naked against the wall, his erection straining helplessly upwards, driven by the vision of her sexuality and by the pervasive sexual pleasure-ache of the clamp about his ball-sac.

She leant back, unfastened her belt and let her trousers fall to her knees. Then she knelt up and began gently to tighten his clamp with very slow turns. Each time his breathing stalled, she pressed her soft full lips to his penis, in the very sensitive place under the head, sucking moistly until his breathing was forced to resume, when she very slowly tightened the screws again, watching his face, waiting for his chest to heave and his erection to stand like a rooted bone, when she again took up the sucking. While she sucked, she was touching herself between the legs, and the wet glans of Ean's penis could feel her agitation through the tremors in her breathing.

His sac throbbed as if trapped between a finger and thumb. But transcending this came a strange feeling, as if the clamp were instead around the gland inside him. The girl was murmuring as she masturbated herself and all the while those soft lips sucked until Ean gasped and groaned and the girl withdrew. 'Wait,' she said, and swiftly tightened the screws one full turn, then slid her lips fully over the head of his penis, enveloping it like a sheath and sliding moistly all the way down until he felt the glans mate to the soft yielding funnel of the back of her throat. She hunched forward, wanting to take it deeper, then gulped all the ejaculate that the pleasure-tortured gland inside him yielded. Through all Ean's agonised spurting she remained impaled by mouth upon his penis, her nostrils flared, groaning, swallowing, her whole body shuddering, as if she were trying to swallow the very flesh that she had forced to subservience in her throat.

When the girl-guard had for the present drunk her fill of her prisoner's semen, she stood up, buckled her belt but left her swollen dark-nippled breasts standing proud. Then she put her arms around his naked waist and her breasts around his standing penis and the pulsing she induced there caused the last dregs of issue to spill upon her velvety nipple-surrounds. As she took suck upon her velvet, the little boat was already pulling through the serpentine portico, and the first rays of sunlight were gleaming on the golden domes and alabaster spires of the Tithe Retreat.

She looked up at Ean again, her eyes glistening darkly and wantonly. 'I might not put you to the boatwomen. I might keep you to myself.'

'As my torturer?'

'As your liberator.'

Over the next few days Ean got to know his guard a little – her traits, her perverse wishes – but he never got to the bottom of that extraordinary statement. She never alluded to it again. She seemed to want to know all he could tell her about Leah but she would disclose nothing concerning Leah's whereabouts, simply saying reproachfully: 'Be assured, my lord master is protecting her.' Then her attention would drift. But whenever she returned from a meeting with her master, she would be brimming with arousal and would want to take Ean there and then, in the little store-room, and have him penetrate her standing, while he was still shackled. She taught him to postpone his climax by withdrawing and clenching the muscle inside. Repeatedly she would make him do this and would watch his penis jerking, then she would slide on to it again and kiss him in the most delicious manner till his climax neared again, when she would slide off him and proudly watch his struggling. Eventually she would instruct him to come and would slide her mouth all the way down his shaft and swallow every drop while touching herself to bring on her own pleasure. Her eyes would be closed and she would be mumbling incoherently around his slippery shaft. The more he thrust into her mouth the stronger her climax and the louder her muffled gasps and cries. Once, amid her shudders, he made out a phrase that afterwards echoed perplexingly through his mind: 'My precious, my only, my lord . . .'

# 13

# The Dresser

Her name was Ulline, though the wealthy merchants who made the journey up to the Tithe Retreat, high above the heat and bustle of the seaport, generally knew her as the Dresser, a title which Ulline preferred, for its formality and its surgical overtones, which instilled an appropriate measure of fear in the potential recipients of her expertise. Put plainly, she got the girls ready – though Ulline's readying had little to do with frippery or attire. Having once acted as surgeon's assistant on the ships, she preferred to think of her suite as a lazaret. It overlooked the staircase of locks that guided the waterway down to the sea and it bridged the ground between the toll-house proper and the alabaster towers of merchant-pleasure. Every girl had to pass through Ulline's surgical fingers and be assessed for possible improvements to the contour or the response of intimate parts.

Every morning she put on fresh white linen – a thin bib to contain her breasts, whose perfect shape shouldered against the sheerness of the material, and a sarong sheathed low about her waist, leaving her midriff bare. In a different setting she would have been thought beautiful. She was tall and graceful, high-cheekboned and with delicate features – small ear lobes, small nose and mouth and slender, adept fingers.

Her hair was silken and long. Like the girls in her charge she went barefoot.

Today, her round would begin with the gentle lacing-up of a girl whose faultless labia had been punctured like the flaps of a boot, with a precision that would do credit to any artisan. Under gentle fingertip pressure, the twelve gold sleepers slid out one by one, showing her punctures healed and nicely open. The flesh of those beautiful labia swelled under the provocation of touching. They felt deliciously alive and very, very warm, like the loose pelt of a naked newborn animal.

Ulline fed the fine, gold-stranded satin cord carefully and delicately through every precisely circular perforation in these soft smooth velvety lips, as the girl moaned faintly, gently drew the cord tight, gently tighter, sealing off the upper part of the vulva, hiding all the pastel pink, then securing the moist warm closure with a perfect bow. The girl's erect clitoris, constrained by the tautness, protruded like a sweetly pushable button from beneath its hood. Though she was sealed by the lacing, still there was space for a finger to get within her sex to test her temperature: in fact there was space for at least three fingers, or perhaps the head of a sufficiently inquisitive penis. Once the girl was laced up, Ulline left her aroused sex to come to terms with its new binding and moved on to check the progress of the others.

She stopped at the third bed. The girl was sleeping. Her wrists were tied above her head and she lay on her side with her knees tucked up. Ulline drew back the coverlet. Lodged between the girl's thighs was the swollen ball-sac of an alabaster dildo. The rest was inside her sex, keeping it open. The insertion had come sweetly – the gentle ritual of it all – the deep examination, then the false starts as the vagina contracted, then finally the delicious sliding up to the balls.

Alabaster was smooth when polished and not too dense and did not in itself cause chafing, though stimulants could be applied if torment was needed. The dildo had a leather loop attached to its ball-sac so that when it was not inside the girl it could be hung at the head of her bed, for the muscle of the vagina benefited from periodic relaxation: then the return of distension would feel more telling.

Her pose was deliciously sexual. Her underarms looked so vulnerably naked. Her hair lay in swirling disarray about her lovely face. Her lips were open, her little tongue protruded, and the mouth of her bottom was a pale velvet funnel. That afternoon, with her dildo bedded firmly, she had come to climax in Ulline's fingers while her bottom was being filled with milk. Or rather, having filled her bottom to the brim, Ulline had sat her on her aproned knee, gently fingered her inexperienced labia and worked her dildo fully home and held her bloated belly, and the girl had finally moaned against Ulline's mouth – her small tongue had come out and pushed between Ulline's lips – and suddenly Ulline's fingers were coated with the warm female oil the girl was exuding around the dildo, and the girl's sex was jerking as if it were a living butterfly being impaled upon a needle.

The milk had been retained in readiness for more to be added so her second climax could be brought on while she was standing, with the dildo still inside her sex and her thighs squeezed tightly round it. This second climax was far more poignant and prolonged. She collapsed forwards against her mistress, whose fingers, drenched in girl-oil, continued at the same pace, steadily clawing that lovely erect clitoris into its plush surround, until her milk was spilled in uncontrollable surges over the balls of her dildo and all down the backs of her legs. Afterwards, she was washed and put to bed to dream about this newfound experience.

Ulline slipped her hand through the leather loop of the bedded dildo. The intimate contact woke the girl. Her eyes were languid; plainly the stimulant that Ulline had put on the head of the dildo had been working. Her mouth was open, her breathing soft. With the tip of her middle finger Ulline tickled the hot inner skin of the pale velvet funnel of that delightful anus. The girl's tongue peeped out and arched seductively against her upper lip. Ulline twisted the balls of the dildo gently, breaking the sexual seal. Female oil exuded and the warm shiny shaft was slowly expelled, the girl shivering as it came free. Ulline looked into the open sex, with its deliciously warm, stretched furrows, the tiny mouth of its urethra, its erect knob. Then she carefully mated the round, warm, oily tip of the dildo to the funnel of the anus and pushed. The girl looked questioningly for a second, then her mouth opened wide in compliance and her head went back, exposing the lovely curve of her neck. With the pressure, that furtive dildo began to slide upwards, inwards. Ulline, watching the fickle muscle continue to distend in hesitant pulses against the repeated urge to constrict, and watching the lovely neck arch tightly back, inserted the dildo to the thickest part and held it, gently twisting to and fro, and listened to the soft moans that so needed quenching. Then, after one more push, she released her grip and gently massaged the clitoris and watched the dildo being gradually drawn by the girl's contractions up into her bottom, all the way up, to the balls. Then Ulline moved on.

There was a special hobby-horse she sometimes made girls ride, its saddle made of alabaster fashioned from a mould of the female parts, with recesses for the lips and clitoris and with a generous, stubby bump for purchase. And on to this bump, after oiling, Ulline would lift the open girl and have her sit and gently rock her little body to nirvana.

Throughout these preparations, the Dresser's reward was the heightened sexuality she induced in her charges and the ensuing gratitude of their lordly masters.

There was one girl who had newly been pierced; in fact her clitoris was still quite swollen and excited. At regular intervals Ulline would gently draw a gold wire through it to keep its puncture open. When she came to this girl for the first drawing of the day, the girl was sitting trembling with knees already held dutifully spread, and Ulline could feel the warmth of her aroused body billowing up from between her legs. Under the gentle drawing and rotation of the wire, little pulses shook her sex and a little of her fluid exuded. So unctuous was it that it lay on the cloth beneath her bottom rather than soaked in, refracting the morning light in pale turquoise and swirling glistening reds, like a bead of precious opal. Ulline moved on.

No two girls were ever the same in their needs or their experience, but the masters frequently ignored this, assuming that every slave girl was promiscuous. Ulline therefore made certain at an early stage that every girl knew how to masturbate herself. Afterwards she would put her to masturbating others, first girls then captive males, not so much as a test but rather as a means of driving that first spark of sexuality into a self-sustaining fire.

But for that first private consultation she would sit the girl within arm's reach astride a tall stool, which was never positioned directly in front of Ulline but always a little to the side. If it was night-time the lamps would be dimmed. She would ask the girl to sit forward. 'Now open yourself,' she would say. She would then comment reassuringly about the development of the girl's inner lips and ask about the ways her current master used her and about her monthly flow, and whether her master used protection. Sometimes she was obliged to explain, for the girl might not properly understand the link between seminal fluid and conception. Then she would ask her to draw her hood of skin back and she would apply a tiny drop of lubricant from the tip of a glass rod on to her exposed clitoris. She would tell her to release her hood and the consultation would be over, and she would have her put to bed or sometimes, if it were daytime, take her with her on her rounds.

But the lubricant would be less than innocent, containing a weak inflammatory agent, a slow sexual irritant steadily working on the clitoris when the girl was trying to sleep or walk. Invariably the girl, if in bed, would be drawn to fingering herself to completion several times. This Ulline knew because she used to watch. Rarely, with certain girls, or if a client required it, Ulline would have her staked to the bed with her ankles fastened open. She would then examine her on the hour through the night and renew the irritant with the little glass rod. Sometimes such girls could be made to come through their breasts, by nipple stimulation with the fingers or the mouth or with the breast-pump; sometimes by the touch of unfamiliar medical instruments between their legs; occasionally simply by the application of the tip of the rod, or by the use of deep fingering to assess the girl's heat at the entrance to her womb.

This day she had a new girl, Leah, who had already attracted the attention of several clients on account of her absence of pubic hair. But Lord Shardlan had spoken up first and had stipulated his requirements. It was undeniable that she was pretty. She wore a broken virgin's chain attached through the labia minora. One of the requirements was that this chain be moved. At present, Leah's clitoris stood freshly primed with irritant and she kept wanting to put her legs together but Ulline made her stand open: desire must be nurtured. However, Ulline permitted Leah to hold the loaded clyster while she attended to the girl who was suspended naked from the ceiling with only the tips of her toes reaching the floor. Another girl, awaiting depilation, lay on a narrow fleece-covered table. Ulline began to put a solid gold ball about the size of an apple into the sex of the suspended girl, who was moaning even before her labia had fully closed round it. 'Anticipation,' Ulline declared. 'She needs to pee.' She knew these words would excite Leah; Lord Shardlan had intimated as much. Ulline therefore brought Leah near and held her naked belly and touched her lovely pierced labia, which were already thinning as her excitement mounted. Thinning of the labia normally accompanied advanced arousal, in this case aided by the irritant's drawing blood strongly to her clitoris and especially to its buried extension. Ulline gently squeezed the punctures wherein the chains were set. The grip of Leah's fingers was weak about the barrel of the clyster.

'It is no harm that you begin to lubricate this way,' she told Leah, wiping her leakage with a soft cloth. Leah stayed guiltily silent. Across the chamber the assistant was fastening the ankles of the girl awaiting depilation. Ulline touched Leah's labia gently; they were thin and soft and wet enough to be moulded into shape, though the chains were an encumbrance. Her breathing was shallow and uneven. Her clitoris had formed a blister-like nodule under her thin-skinned hood. Though Leah did not yet know it, this was to be the site of a new piercing.

The Dresser now left Leah and proceeded with the depilation of the girl on the fleece-covered table. The girl had fine, soft pubic hair. Ulline used a cream and wore a glove on the hand that administered it. She plastered it from the girl's navel, over her pubis, carefully to each side of the lips – not allowing any ingress – then smeared the inner thighs and underneath, into the furrow of her bottom. Then she made her lie completely still.

The first sign that something was happening was the trembling of her thighs. 'Tell me what it feels like,' Ulline said to her.

'It . . . it tingles,' the girl whispered fearfully.

'Cool – like scented water?'

The girl nodded uncertainly, swallowing. 'My bottom feels funny, prickling, pulling.'

'As if a rough-tongued creature is licking it?'

The girl nodded.

'And this?' Ulline pushed a gloved finger up her bottom and kissed her to smother her gasps.

The hairs were breaking away and floating in the cream. Ulline used a thin wooden blade to scrape the girl's belly clean, scraping gently round the lips of her sex, then down her thighs. The exposed skin glowed red and felt as if it was burning. Yet the girl was shivering. Spreading the girl's buttocks, Ulline next scraped into the groove. 'Her anus is a little inflamed,' she observed to the assistant, who swiftly began to wash the girl. Finally Ulline removed her glove and tenderly caressed the girl's smooth pink skin, opening her like a flower. The intimacies of that naked examination made the girl come.

All this occurred while Leah was waiting, her clitoris erect and doubtless trying to shed the coy foreskin of its hood. The Dresser came back to assist, pushing back the foreskin then guiding her slim arms, her nervous hands, directing the shiny, leaking, trembling spout of the clyster up the bottom of the suspended girl. 'Straight up – more vertically,' Ulline whispered, for it had stabbed from behind against the gold ball sheathed within the girl's sex, making her murmur. Ulline made Leah crouch. 'Push the plunger.' As the girl's bottom was being filled, it was in fact Leah who was shaking the most. The Dresser simply clasped Leah's hot, wet, punctured sex and kept easing her foreskin back. She had not time to put her thumb up Leah's bottom before the surplus cream was squirting out round the barrel of the buried clyster and Leah herself came in warm gushes. Ulline carried her to a chair, spread her legs quite fully and her sex very wide indeed, and asked the assistant for something to put up Leah's pee-hole. During the administering of this acutely focused form of sexual pleasure, Leah came again.

When the Dresser looked up, Lord Shardlan was standing quietly watching, his gaze fixed on Leah.

'I thought to pre-empt the others,' he said by way of apology for entering the inner sanctum unannounced.

Ulline stood up and bowed. 'Your wish is her command, my lord'.

He sighed, looking lovingly at Leah. 'Sadly only temporarily. She is betokened.' He went to kiss her and Ulline saw something beautiful and disarmingly inno-cent in the way she offered up her lips. It was plain that Lord Shardlan admired this creature greatly. 'Merek, her master, will doubtless be back for her, though there's no word yet of his return,' he said. 'Something must have delayed him.' She stared up in apprehen-sion. He gazed back at her protectively.

'Perhaps he's been and gone,' the Dresser offered. 'Perhaps he never intended to return. It happens a lot.'

'Ulline – no master in his senses would abandon Leah.' Lord Shardlan lifted his ward gently on to his lap.

'We'll find use for her.' Leah shrank against her protector. 'Don't hide your face, girl,' Ulline said sharply.

'Sit up, turn around, as your mistress requires,' Lord

Shardlan encouraged Leah. 'Don't disappoint me now with wilfulness – not after all the brave and dutiful things you did to please me on our little journey.'

At this mild chastisement, the tears sprang and Leah hurried to make amends. Ulline was impressed by her compliance. She stared at the naked place between Leah's open thighs and sighed.

'Feel free to touch,' Lord Shardlan offered.

'I'd rather whip.'

'Then feel free to whip – for Leah is a good girl, aren't you? Stand up for your mistress. Look, Ulline – these beautiful thighs, this skin, so soft, and this perfect female split.'

Leah was whipped standing – whipped at the front, where it counts best, all upon and around her sex. Throughout, she kept her hands dutifully behind her back, her fingers nevertheless writhing, her naked belly thrust forward and down, seeking to shelter her tenderness, yet with her knees bowed open; and Ulline lashed caustic lines repeatedly between them until the flesh erupted in weals.

'Beautiful, beautiful,' was all Lord Shardlan kept saying as he took Leah's small shivering body back on to his knee. Leah kept open because she surely could not bear to close, to have the raised, stinging, flayed skin pressed between her limbs. Ulline knew this because she too had had a harsh mistress in her youthful training. In part she was now reliving this gift of love through Leah.

'Sit forward,' she instructed. 'Sit on it.'

'Oh no, please,' Leah implored in whispers, tears streaming down her cheeks.

'Mistress Dresser – I've never really taken to this form of play before,' said Lord Shardlan, 'but I must now confess to an interest. I like the certainty and composure with which you deal your strokes. Her flesh is almost burning my thigh.' He started to play with the weals. 'She gains erection quickly – even under these conditions.'

'Because of them. That is the purpose of the whipping, my lord.'

'Not the sole purpose?'

'Leave her with me.'

Lord Shardlan bowed and left for a time. When he returned to that chamber, Leah was coming in her mistress's hands, suspended by her arms with both feet off the floor. Shardlan watched the mistress's slender fist being inserted, post-climax, into the tightness of this beautiful girl. The vision of that pregnant bulge between Leah's legs – her naked lower belly enveloping Ulline's fist – remained with him until his next return. At that time Leah lay on the bed, the ropes that had attached her to the ceiling now loose about her wrists. Ulline moved away to let him examine Leah, whose feet lay pressed together at the soles. 'She looks in prayer, almost,' Shardlan murmured.

Between her legs was sexual mayhem – bright stripes from the whipping, the anus peculiarly swollen, the outer labia wrenched back, the inner ones flaccid, soaking wet, the formerly small vagina now agape. Gently he removed the tiny clamp from her clitoris. Momentarily her knees lifted from the bed. He forced the hood of hot skin all the way back, using his fingernails. Leah gurgled as the blood pulsed into her tortured clitoris, reinvigorating it to a brighter splendour. Shardlan slowly bowed his head into the humid hollow between her legs and entubed the head and shaft of that shiny clitoris with his lips. Her orgasm came swiftly and her hands, still draped with their rope encumbrances, weakly yet somehow wantonly clutched his hair. He felt her knees come up again and her thighs squeezing gently about his ears.

He sat up and gazed at her. Then he lifted her by the shoulders, loosened the ropes from her wrists and kissed her before laying her down. 'What are we to do with you?' He traced the soft lines of her eyebrows with his fingers then turned to Ulline. 'Shall her cunt ever again fully close?'

'Not if I have a say, my lord.'

'Show me again your handiwork, mistress.'

The hand went so far inside Leah's sex that it seemed it must surely burst through into her bottom. And though she lay impaled on Ulline's fist, yet the woman was kissing her so tenderly and Leah's nipples were up so far and shivering, and the pleasure seemed to keep coming, as the fingers in her body kept plucking and pressing at the nose of her womb. 'Men do not know,' Ulline whispered, yet Shardlan had witnessed much, and he tried to gauge from Leah's reaction how this woman made her feel. Leah had grasped and tried to kiss the very arm that fed its hand inside her. Yet when the hand slid out, her flesh looked raw and burning, used and open.

'What will Merek say when he sees it?' Shardlan murmured.

At this point there was an interruption: Lord Shardlan's assistant – the guard, Lirann – had crept into the room and was watching Leah intently.

When his lordship turned, Lirann announced: 'The male prisoner is dealt with, my lord.'

'Thank you, Lirann: there was no requirement to report back – not at this juncture.' He was irked: Leah was disquieted by the news. He started to reassure her. But his guard persisted, and drew him aside to speak privately. Eventually he dismissed her and returned to Leah.

Ulline whispered: 'Your young guard seems quite demanding today, my lord. Do I sense –'

'I trust you sense nothing that does not concern you, mistress.'

Chastened, Ulline bowed.

'Shall we continue?'

Swiftly, Ulline renewed control of master and girl. She made Leah sit forward on the edge of the bed and spread open. Then she said in a conspiratorial whisper: 'Touch her pee-hole. It awaits you, my lord; caress it in the way it needs.'

With those few words he was wreathed in the thrall of obsession. Ulline stood back. In truth it was bewitching to watch a beautiful girl engaged in utter lewdness with a man so driven by depravity that in his breathing one could hear the pounding thump of his heartbeat, as he touched clinically inside her body. Engrossed, he whispered to her: 'It feels like an oyster – when you split its shell and slide your finger in and press the swollen slippery pulp and the little mouth inside squirts its salty fluid in futile defence. But your beautiful inner oyster is much warmer and more alive.' Leah moaned and her knees jerked upwards, as if the orgasm had come through the urethra, where his fingers were focused. Lord Shardlan came very close to her, gently kissing her erect nipples whilst fingertipping between her legs. Then he murmured: 'I have asked Jubal to fashion a little jewelled bodkin to fit inside this tiny place. I want you to wear it to the bacchanal. The Dresser will prepare you.'

# 14

# Jubal

The new piercing throbbed between Leah's legs, where a gold sleeper had temporarily been pushed through, lengthwise under the hood of her clitoris, to emerge a finger's-breadth further up her belly. The sleeper was to be replaced by an insert permitting retraction of the clitoral hood and carrying the two relocated segments of her labial chain. The Dresser had performed the piercing; Lord Shardlan then spent time with Leah before taking her to the jeweller's quarters to be fitted.

Leah stood in front of her master at the entrance to a large, stone-flagged, crypt-like room that tapered towards a glowing hearth at the far end. Extending along one wall was a long wooden bench covered in metalworking tools and unfinished items of jewellery. Spilt gold dust glittered on the floor. A small bed stood against the opposite wall. In the centre of the room was a love-seat upon which a girl was tethered with her ankles apart and fastened in stirrups. On one side of her stood a man as wide as two men; on the other, Ulline.

Shardlan propelled Leah towards the group. Ulline bowed to his lordship and simply said: 'Sara, of the black hair and beautiful pubic bush that our good friend Jubal has just tonsured clean. Now she is being fitted with her pearls.' Ulline's fingers smoothed the freshly naked pinkness with its dusky, shadowy surround.

Leah stole a furtive glance at the wide man holding the callipers and the card of graded pearls. He was balanced on feet too small and dainty for a body so ungainly. He was strangely dressed in a tiny black waistcoat that somehow clung to him yet barely covered a third of his naked chest. His head was completely bald and his skin was pinker than Sara's shaven sex but there were curly black hairs all over his torso. His belly overhung tightly filled leather breeches that extended only to his knees. A thick gold chain round his middle was anchored to a belly stud.

Ulline gently split Sara's labia open and Jubal advanced with the callipers. Shardlan whispered to Leah: 'Her pearls will be fitted inside.' Leah shuddered. Shardlan touched the gold stud in her piercing. Then he said aloud: 'Jubal – I have another patient for you,' whereupon Jubal's head twisted round, tilted and emitted a sneering, knowing smile. Leah turned and pressed herself against her master for protection.

'I shall attend my lord's every requirement directly,' Jubal said obsequiously. But Leah dreaded being handed to a person such as this, who squinted at her with tiny eyes and made her blood run cold. His stubby fingers brandished a shiny metal instrument. Whether it measured Sara or penetrated her, Leah could not tell, but she could hear the gasps and murmurs as Ulline steadied the girl and whispered: 'Good girl. Let him do it,' then, after a long while: 'All done now.' She helped her up and led her away trembling. Meanwhile Jubal waddled over to a small table, slipped the shiny instrument alongside others in a large, soft leather wallet that lay open there, then began scribing something on a slate.

Shardlan gently separated himself from Leah's clinging arms and began to wander inquisitively about the room, leaving Leah alone in the middle, keeping very still, trying to look invisible.

Jubal ignored her and continued scribing until her master drifted over to him; they began conversing in low tones. Then they went over to the workbench and Jubal, opening a little box, said: 'It's ready but might need adjustment. It is better tested with the subject sitting.'

'And what of the jewelled retractor for the hood?'

'The work of but a few minutes extra, if the piercing is healed.'

'Ah . . .'

'No matter, my lord – we shall manage. Let us examine her.'

A high stool was brought and Shardlan sat Leah astride it with her thighs held wide, her sex exposed to Jubal's gaze. She shuddered when those thick pasty fingers touched her and lingered round the piercing, feeling it, stirring queasy sensations in her belly. Before she knew what had happened he had detached the segments of her virgin's chain from the punctures in her labia and, smirking, held them to the light, like trophies. In one quick sweep those callous hands had robbed her of that precious gift; it was the final wrenching parting with the soul of that virgin girl she had once been. Tears of emotion trickled down her cheeks. Shardlan asked: 'What is it?' But Leah could only shake her head, and the tears kept coming, even as he tried to kiss them away. 'You shall not lose these jewels,' he whispered. 'They are simply to be moved to a better place, where their usefulness will increase. You are losing nothing.' But Leah knew she had lost all: Merek had deserted her; Ean had been put in chains to the boatwomen and she herself had been left at the mercy of a new master. He might seem caring but he was also demanding and there was no way of knowing where his demands might take her.

Jubal, having deferred for a few moments to the master, now advanced again and slid a podgy, clammy finger between the lips of her sex and pressed it to her pee-hole. Nausea swelled in Leah's belly; her toes curled; her nipples tightened. She looked away, for fear this tightness might be mistaken for arousal.

'These punctures in her labia, my lord – I might be able to use them to pivot a little gold bit that might enhance the efficacy of the jewelled lodgement.'

'Will the work take time?'

'An hour at most – the parts are stock. Perhaps a little trimming.' Leah wanted to close her thighs to protect her flesh; she wanted to be rid of that dreadful probing finger. 'Stay thus, my sweet! Exactly as put. We must assess you,' Jubal hissed. His lips were wet and pink and she was frightened they would attempt to kiss her. She looked pleadingly at Shardlan as Jubal now lifted her bottom forward on the stool. He drew on to his hand a single silk glove, pulling it tightly over his fingers and flexing them. 'Lie back.'

He had to support her under the shoulders to prevent the stool from tipping. Leah shivered, staring at the vaulted ceiling. At the edge of her vision she could see between her trembling knees his chubby bald head as he bent to examine inside her sex with his gloved hand. She dreaded having pearls attached in there, as had been done to Sara. She felt one smooth fat finger going in a short way, pressing, then two. When he tried to put a third finger into her, her belly tightened in revulsion. He straightened up. 'Good,' he said, nodding. 'Now what of here?' He pointed underneath. 'Tuck your knees up nicely. Support yourself.'

Her head hung down; her hands gripped the legs of the stool. The first feeling in her bottom was a soft insinuation, tongue-like, teasing her anus gradually open, inducing the cloying sinking feeling inside. Her breathing quickened. She heard him sigh contentedly.

Then he gently clasped her closed sex in his bare hand while the gloved finger smoothly entered her anus to the hilt. Through the dread intimacy of that bare-handed clasp came the sweetly lewd urge to pee: she pictured that hand running with liquid while its warm wet fingers provoked slippery perversion from the flesh within her split. Leah shivered at the crude sexuality of such feelings; her bottom tightened round the gloved finger still thrusting inside her.

'Her anus is deliciously sensitive,' Jubal called to Shardlan. All the while, the master had never intervened. Emboldened, Jubal attempted to kiss Leah but she turned her face away. His gloved finger was still inside her bottom and his bare hand was squeezing her sex, softly squeezing until it split and his naked fingertip touched her pee-hole; her head sank back limply and she could not suppress her moan.

'My Lord Shardlan,' said Jubal, 'please bring the instrument. She is ready to test it.'

He raised Leah's head. 'Behold – your jewelled bodkin.' He held up a thick gold pin, in shape resembling the ironstone quills her master had inserted into her, but this one was exquisitely crafted. It bore a spherical knurled gold head at one end and a dark-blue pearl-drop jewel at the other. 'The length, girth and shouldering I have taken from the matched specimen my lord provided from the gauging set. But the size of the pearl is crucial. Each girl is different. I may need to change it – hence the test.'

'Proceed,' said Shardlan.

They carried her to the bed. 'Shall my lord hold her cunny open?' Jubal asked.

Shardlan gently obliged. Jubal held the little bodkin by its knurled gold head and carefully positioned its jewel drop half-way between her clitoris and her pee-hole. Then he pressed and very slowly rotated the smooth hard bead of the bodkin against her. Leah felt a desperate urge to sit up, so invasive was the feeling. She felt Shardlan's lips closing about her nipple, then the bead trailing searchingly down, finding the entrance to her pee-hole, drumming against its tiny mouth. Then it started to rotate, stirring deep, insidious sexual feelings, making her moan, making her master try to tongue the gold sleeper fastened through the skin above her knob. They finally sat her up, shivering, on the edge of the bed.

'She is highly receptive here,' said Jubal, studying the shiny bodkin.

'I know it,' said Shardlan.

They made her spread her legs very wide to grant full access to her pee-hole. The pink inner lips were open with arousal. She felt the little jewel tickle the tiny mouth then press for intrusion. For a second it felt too large and she murmured but Shardlan kissed her, sucked her tongue and whispered to Jubal: 'Persist.' Then he took up the sucking kiss again, gently quelling her gasp as the blue ball passed the tight, tiny rim and slid up inside, causing a cold numb feeling. Jubal withdrew the bead then pressed it home again, triggering a little pulse of pleasure as it spread the rim. Then she felt the ice-cold tightness moving deeper inside her. Suddenly the feeling narrowed down to a pleasure-ache. Leah gasped and closed her eyes but her tongue sought succour in her master's mouth. 'There . . .,' murmured Jubal.

When she found the courage to look, the gold head and a little of the stem of the bodkin projected from her pee-hole; the blue bead was buried somewhere inside her. No fingers held the instrument, which protruded from between her gaping labia, its stem a quivering sexual feeler delving into her body, its glistening gold head trembling with every pulsebeat of arousal moving through her thighs. Shardlan, impassioned by the tremblings, took hold of the head and slowly rotated it, causing the buried blue bead to do its inner mischief, making her moan. He kept turning the instrument very patiently in the same direction and the sexual feeling inside Leah's pee-hole was peculiar and intense.

Jubal carefully opened a small bottle of dense, syrupy liquid. Then he pulled the beaded instrument gently out of her body. Her sex contracted as the blue bead emerged. Jubal dipped the bead into the dense liquid. 'Shall I administer the agaric now?'

'One moment.' Shardlan, sitting on the bed, drew Leah belly-up across his lap. He swept his arm under her knees to raise them. He put his lips to her open mouth and took suck upon her tongue. She could feel his erection stiffening against her back. Jubal's fingers opened her and pushed the blue bead, slippery now with agaric syrup, again through the sensitive mouth of her pee-hole and into her body, smoothly and much deeper than before, until she felt the knurled gold head press against her and the bead touch a place of peculiar pleasure that was locked away very deep. 'Unhh!' she groaned, her tongue still captive in her master's kiss.

'Shhh . . .' Her master, drawing back, gently put his finger over her lips to warn her into still submission. His gaze was fixed between her trembling thighs and his penis was as hard as bone. 'Let him do it to you.'

Leah grunted as the slippery bead of the instrument began moving, twirling against this place deep inside her, stirring a feeling half tantalising, half pleasurable. Then suddenly the sensation changed as the syrup began to work. It felt as if warm water were being squirted slowly into her, filling her, and as if everything between her legs was melting.

With a gentle tug the instrument was slowly with-drawn. But the warm swollen feeling was deepening and spreading. She wanted to be made to come. When her master kissed her, she thrust her tongue far into his mouth. She wriggled to try to get his rigid penis up between her thighs. He resisted her newfound keenness and drew her freshly pierced hood fully and painfully back from her swelling erection. 'See – her clitoris, getting bigger, a nipple almost,' he said. Then he crouched forward, lifted her hips and planted a sucking kiss directly upon it, and Leah almost came. 'Gently,' he teased, breaking the thread of spittle connected to her knob. 'The time is not ripe.' Then he turned to Jubal. 'I think the bit will be needed.'

When it was fashioned and fitted, it formed a gold rod threaded through the lateral punctures in her labia, its ends attached by pearl studs to a bridle. Into the centre of the rod was set a clasp designed to collar the neck of the bodkin just under the knurled head. Thus the bodkin could still be rotated freely but, being captive on the rod, was far less prone to expulsion during prolonged insertion. Then the retractor with its jewelled chain segments was fitted through the new piercing under her hood and tested to full retraction, so her knob remained exposed against the dangling chains. Lord Shardlan stood up with Leah quaking in his arms, her knees tucked up and apart, her sex protruding, her standing knob very wet, her captive bodkin fully re-inserted and her little bottle of agaric clutched in her hand.

# 15

# The Water Gardens

The night was almost gone by the time Lord Shardlan took his new acquisition back to his apartment in the turret overlooking the main portico of the waterway. Plainly she was tired but he found himself reluctant to put her down. He carried her to the centre window and, looking out over the torch-lit enclave of the Tithe Retreat, he pointed out the thread of lights marking the staircase of locks leading down to the distant port and the moonlit sea beyond. He sat her on the balcony, touching her until the arousal broke through her tiredness, then he declared that she must rest before the bacchanal.

A servant brought a tray of victuals and Shardlan made Leah take sustenance before the servant took her to be bathed. Shardlan personally put her to bed, first removing the little instrument of penetration from between her legs, together with its pivot, then the retractor and chains from her prepuce, leaving her sex at last beautifully nude. He could not resist touching it again. He therefore carefully set aside her jewellery, along with the little bottle of agaric, then returned to the delicious business of touching. Her inner lips felt very warm and malleable – enough to retain the slight gape into which he shaped them. All around the entrance to her urethra was swollen and moistly tender. He cooled his fingertips in the water jug before touching her there. Through her murmurs he took firm hold upon the hot little engorgement of flesh surrounding the entrance, as if reaching for the root. He gripped until he could feel the tube inside it, then watched her belly tighten and heard her moan and saw her clitoris pulse and felt the little lump of flesh around the tube trying vainly to withdraw, tugging on his fingers, like an eel writhing on the line. Her climax was so beautifully long-drawn and guttural that he held her little writhing tubule until it was quelled completely and gave not a shiver more. Then he disrobed and came to her naked and kissed her tortured little sex very gently and lovingly, in the atonement that should always follow merciless depravity. Finally she fell into a torpid sleep, which lasted long – through the dawn, past noon and into the late afternoon, threatening to encroach upon her preparation for the bacchanal – but Shardlan was determined not to wake her. Eventually the Dresser arrived with Sara. No sooner was Sara on the bed than Leah sat up with a dream-like sluggishness.

Shardlan sat quietly at the foot of the bed. He simply smiled at Leah. 'You remember Sara – now beset with pearls to make her intimacy so very pretty?' The girl lay still, breathing quickly. 'Open, Sara – let us look.' The girl spread her knees but beyond the shaven sex and a slight puffiness of the labia there was nothing visibly unusual, until Shardlan leant forward and parted the naked lips. Leah gasped as Sara's exquisite treasure was displayed – a nest of glistening pearls that expanded to a circle when she was opened. They were attached to the inner flesh. Shardlan slid his finger through the glistening circle. 'I understand there are others, a little deeper. Let me try to . . . Ah . . .' Sara moaned. There were indeed other delicious little baubles lodged up inside her to stimulate her master's glans.

The Dresser's clear voice sounded from across the room, making Leah twist round in shock. 'Shall I take her for her preparation now, my lord?' Leah looked back at Sara until Shardlan whispered. 'The mistress means you, Leah. Hurry now.' And he nodded to the Dresser.

So now Leah was away with Ulline and Sara lay trembling. She had beautiful black hair and full breasts tipped with black. The shaven skin between her legs looked like alabaster, with a dusky whisper of bluish-black, but her labia remained bright-red witnesses of that inner bejewelling in the furtherance of deviant pleasure. But what an exquisite deviance . . . And why await the bacchanal? Sara's bottom lifted to meet him as his penis slid inside her to the hilt. Her ring of pearls closed like a beaded noose around its base, the deeper pearls studding their pleasure-bolts all the way up the underside to the sensitive frenum, at once triggering climax but impeding flow. The pleasure of so constrained an ejaculation within such a beautiful vagina was deliciously unbearable and exquisitely prolonged.

'You shall leave me naught for Leah,' Shardlan whispered and Sara arched her tongue for him to lick. He felt fortunate indeed to be able to call upon such sensual female creatures. He made her crouch on the marble floor to expel and found it captivating to watch so sexual and primordial an act; he could not resist touching during expulsion. The touching made her tighten but he persevered until she overcame that urge and could push until her little ring of pearls protruded visibly and touchably, shedding the glutinous residue upon his fingers. He smeared that slipperiness all around her clitoris until he made her come and so strong was this climax – taken crouching, with her legs splayed open and her ring of dripping pearls so pushed out and her clitoris so keenly upstanding, like a tongue-tip licking his taunting fingertips – that he was certain she had never been made to come that way before.

His beautiful charge was still quivering on the tips of his fingers. He put her back on the bed, face down and uncovered, with one knee bent, and instructed her to maintain that pressure of pushing. Then he examined her from behind. Her female pinkness was perfectly pushed open and her lovely clasp of pearls was protruding from inside. Again he felt compelled to touch, until the touching made her anus tighten and the bridge of flesh below it, the perineum, turned as hard as polished alabaster as the muscle went into spasm. He slid his hand underneath to stroke the tip of her clitoris one final sticky time, then told her to remain so until he returned. Then he went to ascertain Leah's progress with the Dresser.

By evening the preparations in the water gardens were well in hand. Shardlan stepped on to the back terrace to watch them. The heady perfume of night flowers wafted up to greet him. Torchlight decked the tiers and sparkled in the fountains and cascades. Small personalised tents had been erected amongst the greenery and by the pools. Little fires flickered amongst the alabaster statuary. Servants bustled about their masters. The first of the female slaves were appearing in little groups: Shardlan recognised some of them, even knew them by name. As Marshal of the Fledglings he had supervised their recovery after they had taken flight. He eschewed punishing them for their attempted escape, instead reserving whipping as a sexual tool, to forge a bond between slave and master. The male guards were largely indifferent to such subtleties, which was why Shardlan had chosen a girl as his captain on his missions of recovery. He looked for Lirann now amongst the growing throng; she was due to bring the male slave that had been collected with

Leah. It was important that Leah meet this slave in some circumstance of sexual restraint, in order to spur her arousal to new bounds. For she was unique – sexuality personified. How her original master had come to deposit her here, Shardlan could not begin to guess. But in a few days at most, she would be taken back; the Rule of Tithes was inviolate. He wasted no more time in his musings; there was pleasure afoot and he meant to sample it recklessly.

He went back inside to collect his escorts. The Dresser had just finished breast-pumping Sara. Her nipple surrounds had distended from black to shiny chestnut brown. 'Have you done between her legs, Dresser? Then do that too, before you go down to attend to the males.'

Noting the look of concern in Leah's face at the mention of males, Shardlan took her in his arms to allay her fears while Sara was being pumped between the legs. He cupped her sex in his palm and gently masturbated her while Sara's vulva steadily expanded into the glass dome of the pump. When it was done, the Dresser left, with Leah's concerned gaze following her. 'You shall see your beau again, I promise.' Shardlan pressed gently reassuring kisses upon her anxious lips. 'But first, your bodkin.' There was surely no intimacy more pertinent to the master-slave indenture than this. What pleasure could bring deeper satisfaction than to kiss his naked girl and in the kissing to give a tiny tug upon her bridle or a minute twist upon that little bodkin and know by the depth of her murmur that it had moved inside her, drawing delicious belly-quivers?

Shardlan dipped the beaded tip of the bodkin into the agaric syrup. 'Open,' he whispered. Her thighs and naked sex obeyed. He held the little insert poised at the mouth of her pee-hole. 'Now push your tongue out, as in wanting.' As Leah's small tongue peeped, so Shardlan very gently pushed the bead-tipped shaft up inside her beautiful body until he heard her first shocked murmur and felt the soft resistance of the tiny inner muscle. Then he gently twirled the spindle of the bodkin until that inner muscle yielded and she gasped as the beaded head went right inside and a tiny dribble of her precious liquid leaked. But her lovely little tongue still peeped seductively and Shardlan kissed it and very slowly twirled the knurled head of the bodkin and she shuddered as if she might come.

'Now I control this lovely part,' he said. 'Nothing comes without my permission. Do you understand?'

Leah, trembling, nodded.

'Slip your tongue away, though I find it quite beautiful in its lewdness. When anyone touches your bridle, whenever you feel the bodkin move inside you, in whatever company you find yourself, then your tongue must protrude in delicious insolence. Is that clear?'

Her body seemed beset by shivers, though the air was warm. Carefully, Shardlan fitted the gold bit to the bodkin and secured it through her labial punctures. He was pleased to note that, throughout the fitting, her tongue would now and then poke. Then he fitted the stiff little bridle to her bit and made all secure with its pearl-headed screws. Finally, through the piercing in her hood, he fitted the gold retractor and its dangling jewelled chains. 'There . . . let this treasure never hide its lovely head again.' He gently tightened the retractor and her clitoris burst forth, glistening with arousal: the agaric was already working its inner charm. Every slight movement of her body would stir a little pull or push or twist upon the tiny tight muscle of the urethra that held the bead of the bodkin secure; and every tremble of her chains would spur another pulse into her swollen nubbin.

Both girls were now ready – Leah bridled for perverse pleasures and Sara with her nipples and vulva pumped up to grotesque yet profoundly sexual beauty. He took a girl on each arm and led them naked on to the terrace, then down the alabaster stairway towards the sounds of the lutes and into the jasmine-scented warmth of the evening air. 'Breathe deep, my little cherubs,' he whispered and was pleased to note how docilely his charges obeyed. He chose a circuitous route through the voluptuous greenery, pausing at an arbour or an arch to kiss and touch his girls or just to look. He put fragrant blossoms in their hair. At the springs and fountains he made Leah drink and Sara dip her swollen nipples into the cooling pool; then he ordered Leah to suck them. While she sucked he gently twirled her bodkin from behind and was pleased to see her small tongue pushing out lewdly to the side of that turgid nipple. His purpose was to bring his charges to a suitable state of arousal and then to push them beyond it. He therefore led them on towards the sounds – the sighs and sexual murmurs coming from the surrounding greenery.

When they emerged into the colonnaded clearing, Leah was already in Shardlan's arms: he had taken the precaution of lifting her in anticipation of the shock of reunion. The three naked male slaves were standing in a line facing away from her, their ankles wide apart and their arms roped behind them over a long wooden bar at shoulder height. Leah drew breath sharply but the surprise was Shardlan's, for the slave called Ean was not there; neither was Lirann.

Lirann was watching from the bushes. Ean was with her; she had released him from his shackles and garbed him as a servant. In the dark he would never be noticed as being out of place. She put her finger to his lips to silence his gasp when he first saw Leah in the master's arms. So long as that girl was indentured to this place Ean needed no shackle. He paid no attention to the other girl; he remained focused on Leah. Lirann meant to seal that bond. Before bringing him here she had taken care to arouse him without fulfilment. That arousal would now be redoubled by having him watch the proceedings. 'Her master intends no harm, but he will surely train her to his ways,' Lirann whispered, adding, 'whatever they might be.' And sure enough, the spark of jealousy glowed in Ean's eyes, still fixed on the colonnaded clearing.

The Dresser, Ulline, walked slowly behind the male slaves, directing them to obedience with the handle of her whip. Her white bib was undone and her breasts were exposed. She was plainly drawing pleasure from flaunting herself. The master lifted Leah's chin and deliberately kissed her. Ean winced. Lirann slipped her hand under the breast of his tunic and caressed his nipple; his heart was thumping – all was well. 'What has she in mind, the Dresser?' Lirann whispered.

Ulline was holding a device of shiny metal that looked like the long curved bill of a bird. She cocked the bill slightly open and loaded into the end a white cylindrical charge. With the charge held firmly in the tip of the beak she walked to the first slave and crouched behind him. 'You know where that is going?' Lirann whispered. Lirann knew; she had seen it often; she knew that men could experience pleasure there as much as girls. At first Ean looked away, until the slave began to moan. Lirann, reaching down, could feel Ean's penis becoming restive. She glanced across and saw the shiny bill stretching the slave's anus, with Ulline still pushing, forcing him to take yet more. It pressed his penis to full and trembling erection before being withdrawn. And Ean's erection trembled too.

'The little gadfly is deep inside him,' Lirann whispered. Soon the slave began to breathe just as men do

231

when seeking satisfaction with girls. Quickly Ulline reloaded the device and slid its shiny length inside the second slave, whose anus tightened against the insistence of the insertion, making Ean shiver. Quicker still, Ulline did the third. Then she stood up, leant against the wooden bar and watched their erections harden. The master had fastened the girl Sara to one of the columns, as if in offering before the men. Her sex was extravagantly swollen. 'Look, he has pumped her up,' Lirann whispered. 'But what has he done to Leah? I cannot see.' Ean's tortured gaze tracked across, intently following the master back to Leah.

'Before long the males shall need to shed their burden,' Lirann whispered. She slipped her other hand down the back of Ean's trousers, seeking the place of male penetration. He was trembling. The master had set Leah down by the men. 'My lord keeps Leah watching, perchance to handle them while they are in heat? "Go on, little one," he urges her, "Do as the good Dresser bids."' Shyly, Leah crept closer. Lirann gently fingered the root of Ean's penis and thumbed the place where the males had been penetrated.

Leah had crouched behind the first slave. Her hand reached up, her fingers gently flexing; she kept looking to Ulline for directions. Lirann's fingers closed in a ring about the root of Ean's penis; it made his anus pucker against the stroking of her thumb. She had dropped his trousers and his erection was curving like a polished bone. His balls had tightened. Leah, clasping her hand round the wooden bar, swung tentatively under it, to crouch now in front of the slave and to look up between his legs. Her other hand returned to finger his anus. His penis throbbed and pulsed above her face – blind-pulsing, Lirann called this, where the male is close to spillage but no liquid issues and the penis gulps as if gaining strength.

Lirann could feel Ean's ball sac moving, wrinkling. There were two plums inside the skin which lifted and sank as Ean wrestled with his feelings. Lirann could feel the warmth exuding from his straining flesh, and smell the strong scent of his sweat. Her thumb kept working in his open groove, stroking, teasing and poking his anus.

Suddenly Ean groaned. The master was playing with Sara's swelling and Leah was kissing the slave, pressing her open lips against the bare, warm, vulnerable place where his balls adjoined the base of the penis. Lirann held Ean very close now, ringing his penis tightly, stroking his anus very softly, murmuring in his ear: 'Is she not warm and loving?' The slave began to ejaculate over Leah's face but her lips kept kissing the root of the penis. Sounding across the clearing came Sara's plaintive cry of deliverance. Ean groaned and shuddered as if he would die, and the pleasure Lirann then experienced was acute: her collaring finger could feel his fluid – while it was still inside him – coursing upwards within the stem. Then she felt it coming out, splashing hot against her bare arm, running over her hand.

Leah kept sucking under the slave's penis; there were splashes now on her naked shoulder and it was running down her back. Then she sat back, resting on her elbows, glancing up at the master, who was now back with her. 'See – her master approves,' Lirann murmured mockingly. Ean's penis had not softened. A trail of densest white was strung down its length like candle-wax. Lirann crouched and licked it clean and swallowed, then licked her arm and the back of her hand. When she stood up again, she took up that same grip about the root of his turgid penis, keeping it strong.

Ulline was putting another charge into the slave who had climaxed. The master took Leah's chin in his hand

and kissed her lips. Her cheeks were flecked with slavish semen. His rigid penis brushed her naked breasts. As Leah's lips closed lovingly about the head of the master's penis, Lirann suddenly experienced a dread cramp in the pit of her belly, then a wave of rising revulsion. His eyes had closed in ecstasy as he caressed that little trollop's promiscuous face.

'What is it?' Ean suddenly asked.

'Nothing.' Yet this stranger was more aware of her feelings than her own master for whom she had sacrificed all. She kissed Ean. 'Put your cock inside me – now, this instant.' Lirann climbed on to it. 'Just hold me and kiss.' It felt bone-hard inside her where she was slowly melting to anguished jelly. As he glanced over her shoulder to watch, he was becoming more and more aroused and trying to make soft thrusts. 'Shh . . . Stop. Stay still inside me. Just hold me. Shh . . .' She squeezed him with her muscle and held him tightly, in the way men liked, so tightly that she could feel the shape of his glans inside her. Suddenly he groaned and the bulb of his penis seemed to swell and struggle. 'Still,' Lirann whispered, kissing his neck, squeezing steadily with her sex until she was sure his fluid was contained. Then she slid off him and gently sucked the head of the penis – lovingly, truly lovingly. Then she clasped her fingers once again round its root.

She saw that the other two slaves had been made to ejaculate. The trollop was now standing up, with streaks and runnels of fluid all down her front from her shoulders to her knees. The master was talking to her, encouraging her, touching her between the legs until her tongue poked out. Lirann wanted to kick him. Trembling, she glared at Ean. 'He has put an instrument inside her, where she pees from. She cannot pee properly with it in – just as you cannot pee with your erection. And I mean to keep your erection hard.'

'What is it? What irks you?' Ean whispered.

'You do.'

So he took her in his arms and laid her gently on the grass and tried to go inside her again and she said: 'No.'

He was staring at her belly. Then he whispered: 'There's a beautiful dark line right down the middle; it's your delicious wantonness coming out. Let me kiss it.'

'No. Take me to bed. Take me away from here now.'

And he said: 'But what of Leah?'

# 16

# Privileged Usage

Leah shivered, even in the warm air. Her master had temporarily returned to play with Sara, still tethered naked to the column. He was applying the breast-pump between her legs.

The men's spilt pleasure-fluid tickled Leah's body, causing tightness where it had begun to dry. Her nipples stood hard and the instrument between her legs taunted her with arousal where the agaric-coated bead held the inner muscle of her pee-hole open. The sensation was like no other, melding the need to pee with the need to come. She heard Sara's gasping then the master handed her over to Ulline for sexual smacking while he returned to Leah.

He made her spread. Then he gently tightened the retractor, drawing the hood of her clitoris far back, exposing the sensitive glans to the taunting of its dangling jewelled chains. 'We might need to fashion a little pump just for this,' he said, touching her erection. Then, gathering semen from the streaks upon her breasts and face, he smeared its glueyness round the glans, then gently impressed the gathered chains into its swelling. Through her shivers, he kept saying she was beautiful. 'Let me look at you.' He opened her wet sex with his semen-slicked fingers and nuzzled them gently round the entubed bodkin. 'Beautiful.' He rubbed her anus steadily with his thumb.

The slave who had ejaculated first had been recharged with a new slug of agaric inside him. His swollen penis was already leaking clear sap. 'Make him come again,' murmured Shardlan, his eyes glittering at the prospect of renewed spillage upon her face and breasts.

He stretched Leah out on her back, her head towards the slave and between his ankles. When she looked up she could see his swollen sac and the line of clear sap flowing down the underside of his stem. She knew that if the stimulation could be controlled then his fluid would remain as clear as pouring-honey, but with a taste more astringent and strong. So she started slowly. Her fingertips found the smooth waxy skin in the creases of his thighs and gently pressed there. Then all eight fingertips cupped his sac. It felt alive; the skin rippled; the balls inside felt like heavy weights. Lifting his sac, she pressed just the tips of her little fingers into the base of his swollen penis. It wavered like a laden boat pitching in the swell. She heard his catch of breath; his clear sap started to drip upon her chin. Her thumbs pressed up behind his sac and she could feel the buried extension of his penis, like a fat hard tube extending into the groove of his buttocks then up inside him. The root of his penis was in there, with the slug of agaric steadily stimulating it.

Gently she slid the two middle fingers of her right hand back along the smooth buried tube, pressing until she felt the skin texture change from smoothly waxy to velvety hot. He moaned when she touched and tapped there. A single heavy drop of his hot, clear sap spilled on to her neck and ran down warmly under her ear lobe. She caught the next one, hot and musky, in her mouth. She heard her master's whispered approval. She kept pushing gently. Little hot tickling drips slid down her up-arched tongue, imparting a faint taste of the sea. Her master touched between her legs, imparting delicious feelings. Her two middle fingers slid inside the slave, where he was red hot. There was no trace of the slug of agaric, which must have melted. She curled her fingers inside, pressing up behind the penile root, and suddenly his back hollowed deeply and he froze: she had found the gland, that swollen lump filled with sap, and her fingertips were gently compressing it, trying to drive that luscious sea-scent up the spout of his penis to drip upon her tongue. Suddenly he gave an anguished cry; his anus tightened sexually round her fingers once, then went into spasm. The first forceful spurt of true semen fell hot upon her belly. She felt Shardlan spreading back the lips of her sex, and the bodkin tugging inside her, then the thick gobbets of fluid slapping down upon her belly and drenching her open sex in heavy scalding pulses.

Ulline hurriedly knelt beside Leah's head and forced her fingers into the slave, alongside Leah's, to ensure a full expulsion. 'You know what his cock is shedding?'

'Semen,' Leah lisped, writhing under Shardlan's slippery fingers as the last warm globules sank silently on to her quaking breast. Ulline reached down to squeeze the semen-coated nipple. Leah reached up to kiss Ulline, her lips and tongue showing Ulline just how wanton was her craving. Then she shuddered as she felt her master twirling the semen-soaked bodkin within the sensitive burrow of her pee-hole, while Ulline gently nipped and nuzzled her tongue as if milking it with her teeth.

Shardlan drew Leah's shaking body upright. 'Stand open and still,' he told her, his eyes burning with excitement at her nearness to coming. She so wanted to be kissed and held, but the only point of contact was that cruel slippery bodkin – twirled, then gently withdrawn and pushed back into her body, repeatedly opening and closing the tiny muscle, stimulating it until her tongue thrust out and her climax came in shudders and groans, wetting his taunting fingers with unstoppable squirts of pee.

And with her dripping body now helplessly slumped against her master, an anguished cry beside her signalled the wringing of ejaculate from the next slave in line. Ulline was capturing it in a small gilded goblet.

'Quickly,' said Shardlan. 'Put it to her lips. Let me see her drink.'

It was warm, glutinous and powerfully aromatic. It flowed as a single large coalesced globule. Leah sucked it up, holding it proudly in her mouth before swallowing as she watched her master. Her tongue was coated; her lips were sticky. Her master's response was to press the bead on its fine gold shaft gently deeper into her. When she moaned again he murmured: 'Hush,' kissed her quaking breasts and thrust the love-bead to the limit. She felt his fingers seeking her anus, opening it, making it an acute accomplice to her second pleasuring. Leah finally slumped against him, his fingers up inside her bottom, his thumb inside her sex, her tongue poking out and her contractions tugging upon that little instrument of luscious sexual torture threaded up inside her.

Ulline said: 'You can wash her down in the fountain.'

Shardlan answered: 'But who would want to sluice the perfume from so perfect a flower in open bloom?' With that, he carried Leah off through the gardens, leaving Sara to take Leah's place with the slaves and Ulline.

The pathways twined amongst braided rills, small cascades and broad pools with ornate fountains. Little groups of masters and female slaves were everywhere. In the grottos and secluded clearings, girls were being tied to trees and held in common; sexual whippings were being administered; girls were being mated with

statues. Shardlan directed Leah to one such place of
statues. There were eight or ten masters, three girls and
several servants. The place was torch-lit; there were
braziers and some tables and chairs. Shardlan set Leah
down and took a chair for himself. The servants
brought him a tray of delicacies and drink and asked
if anything more was wanted. He said: 'Minted water
– a large flagon, with a touch of bitters – very weak.'
Then he turned to Leah. 'The water is for you to drink
while I savour my wine and play with you. Come here.'

He began directly, obsessively, exploring between
her legs, between the outer lips, between the inner
ones, finding the place where the gold shaft of the
bodkin entered, gently gripping the distended surround, gently squeezing the flesh tight, gently trapping
the tube of her pee-hole against the rigid gold spindle.
Her tongue slid out; he sucked the tip; her breath was
shed in little shudders through her nose. She could feel
the bead of the instrument, like the head of a little
erection, simulating the penetration of her sex but
coming inside her pee-hole. The sucking tongue-kiss
continued until the servant returned. Then her master
made her start drinking the mint-water. He let her
swallow at her own pace, provided that she continued
drinking. All the while he held her bodkin and gently
stimulated its fleshy surround. He recharged her cup
using his free hand, for he would not relinquish that
special contact.

'Shall my lord let me . . . when it comes needed?'
Leah whispered.

'Let you what?'

'Pee,' she murmured, shivering softly.

'Sweet girl, all your wishes shall be granted –
in time,' he answered, caressing the drying rivulets of
semen, tracing their paths down her breasts and belly.
Already she could feel the burden of need slowly
swelling. As if in response, Shardlan dipped his fingers

into the mint-water and gently stroked its cool wetness round her knob: one hand kept hold of the bodkin, while the other gently turned her to warm her back against the brazier, which caused her nipples to erect, which meant that he could the more readily kiss them. The dried semen turned glutinous, slippery.

'Oh please, master, please . . .,' Leah begged.

'Turn your front to the fire.' Her legs were trembling. Slowly, purposefully, Shardlan spread her sex, the outer lips then the inner, until the radiant warmth of the brazier bathed the sensitive inner pinkness and the gold insert gradually warmed and a new sensation came as this gentle warmth spread up the shaft inside her. And when he twirled the bodkin anew, she desperately wanted to come – against all that sweet warm pressure of pee inside her. 'Let's get your knob up,' he coaxed, though it was already up. One hand fingered her erection and the other twirled her bodkin round and round inside her, until her breathing suddenly snagged and she felt as if she were peeing, each stabbing pulse pushing the pleasure of an orgasm down the tube of her pee-hole. But nothing save a little oil had come out and the master was whispering: 'Good girl, good, sweet dirty little creature. Your little knob is jumping like a strangled cock trying to squirt out semen.' He held the bodkin rigidly still and wiped her oil around her pulsing clitoris, then tugged it as if milking a teat.

Leah tried to hide her face: there were masters watching nearby. Shardlan turned her to face them. 'Just some colleagues here to see you,' he whispered. Suddenly, a tall grey figure of a lady accompanied by a servant broke through the group and marched over to Shardlan.

'My lord – I have been looking for you. Both of you. I take it this is she?' Her cold grey gaze made Leah recoil.

'Leah – may I introduce you to Lady Tellen? Lady Tellen is my sister.' Shardlan smiled wanly.

'Not quite, my friend. Soulmate, perhaps – the rest is idle speculation. But let me look at her. Leah, of the hairless cunt. And now she is affronted. Stand straight, girl. Do I speak too plainly for the sensibilities of a slut bedaubed with spunk? Give me charge of her, Shardlan, this instant – I demand it.'

Bowing, he stepped back. Lady Tellen turned to her servant. 'Get me a male. Be quick. And you' – she turned on Leah – 'bring your flagon.' She led her by the ear into the bushes.

'Now we are alone – girl to girl.' Suddenly her mood had changed: her breathing was stilted, her manner nervous, her eyes glittered. She took the cup and flagon almost gently from Leah's fingers and set them down. She was trembling as she took Leah's hands and kissed her fingers. Then she kissed her on the lips, long and gently. Finally she whispered excitedly: 'Ulline fisted you? She made you come? Shardlan told me. Oh, you beautiful sexual creature. Let me touch you, inside.'

Leah whimpered in fear.

'Shh, I know. You cannot take a fist in there, not now, all bridled up and with all this drinking. Tellen will be gentle. Shh . . .' When Leah began to squirm, the lady sucked her shivering nipples and gently cupped her distended belly. 'These lovely thighs are trembling.' Crouching, she planted gently dabbing kisses over their inner surfaces. 'Did Shardlan make you drink too far? But it makes you that much more deliciously on edge. It makes these lips so soft and hot – so trembling, kissable . . . And this bridled little pee-hole – so delectable – let me tongue its tiny rim.' Leah groaned; the lady's cool tongue gently nuzzled and licked. 'Every part, made so receptive and keen . . . Let me push this hood back a little further, get you out

242

a little more.' She tightened the already tight retractor. Leah's clitoris felt as if it would burst; its buried swollen root throbbed against the rigid shaft of the retractor. And all the while there was that pressure to pee; a pervasive numbness thwarted by licking waves of hypersensitive sexual feeling.

'Oh, but you are beautiful, like this, with your bridled little cunt . . .' She kiss-sucked Leah's knob up to a rigid point then brushed her lips back and forth across it until pleasure pierced Leah and electric pulses stabbed up the tube of her pee-hole and her knob turned numb from the over-pleasuring lip-brushes. Then Lady Tellen stood up and urged her backwards against the base of a young tree. 'Sit. Stretch these lovely legs out – wide.' She filled the cup from the flagon. 'Now drink.'

'Oh, please – no more. I cannot.'

Tellen slapped her breasts. 'Do it!'

Leah's breasts were still shaking. Tellen milked the nipples. 'How soft and stretchable they are becoming now. There, do it for me, sweet beauty – keep drinking.' The empty cup finally slipped from Leah's fingers. She started shivering, moaning. Tellen kept touching her – from nipples to clitoris to pee-hole and back again. Then she thrust three fingers in and smothered Leah's gasps with kisses. 'Oh – so swollen up to bursting, now . . .' The fingers repeatedly trailed warm wetness up Leah's belly to her nipples. Then suddenly Tellen stood up, casting aside her cloak and spreading her split skirt – 'Now, come close, my precious – kiss your mistress, in here, kiss it. Oh yes . . .' She mounted Leah's face, forcing her small, cold, thin-lipped sex into Leah's open mouth – riding it, one hand braced round the narrow tree-trunk, the other reaching back, tugging at Leah's bridle, until Tellen's climax squirted into Leah's mouth, drenching her tongue. Leah, shuddering, felt her own warmth flooding out between her legs, felt an unbearable pleasure that drew down inside her, all the way from her shivering nipples to the overstretched muscles of her inner thighs.

The mistress stood up, breathing heavily, and wiped herself on Leah's hair. Then the servant appeared with a naked male slave bearing a collar round the base of the penis.

'You're too late. Take him away. No, wait.' Leah was slumped naked, wet all down her front and shivering. Tellen removed the saturated bridle and bodkin from between Leah's thighs. She dragged the slave to his knees by his leashed penis. 'Now kiss her. Kiss it. Suck it up to goodness.' While he sucked, she steadily tightened the collar round the base of his erection, then pushed the beaded bodkin as far as it would go down the tube of his penis, triggering swift ejaculation. Then she dragged him off and pushed the semen-coated bodkin back up Leah's pee-hole, all the way up, rotating the smooth bead until the tiny muscle gave way to a pleasure so focused and intense that Leah thrust against the instrument; but Tellen controlled and extended the climax, slapping all the pee-wet places, labia, belly, breasts and clitoris, until Leah fell back, helplessly twitching, against the trunk of the tree.

When she finally looked up, Shardlan was watching. Tellen calmly put her hand up through the split of her skirt then pushed the fingers into Leah's mouth.

'You have made a sound start, my lady: pray continue,' Shardlan murmured. 'Perhaps show her the others.'

Together they took her to see the girls and the statues. The carvings were larger than life-size; their erections seemed larger still. Lady Tellen made Leah kiss one. 'Take it fully in your mouth. Deeper . . . Try to swallow.' She touched between Leah's legs: all the feeling was still there. They decided to recharge the bodkin with agaric and made Leah sit open for it. A girl opposite had been made to climb on to the alabaster phallus of a statue. She stood on tiptoe, mating. The penetration by the oversized phallus had pushed her anus back.

'Hold still, Leah,' Shardlan said as the coated bead was reintroduced inside her. Then the rush of new arousal struck. She wanted to close her legs. 'Stand up.' They helped her, leading her over to the girl. 'Push your fingers up her bottom,' Tellen said. Leah hesitated, her legs shaking, the bead of the bodkin throbbing inside her. Tellen wetted Leah's fingers with spittle. The girl moaned as her tight little rubbery anus opened to Leah's slippery fingers. Leah could feel every detail of the stone phallus inside – the shaft, cap and rim – tightly sheathed in the girl's inner skin. And the girl was coming to climax. 'Help her – touch her lovely knob.' Leah reached round and all the girlish honey was already running down to the base of the phallus. As the girl cried out in pleasure, Tellen's slim cool fingers found the little knurled knob of Leah's bodkin, gently rotating and pushing it till Leah's tongue protruded and her knees buckled and the bead inside her popped the tiny muscle open and she came to climax, squirting pee around the shaft of the bodkin and down the back of the girl's trembling leg.

Leah was led onwards, to witness a girl with eyelets and laces through her labia being laced to a phallus. The girl's master then proceeded to whip her. Shardlan edged Leah forwards. 'Kiss her lacing.' Leah knelt shaking in front of the punished girl. Her tongue was trembling as it placed the first nervous caresses on the soft flesh pushing through the bedded thongs of leather. The lovely clitoris lay trapped between the inner pressure of the phallus and the tight, stretched shelter of the hood. Leah gently sucked it out and the girl's pleasure came wetly, thin honey bubbling through her lacing. Shardlan drew Leah down on to the grass, kissing her honeyed lips; Tellen kissed the moist erection between her legs and gently twirled the slippery bodkin; the girl's owner recommenced her whipping. Then, amid the kissing and the twirling, Shardlan whispered: 'Shall we take you up to the orangery now?'

And so it was that Leah's needs were attended to, in an environment of relative seclusion where a group of interested men had gathered and the scent of beautiful plants mingled with the scent of beautiful girls arrayed on simple flower-strewn narrow daises among trickling fountains.

Two young men approached as Shardlan laid Leah on her dais. 'No bottles,' Tellen warned. Then she relented: 'But go gently – not too far.'

Shardlan stood back, watching and musing. 'Is she not beautiful, Tellen? See how deeply his cock is being throated. Let me touch her breasts ... You there – gently with that bottle.' Shardlan worked her nipples wetly but tenderly. As he reached to caress her erection, her belly lifted; the young man with his penis in her throat groaned in climax; the bottle between her thighs was expelled. But her labia stayed beautifully open. Shardlan stroked their sensitive edges. Tellen motioned the young men away. Shardlan took Leah's lovely body in his arms, kissed her, tongued her, even through the stranger's semen, gently twirled the bedded instrument into play inside her lovely body and held her for a sweet few minutes, then offered her for privileged usage.

She shivered sexually as the sheaths – velvet, silk, ribbed, and beaded – were spread out in line by her cheek. Shardlan remained stationed by her head, whispering encouragements, as a master must, and kissing her open mouth. Tellen occasionally touched her or aided a penetration or stripped away a sheath and forced an ejaculation. Semen spilled freely into Leah's thirsting mouth. Her lips glistened with it. It hung pungently at the back of her throat. Shardlan tasted it and still he continued to kiss – who would not, when a girl is so aroused? The burning droplets shed on her body he gently massaged into her skin. He gently grasped her open sex and toyed with the head of the little bodkin while Tellen held open Leah's anus so that living semen hotter than her vitals could be squirted up inside her. Masters of various ages took turn without priority.

In time her naked body became covered in semen. Still her master would not let her be – his fingers were perpetually between her legs, gently parting her labia, stimulating her clitoris, toying with her tiny gold insert, exploring those exquisitely sensitive female folds. Why were those pleasure centres cloistered there, if not for the seeking and taking? He said he wanted to cultivate within her the need for this protracted stimulation; he said it made her that much more craving of love and that much more permissive in giving. He said he would play with her through the night: while she slept, he would remain, unsleeping and worshipping her flesh, and when she awoke in the morning he would be worshipping it still.

Leah kissed her master and caressed his neck and ear lobe and kissed his lips again and he lifted her and carried her to bed and, true to his word, he remained unsleeping, touching, taunting, kissing, torturing her exhausted body with pleasure through that night.

On the morning following her sweet ordeal, Leah lay in gently exhausted sleep, stretched out face down in beautiful nude abandon upon Lord Shardlan's bed. Her untrammelled carnality had wooed him. He sat upon the edge of the bed and laid his fingertips very softly on the hollow at the base of her spine. She murmured in her sleep and her face turned to the side. He kissed her lovely eyebrows. Her eyelids opened.

'Does it hurt, still?' he whispered.

Leah nodded, but held her chin up bravely on the tips of his fingers while he touched the tortured, opened place between her buttock cheeks.

'Does it sting?

'Yes,' she murmured. 'Ohh!'

'There are some tiny lesions. My friends were too harsh here.' The muscle of her anus was hot and swollen, and, though her bit and bridle had been removed, her sex was raw: most of that was his doing. He took her lovely used, naked body in his arms and lay alongside her, just to feel that smooth perfect belly against him. He kissed her and found her lips so softly delicious, carrying all the nervous weight of girlish fear of what he might next want to do. Yet her arms, already complicitous, were around his neck, though her anxious fingertips barely touched his skin. It was these contradictory sexual signals that made these girls so very special. The kiss was scarcely complete before the servant entered the bedroom. 'My lord, Lirann is outside.'

'What does she want?'

'The male slave, Ean, cannot be found. It seems he has escaped and –'

'That is of scant concern.'

But Leah sat up looking fretful and tense.

Then Lirann strode defiantly into the room. 'My lord – Merek is back to claim his girl.'

# 17

# A Reunion

'Merek is at the wharf. He is asking for her,' Lirann announced bluntly, staring coldly and smugly at Leah on the bed, as if to say: 'Yes, your master is back now, girl, and he will surely vent his wrath upon your profligate hide.' But what she said was: 'I can take her to him, my lord.'

'No – keep her safe here for the present.' Lord Shardlan had paled.

'But –'

'I shall speak to him.'

'But my lord, under the terms of her tithe –'

'Please do as I say!'

Lirann bowed silently and remained with head hanging, uttering not another word, until Lord Shardlan had dressed and hurried from the room.

Then she glared at Leah. 'Get some clothes on.' Leah froze. Lirann took three steps forward and, raising her arm as if wielding an axe with which to fell a tree, she delivered one dreadful slap across Leah's face, then another that was harder still. Then she grasped her by the hair and dragged her off the bed. 'Get some clothes on – now!'

When Lord Shardlan returned, having asked in vain at the wharf for the elusive trader Merek, and finally having guessed what was afoot, he found Lirann alone in the bedroom.

'Where is she?'

'She has gone, my lord. Her lover took her.'

'Ean? You didn't try to stop him?'

'I could not.'

'You mean you would not.' Seething, Shardlan strode out on to the terrace and clutched the balustrade. Lirann meekly followed. He did not look at her but stared out over the gardens and the hillside beyond. 'Perhaps I should send a party in pursuit? I think I shall. What say you to that?' He scowled at her.

'Surely, the party designated to hunt down runaways is you and I, my lord?'

'I should have you flogged for this, Lirann.'

'As it pleases, my lord. But do not harm your child.' She unbuttoned her tunic top and dropped it to the floor, leaving her swollen breasts naked and her master utterly speechless.

He did not flog Lirann. He carried her to his bed and sealed the peculiar bond that tied them, lord and pregnant girl-guard. All thought of pursuit was put aside for a precious time of sharing. Then, just as all seemed settled for Lirann, Ulline came knocking at the bedroom door. Shardlan drew the sheet completely over his naked assistant.

'There is a girl asking after you, my lord,' said Ulline.

'Truly, I am having to fend them off, today, Mistress Dresser. Pray put her to someone else. As you see, I am beset.'

'She will see no one else; she seeks work; she says you promised to take her on if she chose to ask.'

'I promised no one. Who is this barefaced individual?'

'She says her name is Deneca – Denni.'

'Ah . . .'

\* \* \*

In the late morning sun, two breathless figures stood at the top of the staircase of locks.

'Don't stand in the open, Leah. We may be seen from the Retreat,' Ean said.

'I want to look – just to look at the view.'

'But we need to keep moving: they will surely come after us. I don't trust Lirann.'

Leah didn't answer. She was strangely quiet and calm. He looked upon her delicate features, her soft blue eyes staring ruefully out across the sunlit landscape.

'Are you thinking of Merek?' Ean asked apprehensively.

'My destiny does not rest on Merek – not now.' Leah turned. The slave-token was no longer round her neck: it slid from her fingers into the water. She looked at Ean searchingly for a long while. Then she said: 'How many times did you seek to save me?'

'And failed each time . . .'

'And still you persisted.' Her eyes were now moist with tears. 'Come here, Master Ean.' Leah took him in her arms and kissed him, through her tears and with them. Then, still holding him, she turned and looked wistfully down upon the beautiful, vast expanse of the bay and the open sea beyond.

nexus

The leading publisher of fetish and adult fiction

## TELL US WHAT YOU THINK!

Readers' ideas and opinions matter to us so please take a few minutes to fill in the questionnaire below.

**1. Sex:** Are you male ☐ female ☐ a couple ☐?

**2. Age:** Under 21 ☐ 21–30 ☐ 31–40 ☐ 41–50 ☐ 51–60 ☐ over 60 ☐

**3. Where do you buy your Nexus books from?**

☐ A chain book shop. If so, which one(s)?

_____

☐ An independent book shop. If so, which one(s)?

_____

☐ A used book shop/charity shop
☐ Online book store. If so, which one(s)?

_____

**4. How did you find out about Nexus books?**

☐ Browsing in a book shop
☐ A review in a magazine
☐ Online
☐ Recommendation
☐ Other _____

**5. In terms of settings, which do you prefer? (Tick as many as you like.)**

☐ Down to earth and as realistic as possible
☐ Historical settings. If so, which period do you prefer?

_____

☐ Fantasy settings – barbarian worlds
☐ Completely escapist/surreal fantasy
☐ Institutional or secret academy

- ☐ Futuristic/sci fi
- ☐ Escapist but still believable
- ☐ Any settings you dislike?

_____

- ☐ Where would you like to see an adult novel set?

_____

## 6. In terms of storylines, would you prefer:

- ☐ Simple stories that concentrate on adult interests?
- ☐ More plot and character-driven stories with less explicit adult activity?
- ☐ We value your ideas, so give us your opinion of this book:

_____

_____

_____

## 7. In terms of your adult interests, what do you like to read about? (Tick as many as you like.)

- ☐ Traditional corporal punishment (CP)
- ☐ Modern corporal punishment
- ☐ Spanking
- ☐ Restraint/bondage
- ☐ Rope bondage
- ☐ Latex/rubber
- ☐ Leather
- ☐ Female domination and male submission
- ☐ Female domination and female submission
- ☐ Male domination and female submission
- ☐ Willing captivity
- ☐ Uniforms
- ☐ Lingerie/underwear/hosiery/footwear (boots and high heels)
- ☐ Sex rituals
- ☐ Vanilla sex
- ☐ Swinging
- ☐ Cross-dressing/TV
- ☐ Enforced feminisation

☐ Others – tell us what you don't see enough of in adult fiction:

_____

_____

_____

8. Would you prefer books with a more specialised approach to your interests, i.e. a novel specifically about uniforms? If so, which subject(s) would you like to read a Nexus novel about?

_____

_____

_____

9. Would you like to read true stories in Nexus books? For instance, the true story of a submissive woman, or a male slave? Tell us which true revelations you would most like to read about:

_____

_____

_____

10. What do you like best about Nexus books?

_____

_____

11. What do you like least about Nexus books?

_____

_____

12. Which are your favourite titles?

_____

_____

13. Who are your favourite authors?

_____

_____

14. Which covers do you prefer? Those featuring:
(Tick as many as you like.)

☐ Fetish outfits
☐ More nudity
☐ Two models
☐ Unusual models or settings
☐ Classic erotic photography
☐ More contemporary images and poses
☐ A blank/non-erotic cover
☐ What would your ideal cover look like?

_____

15. **Describe your ideal Nexus novel in the space provided:**

_____

_____

_____

_____

16. **Which celebrity would feature in one of your Nexus-style fantasies? We'll post the best suggestions on our website – anonymously!**

_____

## THANKS FOR YOUR TIME

Now simply write the title of this book in the space below and cut out the questionnaire pages. Post to: Nexus, Marketing Dept., Thames Wharf Studios, Rainville Rd, London W6 9HA

Book title: _____

# NEXUS NEW BOOKS

*To be published in April 2008*

## NEXUS CONFESSIONS VOLUME 3
### Various

Swinging, dogging, group sex, cross-dressing, spanking, female domination, corporal punishment, and extreme fetishes . . . Nexus Confessions explores the length and breadth of erotic obsession, real experience and sexual fantasy. This is an encyclopaedic collection of the bizarre, the extreme, the utterly inappropriate, the daring and the shocking experiences of ordinary men and women driven by their extraordinary desires. Collected by the world's leading publisher of fetish fiction, this is the fourth in a series of six volumes of true stories and shameful confessions, never-before-told or published.

£6.99 ISBN 978 0 352 34113 6

*To be published in May 2008*

## PORTRAIT OF A DISCIPLINARIAN
### Aishling Morgan

Stephanie 'Stiffy' Truscott has a talent for trouble and no less than six aunts, every one of whom considers the best place for her to be over the knee. They object to her driving, her dancing, but most of all to her choice of fiancé, and as she attempts to evade their preferred form of justice she only manages to dig herself in deeper. After stealing her prospective father-in-law's prize pig and being tricked into joining the local fascists, she knows that the least she can expect is to have her bare bottom caned in front of a large audience, but still she tries to wriggle free.

£6.99 ISBN 978 0 352 341792

If you would like more information about Nexus titles, please visit our website at www.nexus-books.co.uk, or send a large stamped addressed envelope to:

Nexus, Thames Wharf Studios,
Rainville Road, London W6 9HA

# NEXUS BOOKLIST

Information is correct at time of printing. To avoid disappointment, check availability before ordering. Go to www.nexus-books.co.uk.

All books are priced at £6.99 unless another price is given.

## NEXUS

| | | |
|---|---|---|
| ☐ ABANDONED ALICE | Adriana Arden | ISBN 978 0 352 33969 0 |
| ☐ ALICE IN CHAINS | Adriana Arden | ISBN 978 0 352 33908 9 |
| ☐ AMERICAN BLUE | Penny Birch | ISBN 978 0 352 34169 3 |
| ☐ AQUA DOMINATION | William Doughty | ISBN 978 0 352 34020 7 |
| ☐ THE ART OF CORRECTION | Tara Black | ISBN 978 0 352 33895 2 |
| ☐ THE ART OF SURRENDER | Madeline Bastinado | ISBN 978 0 352 34013 9 |
| ☐ BEASTLY BEHAVIOUR | Aishling Morgan | ISBN 978 0 352 34095 5 |
| ☐ BEING A GIRL | Chloë Thurlow | ISBN 978 0 352 34139 6 |
| ☐ BELINDA BARES UP | Yolanda Celbridge | ISBN 978 0 352 33926 3 |
| ☐ BIDDING TO SIN | Rosita Varón | ISBN 978 0 352 34063 4 |
| ☐ BLUSHING AT BOTH ENDS | Philip Kemp | ISBN 978 0 352 34107 5 |
| ☐ THE BOOK OF PUNISHMENT | Cat Scarlett | ISBN 978 0 352 33975 1 |
| ☐ BRUSH STROKES | Penny Birch | ISBN 978 0 352 34072 6 |
| ☐ CALLED TO THE WILD | Angel Blake | ISBN 978 0 352 34067 2 |
| ☐ CAPTIVES OF CHEYNER CLOSE | Adriana Arden | ISBN 978 0 352 34028 3 |
| ☐ CARNAL POSSESSION | Yvonne Strickland | ISBN 978 0 352 34062 7 |
| ☐ CITY MAID | Amelia Evangeline | ISBN 978 0 352 34096 2 |
| ☐ COLLEGE GIRLS | Cat Scarlett | ISBN 978 0 352 33942 3 |
| ☐ COMPANY OF SLAVES | Christina Shelly | ISBN 978 0 352 33887 7 |
| ☐ CONCEIT AND CONSEQUENCE | Aishling Morgan | ISBN 978 0 352 33965 2 |
| ☐ CORRECTIVE THERAPY | Jacqueline Masterson | ISBN 978 0 352 33917 1 |
| ☐ CORRUPTION | Virginia Crowley | ISBN 978 0 352 34073 3 |

**NEXUS NON FICTION**

- - - - - - ✂ - - - - - - - - - - - - - - - - - - - - - - - - -

Please send me the books I have ticked above.

Name .........................................................................................

Address .........................................................................................

.........................................................................................

.........................................................................................

.................................................... Post code ....................

Send to: **Virgin Books Cash Sales, Thames Wharf Studios, Rainville Road, London W6 9HA**

US customers: for prices and details of how to order books for delivery by mail, call 888-330-8477.

Please enclose a cheque or postal order, made payable to **Nexus Books Ltd**, to the value of the books you have ordered plus postage and packing costs as follows:

UK and BFPO – £1.00 for the first book, 50p for each subsequent book.

Overseas (including Republic of Ireland) – £2.00 for the first book, £1.00 for each subsequent book.

If you would prefer to pay by VISA, ACCESS/MASTERCARD, AMEX, DINERS CLUB or SWITCH, please write your card number and expiry date here:

.........................................................................................

Please allow up to 28 days for delivery.

**Signature** .........................................................................

**Our privacy policy**

We will not disclose information you supply us to any other parties. We will not disclose any information which identifies you personally to any person without your express consent.

From time to time we may send out information about Nexus books and special offers. Please tick here if you do *not* wish to receive Nexus information.  ☐

- - - - - - ✂ - - - - - - - - - - - - - - - - - - - - - - - - -